YOUR

TRUE

COLORS

COPYRIGHT

For Mom, Carla Jenkins Martinez, who always raised me to make sure my "true colors" were never too horrific.

The real you is not what you show to the world, but what
you are when no one is watching.
—Unknown

I was ashamed of myself when I realized life was a costume
party; and I attended with my real face.
—Franz Kafka

I was cured all right.
—Anthony Burgess, *A Clockwork Orange*

PROLOGUE

Her screams were muffled in between the songs, which is how Lance liked it. He knew his subwoofers were located in the back, near the trunk, and was secretly hoping that that would shut her up, but she was insistent on screaming until her vocal cords gave out. These were minor miscalculations on his part. He thought he had done his homework when searching for his first candidate, but he didn't expect her to put up this much of a fight.

*   *   *

No one noticed Lance at school because he was like a fly on the wall: a janitor for nearly twenty-eight years, and the only friend he had was another hideous guy named Earl. Sometimes he had to count his blessings, though, because Earl was twenty years his junior, already balding, and in even worse shape than he was.

They tried to have their meals during lunch hours with the rest of the faculty, but the teachers could think of (and had used) every excuse in the book to not include them. They were treated like they were contracted workers when, in reality, they were all employed by the same school district. Hell, he had more tenure than the majority

1

of the teachers. Maybe he didn't have a fancy four-year degree, but he was still valuable. And you bet your ass these people would contact him when they had a leaking faucet or needed something cleaned up.

After his mom passed, Lance was contemplating ending it. He even had the noose ready in his garage. The house was too quiet after her long, hard-fought battle with cancer, and he didn't have any kids of his own. No woman would touch him with a ten-foot pole. As he was testing the strength of the rope, he got a text from Earl. Lance was annoyed. It was his turn to be on call this weekend, and he didn't want to go check out some flooded pipes in the boys' bathroom. Begrudgingly, he read the message anyway.

This was out of the ordinary.

Earl wanted to meet up for drinks. The text was vague, but it seemed like his only friend wanted to get something off his chest. Lance figured the hanging could be put off for another hour. He showered and put on some nicer clothes. Not as nice as what he wore to his mother's funeral, but better than what he wore to the high school every day.

He found out early on that working his job with nice clothes was pointless. A lot of the time he had to get stains out of the shirts and jeans. Sometimes even the best bleach couldn't fix the problems. When Lance raided his closet, he found a nicer dress shirt but was a little

2

embarrassed when he wasn't able to button it down completely.

It had been a while since he'd gone out.

Instead, he opted on wearing a wifebeater underneath with all the buttons loose. It was an okay compromise. It's not like he wanted to impress Earl, but he still had some dignity left when going out to a bar. He put on some deodorant and cologne and passed his mother's room. It still didn't feel right not having her in the house, and he couldn't bear the silence anymore. For a while he even had those cheesy nineties sitcoms playing in the background because it at least filled the house with some sort of noise; but without her laughing along with the laugh tracks—it just felt empty.

He got to the sports bar and felt ridiculous for putting any effort into looking the part because Earl was his same old self, and it looked like the same outfit he had worn the day before. Of course no one would notice. They were both invisible at that job, and no one here at the bar would look twice at them. He pulled up a seat next to him and noticed that his friend was nose deep in a book.

"Reading at a bar?" Lance joked.

"I'm almost done with this chapter. Hold up for a sec." Earl doesn't look up. Not even once. Lance sat there awkwardly and didn't know what to do, so he ordered a beer from the bartender, and only when it was being brought back did Earl finish.

He read the rest of the chapter and put a bookmark in it like he promised. When he looked up at Lance, he had the biggest smile Lance had ever seen from his only friend.

"Everything alright?" Lance had to ask even though he seemed more than okay.

"I got you something, man." Earl reached into his backpack and grabbed another copy of the same book that he was reading. He handed it over, clearly ecstatic.

"You brought me to a bar to give me a book?" Lance arched an eyebrow and couldn't help hiding his laughter.

Even the bartender overheard the conversation and joked with them that the library was down the street. That brought a new wind to Lance and soon he was holding both of his sides. If anything—at least this night was a nice send-off before leaving this world, he thought to himself.

But Earl didn't laugh during any of this and waited for him to get a grip. When Lance's laughter finally died down, Earl insisted that he had to give the book a shot.

"I know you're skeptical now, but I promise you that it'll be a game changer," Earl explained and then ordered another beer.

Lance swigged his sixteen-ounce down and looked at the cover. Flipping it around to inspect the back, he read the testimonials from people who claimed that it had changed their lives for the better. He gave a humorous grunt and turned back around to Earl, who studied him.

"I'll read a few chapters because you're a friend," Lance promised, and it seemed to be all the affirmation that Earl needed.

The two ended up talking about how horrible their sports teams were, and, of course, the work talk ended up being the focal point of their conversation as they vented about how their district was too cheap to shell out the money for the proper tools they needed. The pair discussed how shitty their coworkers were and how their boss didn't even monitor them because he was too busy cheating on his wife with half of the teachers there. They both made fun of him the best they could, but they couldn't mask how jealous they were that Jalen was good looking and charismatic.

In reality, Jalen actually treated them with dignity when alone with them, but he wasn't as chummy when the rest of the colleagues were around. Outside of giving them orders, he typically distanced himself from them like everybody else did. The two of them were not stupid and had pointed it out in the past, but Jalen had been insistent that it was because he wanted to maintain a professional atmosphere in front of the rest of the staff.

Whatever.

"Justine Baker is still missing," Earl reminded Lance after they were a couple of beers and a few shots in.

"Oh . . . yeah . . . that's crazy." Lance hadn't even thought about the missing student until now. Sure, he remembered her . . . who wouldn't? She was one of the most beautiful girls in the school. He'd even seen the principal and a few of the other teachers look the other way whenever she would cause problems.

"Something tells me she's just fine." Earl smiled to himself, and Lance observed him closely.

"You want to tell me something, man?" Lance whispered, excluding the bartender from their conversation.

"Just read the book," Earl responded, like it would answer all of his questions.

What a weird thing to say. The two ended up going back to sports talk and soon closed their tabs. Because Lance knew he didn't have much time left on the planet, he went ahead and left the bartender a hundred-dollar tip.

He was halfway across the bar when the bartender realized this and voiced his gratitude to Lance, who just threw up his hand in the air and waved him off. It didn't mean anything to him. Shit. He could've left five hundred dollars but didn't know how much their credit card transactions allowed, so he decided to play it safe. He considered it a parting gift to a cruel world.

When he got home, he was too tipsy to continue with his original task. It would have to wait for the morning. He tripped into his bed and the book fell to the ground. Lance slept well that night despite all of that, though his head was pounding when he woke up.

The smell of puke was his rude awakening; he looked down at the stained carpet in disgust. Fortunately his projectile vomit missed the book Earl gave him. Lance wanted nothing more than to end it already so he didn't have to smell any of the mess, but having made a promise to his friend, he picked it up and began to read the first couple of chapters. He didn't put it down for the rest of that Saturday.

Lance completed it in three days, even taking off of work to finish it. The world had opened up to him, and he was genuinely surprised at his newfound purpose in life.

*   *   *

His first kidnapping was sloppy, and he later told Earl that they needed to focus on girls from other districts, but his friend didn't seem too concerned with being caught. He explained that whatever happened, happened.

7

Lance reminded him that law enforcement would eventually catch on to them, and it wouldn't take long for them to get a search warrant for both of their places.

"Which is why you should choose the ones you want the most," Earl explained. "We don't have much time left, so make sure it counts."

He's right, Lance realized. Why worry about the consequences? Lance had been eyeing Annmarie Gonzalez ever since she stepped foot there her freshmen year. She kept to herself and also read a lot. He liked that she was the shy and quiet type. Plus, she dressed conservatively, which made him fantasize more about being intimate with her and the fact that she'd only be his.

He studied her routine and made sure to take his break when she walked out of her classes and went to her car in the crowded parking lot. He tailed her white sedan and noticed she lived a little further away from the school than he expected. Both of her parents worked late shifts, so it wasn't too hard to snatch her early in the night; however, the chloroform didn't knock her out completely, and she thrashed heavily when he put her in the trunk.

Her screaming was loud. So loud that he had to turn up his music all the way and hightail it out of her neighborhood. He then had the not-so-brilliant idea of taking a long, scenic route home that added another hour to his trip, because he halfway hoped that she would tucker herself out by then, but he had no such luck. She was a screamer, and even though he soundproofed his house and built the spare bedroom with reinforced steel, he was still worried.

His vehicle started shaking, and he looked at his dashboard when the tire pressure indicator started blinking.

"Shit," Lance muttered.

A blown tire. On the highway. That's just great, he thought. Lance realized he was going to have to move her to the backseat while he fixed it and was aware she'd have a lot of fight in her. He pulled off to the side of the road and braced for her to jump out, but that didn't happen.

He looked down at her as she shook uncontrollably.

"I'm not going to hurt you unless I have to," Lance explained. He reached into the trunk, and she shrieked before he even touched her.

She started rambling in Spanish and English for him to not hurt her, and she truly could not stop quivering. He told her to get out of the trunk and to go to the backseat. She slowly exited the trunk, and to Lance's surprise, Annmarie actually started to obey his instructions. But before she got into the backseat, she made a break for it and started to run.

"Aw shit." Lance groaned and began to chase her.

She looked behind her and twisted her ankle when tripping over debris left on the side of the road. She screamed in agony and fell to the ground. Lance was able to catch up to her and lifted her over his shoulder.

She kicked and clawed, breaking his skin and drawing blood, but he was able to successfully get her back to the vehicle and throw her in the backseat. Afterward, he took the spare tire out and began to fix the flat as quickly as he possibly could. It was hard to steady the car with her kicking around, but he was able to make it work.

It was a miracle that no one else had joined them on the roads that early into the night. It was as if God was on his side. It wasn't until she was back in the car that a couple of vehicles passed by them. Lance crossed his fingers that no good samaritan would stop to try to help him out.

Then Lance's heart sunk to the pit of his stomach: police lights. A trooper slowed down. Annmarie saw this, and with rejuvenated energy and a profound new will to survive, she screamed at the top of her lungs as the trooper got out of his vehicle and approached Lance's car. The young kid behind the badge was not the best looking of the bunch either. He assessed the situation.

Lance knew the end of his road was here before he even began. Oh well, he thought, maybe he could hang himself in the prison cell.

"Evening, sir."

The trooper looked to the backseat at the screaming girl and back to the aging janitor fixing the tire. Then he bent down, looking Lance eye to eye while he took off his shades.

"Chapter eight says that there will be speed bumps, but you cannot let them slow you down."

He's a fan of the book too, Lance realized. And with that, the officer walked back to his unit, turned off his lights as he passed them on the highway, and drove away.

Back to work.

Your True Colors

PART I

ISABELLE

Your True Colors

CHAPTER ONE

Trey is early as usual—a full half an hour before his shift starts. I know that I am the last person to judge, but to be fair, I already know that I have no life outside these walls. His marital problems have been going on for over a year now, and I know he comes in earlier than everyone just to leave two hours later too. Off the clock. Charity work. Anything just to be as far away from her as possible. I envy him. Even if it's an emotion as negative as resentment, he's still on someone's mind.

I join him in the break room where I wait for him to pour his black coffee. The majority of the time, he doesn't even notice I'm there, waiting to use the company's espresso machine next.

"Jesus Christ, Beth, just give it a damn rest," he mutters under his breath as he checks a recent text on his phone. He looks up and locks eyes with me. "Do you ever get the idea that someone is just waiting for you to mess up?"

This is out of nature. Normally, he just walks right past me. I stare at him, dumbfounded. Not only because this is a first, but also because I don't really know how to answer his question. My mouth feels like cotton is stuck at the roof of my mouth. "I—"

16

"Why don't you just end it already?" Behind me, Jackie Roberts attempts to keep a straight face, but a sly smile touches the corner of her lips.

This is a contagious smile she flashes, which eventually also earns a smile from Trey. "You're just loving this, aren't you, Jackie? I may be married to Satan herself, but at least I am not dating half the men in the city."

"Low blow. You're not wrong, but still—that's beneath you, Trey," Jackie teases him and is clearly not offended. She turns to me, "Bella, are you using the machine next?"

My name is Isabelle and I was waiting next with my mug, obviously, but I don't voice any of this and just shake my head.

"Cool." Jackie fills up her mug and continues her playful conversation with Trey. I've been used to her type since high school. The popular kids whose biggest cardinal sin is not to be liked by nearly everyone they meet. Especially when it comes to the athletes. And although Trey is far removed from his peak tennis-playing years— he's still not bad on the eyes for being in his midthirties.

I stare off into space and miss the insult Jackie gives about Trey's aging wife. It is odd that he married fifteen years his senior and had two kids with her, but, if I had to guess, he didn't know how much value he'd have this early in his life. I hear all the rumors in this building,

17

and the word on the street is that Trey met his wife through one of his dad's coworkers. What teenage boy wouldn't want to reenact the whole Mrs. Robinson fantasy? Predatory or not, Beth sank her claws into him, and while Trey had a mom who dipped out on him during his developing years, Beth offered a very voluptuous body and attention. Trey's Mommy issues were resolved.

But he's not a boy anymore.

I watch as Jackie, ten years younger than Trey, lightly touches his chest at a cheesy joke he says. I attempt to not stare for too long. Even though I don't think they'd notice to begin with. I'm a ghost. This isn't anything new. A lot of women think that being skinny automatically makes you attractive. They couldn't be further from the truth.

I'm far skinnier than the average woman. My hair is practically a bird's nest and I am deathly pale. I hide most of my face with my outdated glasses and have been told on some occasions that it looks like I shop at a thrift store.

It also hurts that I am beyond average. Everyone likes to think that they are, but I think ugly people are at least treated nicer by the pretties because there's a sense of pity. I'd be perfect as an extra on a movie set because at least then I would just blend with the crowd.

Even the tiny room I work in wouldn't be noticed if someone didn't point it out. No, that's not a closet. That is actually where I work. Away from the others in the office.

I know that the company has changed drastically since its start-up days and I never spoke up about being reacclimated back in the office with everyone else, but there was a good reason for that. I knew when I first started that I could be a bit of a distraction.

I'm dyslexic—actually dyslexic and not just saying that like most millennials toss around conditions like ADHD or depression. Since my college years I've used software that I speak into so I can print out the thoughts that are in my head. And it's gotten me far. But I understand from management's perspective that they couldn't have someone mumbling every ten minutes into an app just to get their workflow done.

"That's a new mug." I jump slightly and look over my shoulder at Santiago, who observes the old mug that I haven't taken out in a couple of months. The truth is I haven't cleaned my current mug in two weeks, and I was beginning to wonder whether it was a stain or actual mold. Please don't judge.

"You're early, Santiago." He winces a bit at hearing his name. Santiago, or Santi, as he prefers to be called, is the social butterfly in the office. I made the horrible mistake years ago of interpreting his friendliness for flirting and asked him to dinner.

19

He was polite and dropped another woman's name, telling me he was flattered but was in a new relationship. His social media profiles were open, though, and it was obvious he was just being nice, but I took my loss and moved on. It was uncharacteristically shortsighted on my part. Had I not been so flattered with any little human interaction, I would've clearly seen that he talks with nearly everyone in the office. Even the grumpy ones let their guard down around him.

"Or have I seen that mug, Isabelle Claire Dunham?" His light flirting does cause me to snort every time. He prefers his nickname, so when I call him his actual name, he comes back at me tenfold with my full birth name. He has even included ridiculous additions like miss, your highness, or a fictional lineage like saying "Isabelle Claire Dunham the Fourth." Today, I snorted some coffee into my nose. Great. He's charming, I'll give him that.

He smiles. This is a victory for him.

"Why were you not at the company picnic this weekend?" he inquires.

"That was this last weekend?" I genuinely forgot and inadvertently broke the promise that I made to myself that I would attend. A goal to get myself out there more. Even if it was some stupid company picnic.

"Well, yeah. They reminded us at the end of our shifts on Friday," he continues. Last Friday, right, the one day I had a dentist appointment and had to duck out early. I didn't even have cavities, which normally is a good thing, but now it feels like a waste of time and a missed opportunity to get myself out there. Ugh.

"Was it fun?" I try to hide my disappointment but fail to do so. Even Santi senses this, and whatever juicy story he was about to tell me quickly changes.

"No, of course not." Santi waves his hand dismissively. "You know how lame it is watching Tyreke try to rally up the employees." Tyreke's our boss. He means well but tries too hard to get approval from everyone. The popular kids never change.

Jessica Cho bulldozes into the room, and her face lights up when she sees Santi. She mimics Tyreke's voice like a natural impressionist: "This is how we do the three-legged race." Jessica tilts sideways in an obvious reenactment of an event over the weekend. Santi loses his shit and gasps for air. The two lean on each other for support, laughing.

I don't want to make things awkward, avoiding confrontation as I always do, so I exit the room silently and set up my work station. When I look up from my desk and through the window in my door, I see Jessica still leaning on Santi for support. She has a boyfriend who's obviously way hotter than Santi, but most women would choose Santiago over whoever they are dating. He's not the most attractive with his goofy 'fro and obscure band

T-shirts, but he truly excels at making you feel like you're the only person that matters in the world.

To be seen. Something I'd like. Who wouldn't want that? Maybe one day I can talk to him like a normal human being.

Two hours into my shift, I'm already focused. I don't hear the footsteps approaching or the light knocking on my door. I look up and am startled to see Tyreke looking at me with an awkward smile.

"Sorry to interrupt.". I compose myself and put on my best fake smile, which I had to perfect in the mirror.

"You're not interrupting anything too important. What's up?"

Moments later we're in his office, which under normal circumstances is never a bad thing for me. I've been told in recent meetings that I meet numbers better than any other employee and, if anything, should have renegotiated my salary numerous times. There have also been rare instances where other employees have not been getting along, and I've been sent in as a "neutral" third party, but I had to play dumb and act like I knew nothing. It's best to stay out of the drama as much as possible to maintain that reputation.

The strangest thing is that his computer is tilted outward so both of us can look at it. When the blinds are shut, this gesture usually sends the alarms to the office that someone is in trouble. The problem is that his blinds don't necessarily hide everything like he thinks they do. Gossip usually spreads within seconds.

This time, however, he double-checks the blinds and actually does close the room completely. I begin to worry.

"Isabelle—where would we be without you? How many years have you been with the company now? Seven?" His light tone seems disarming enough, but I sense another emotion as well.

"Eleven," I reply. Most people don't know this, but I'm actually the highest tenured in the short life of this company—minus the shareholders, of course.

"Eleven! Holy smokes. I should be working for you at thit point, amiright?" His tone has shifted, and I do know that emotion after all . . . it's nervousness. Because I don't know how to respond to this, I just sit there with a blank face, and the uneasy silence fills the room. I am genuinely not trying to be intimidating, but I am too much of a freak to know what else to do.

Tyreke composes himself the best he can and starts typing on the computer for both of us to see. He begins talking rapidly as he walks us through what he is visually showing us on the screen. "In your recent report, you noticed a shipping error with our last products," he laughs nervously but lightly nudges me on the shoulder, "which is great of you! That's not even your department."

I remember this report. It did affect me, because with the improper funds in the shipping area, it directly affected where I was pulling my numbers from, and I forwarded it to the manufacturers, thinking it was a typo on their part.

"Nothing special on my part. It just helped me reach my goals." I shrug my shoulders.

"Yeah, and I get that. I really do. But I deleted that email you sent to Pyrochonics and was able to free up space where you could get your product again." He's pointing with his mouse at the itemized documents. Maybe that coffee wasn't that strong this morning, but I'm finally coming around to what all of this is about. I'm not in trouble. He is.

Tyreke keeps mumbling on, which only digs him further into the hole. I don't know why he's so nervous around me. It's not like I have any authority around here. "Listen, your report goes back to the previous three years, and obviously it is a problem to be missing funds from there, but we have an ample amount of stock over in the Trenton lot. There's really no need to look into this further."

This time around, my silence is on purpose since I have to assess the situation and convey myself as clearly as possible. He's holding his breath, awaiting my response.

"The way I see it, Tyreke,"—just like Santiago, Tyreke insists on a first-name basis for the office space; he believes it creates less of a boss-employee dynamic—"I accidentally stumbled in the wrong department and will not look into this further."

The moment of silence seems to last forever. He exhales rather loudly.

"That's good, Isabella, very good." There he goes forgetting my name again. He continues, "Your performance review is coming up, and I'm a little curious about what competing companies might offer for someone with expertise like yours?"

Nope. Uh-uh. I'm not getting entangled in this further than I already have. I'm definitely the type to avoid drama at all costs, but now I'm starting to realize even if shit goes down . . . I'm still a witness to some sort of a paper trail. He waits for my response.

"Really, Tyreke, it's nothing. My standard three percent annual increase I always get is more than generous enough."

Tyreke is in deep thought. He is going back and forth in his head on whether or not I'm playing hardball. Which I'm definitely not, but now I'm beginning to appreciate those who would take advantage of this unique situation and attempt to squeeze something out of him. Finally, he responds.

"Very well, Isabelle, I think we're done here." Oh, *now* he gets my name right. Well, now I'm attempting to get out of there so I don't have to be there longer than I need to.

I almost reached the door.

"Isabelle." I turn to face him, and I look from the floor to his eyes. They're grateful. "I appreciate you. Really."

"It's nothing, really." I scurry out of his office, and, no surprise, no one is paying attention. In fact, Santiago has half the office hunched around his monitor as they all look at a viral video and burst out laughing as the punchline is delivered.

I am a ghost. And although I consider it a curse, right now it's a blessing—and, for once, I'm grateful to be on nobody's radar at all.

CHAPTER TWO

Traffic is light when I get off, which is normal because I tend to finish my workload about three hours earlier than any other employee, and, therefore, I have the luxury to get out before rush hour. Today, Tyreke must be loving it because even though our conversation had "an understanding," he still seemed a bit on edge when we passed one another in the office a couple of times earlier today. This could've just been my perception too. I live rent free inside my own head and often don't know what to do after confrontations. The few I've had in life.

My ex-boyfriend used to point out how odd it was that I would drive without listening to anything—the ambiance of the bustling streets around me versus modern music, podcasts, or even NPR. There's usually a serenity to just letting the world reveal itself around you, but I couldn't seem to shake off the meeting I had with Tyreke; today I try to get my mind off of everything and open a music app on my phone at the next traffic light.

It doesn't take a rocket scientist to open a preinstalled music app. I don't know what modern music sounds like even though Tricia sometimes plays her computer's music a bit too loud. I often walk past her

27

cubicle, which typically features artists who are invited to perform in the Super Bowl halftime shows. I recognize one of their names and allow the music to fill the car.

The music bleeds into the seats, and I attempt to focus on the lyrics. I'm not a poet by any means, but it really does surprise me that many people call this art. So, singing about a one-night stand is really something most consumers eat up? And if I'm getting the lyrics correct, it sounds like she's a homewrecker on top of it? Classy.

A couple more songs play, and they serve their purpose of distracting me from my off day. But then the ads come on. I guess this was bound to happen. I don't ever use this app in my car and should've expected some sort of annoying advertisement. The first one is for laundry detergent, but the next one is off. Like really off.

There's light breathing, almost as if it isn't playing from my speakers but rather that there's someone in the car with me. A man speaks in a soothing voice, asking if I have met the most important person in my life. I'll hand it to whoever edited this ad: it doesn't sound like a fake voice actor. It sounds like someone who's having a genuine conversation with you.

"Your life is your most precious asset, but how have you been living this long without meeting the most important person in your life?" Great, I have a feeling now that this is going to be an ad for a dating service. I'm not interested in seeing more unsolicited dick pics or meeting someone blander than myself, but for some reason this man's silky voice sounds different. "The most important person you'll ever meet in your life is not a romantic partner, your parents, or God . . . it's yourself." How long is this ad? And why am I so drawn to it? "I'm here to help you unlock the real you. To really embrace the person you were meant to be—"

HONK!

I look up and notice that not only have I missed my exit, I've nearly collided with oncoming traffic. I swerve at the last second and realign into my own lane. A couple of middle fingers fly out of people's windows, and there is added road rage to those around me, but everyone is still in one piece.

"Dammit," I swear only to myself, but I turn back to the radio. The ad is long over and the next generic pop songs continue to play as if the ad was never even there. The worst of it is this: I didn't just miss my exit but am nearly five miles away from where I normally get off. Fan-fucking-tastic, Isabelle.

My father is waiting outside. Another anomaly. His respirator and oxygen tank is with him, and his back stiffens as he sees me pull into the driveway. It's odd to not see him in the living room rewatching the glory years of the Spurs from the early 2000s.

29

I attempt to act casually as I wave to him while I pull in. I really need to watch more sitcoms just to get a better grip of how people are in real life. I have to be on the autistic spectrum or something on top of being dyslexic, because no one goes through life as awkwardly as I do without something being wrong with them.

I'm not even halfway out of my car when my father hollers to me, "You're late."

"Good to see you too, Dad." My dad chews this over and nods to himself.

"Got a little worried is all." I've lived with him long enough to know that this is a lie. But I'm willing to overlook it. My dad is not as clever as he thinks he is, but at least he's not an abusive asshole. Just one of those self-centered ones. Tanner Dunham has always cared about one person: Tanner Dunham.

"What do you want, Dad," is what I want to say because at least it cuts to the point, but the prolonged conversation is something that will help me get back into my rhythm of normalcy. Instead I play along with the caring father act. "That's nice of you, Dad. Traffic was just off today. I think there was an accident off the interstate."

My father nods, clearly not paying attention, and feeling he's far enough off the hook. "Hey, Izzy." Oh man, he must really want something. He hasn't called me Izzy since I was a teenager and he pawned off my cello. "I was thinking we could go to that restaurant tonight. What was it? Lucky's?"

Between the servers in skimpy clothing and the overcooked bar food, I couldn't think of a worse place to eat. It'd be one thing if I could go there and my dad could act like a normal human being, but the secondhand embarrassment of watching him act like he's thirty years younger and more attractive than he is as he does his habitual train wreck performance of flirting kills me. Of course they humor him every time we go, though. You just can't turn away a paying customer who's willing to overtip.

"Dad," I protest, "I think we still have leftover pizza from Vinney's that we should get through first." I have to add my most gentle voice that I managed to steal from Mom before she passed. It's firm but still reasonable.

"I'm getting to it. I was actually going to eat it tomorrow while you were at work." He studies my body language and can see that I'm not going to budge.

"Well then. In that case, this gives me an excuse to make that pasta before the sauce expires—"

"Such a fucking brat! Why can't you just take me to Lucky's?" he snaps abruptly.

My jaw drops. Never in my thirty-five years have I heard him swear at me. Even when he was first going through his twelve-step program. Moments seem to pass,

31

but neither of us says anything. I cannot believe I have to be the one to break the silence.

"Dad. It's been a tough day and—"

"You're right, sweetie." He's on the losing side and changes tactics as quickly as he can. "Sweet T, I apologize. I've been cooped up all day, and there's only so many Popovich wins I can watch. We both know I live a pretty pathetic life. Come on, Izzy. Don't worry about making any food for your old man. I can cover us both and we can even swing by and get ice cream from that shop you like."

That ice cream shop that's been closed for five years, but like Dad would notice a detail like that. I sigh heavily because I don't want him sulking the rest of the week over something like this. Sometimes when picking battles, it's better to just cut your losses for a short amount of time than have to deal with the repercussions in the long run.

"Let me shower first," I grumble, but Dad chooses to ignore my sourpuss mood and practically backflips on the front patio.

"You're the best daughter a father could ask for. You really are." I turn my head so he doesn't see me roll my eyes.

I sift through the mail when I get in and notice by Dad's recliner there's a book. Did Eddie, his military buddy from their time in Iraq, leave it? I guess that's honestly more laughable than Dad reading. As dumb as my father can be, Eddie is the dullest crayon in the box.

I get closer to the book and see the page's cover, which is a question mark with a silhouette of the words "Your True Colors." Of course, even when reading the title, it reads to me as "Color Yours Truly." The mental gymnastics I have done in my head grammatically correcting what would sound right can be maddening, but with small titles like this I can handle it. "Your True Colors" with a question mark. What an odd title for a book, and what's my dad doing with it?

This would be the perfect opportunity to open up some dialogue with my father and have a normal conversation while I drive us to Lucky's, but I'd rather listen to home-wrecking pop stars than have to engage with my dad more than I need to. Lucky's does have alcohol, so thank God for that.

CHAPTER THREE

It's a Monday night, so I suppose I should've guessed that it would be slower than usual, but I'm actually saddened there's not more of a crowd. Fewer customers means these poor women have to spend more time with my dad, and hold the Viagra, doctor, because my old man is already naturally revved up. His eyes wander, and I do my best impression of not noticing.

The server has already brought my third drink, and I tell myself to slow it down because Lord knows my dad's not going to say anything. If Mom were still alive, she'd have my back, but then again, if Mom were alive, we wouldn't be at Lucky's to begin with. My Dad's always had wandering eyes but never overstepped his boundaries. Especially since she was the breadwinner in the relationship. Our house, cars, and pretty much anything of value in our lives was thanks to Mom's work as a doctor.

Of course Dad would always tell his friends and family from his side that she was a registered nurse. Like having a wife that is a doctor would somehow emasculate him. But you know he would never turn down her paychecks that came in, and with her on call all the time, he also didn't mind how little time she spent in the house.

34

She was definitely a stronger woman than I would've been. Despite only having one kid together, my father was notorious for blowing through a lot of her money as if she had to support a family of five. He was always enamored with stupid investments and gambling. Had he been born fifteen years later he would've easily been a cryptobro who would be the only shareholder in companies that were going nowhere.

I often wonder if I'm low maintenance because I enjoy living a relatively minimalist life or because subconsciously I was unwilling to put more of a burden on Mom's life. She already was taking care of this man-child, and I will give her some credit: when I turned sixteen, we opened a checking account together that he was completely unaware of. It's not a gold mine, but with the correct kind of investing, many would wonder why I even work at all.

"Boyfriend?! That's ridiculous! How has this loser you're with not put a ring on your finger yet? I know that would be my top priority." Mercedes (obviously not her real name) glances over at me, and she can feel me wanting to disappear into the booth.

"You think I would say yes to him so easily? I got to make him work for it." She winks at my father, which that gesture in itself gives me goosebumps. You know, maybe I should keep the drinks coming because I'm pretty sure I'm about to vomit. "Honey, are you okay on that margarita?"

No. It's watered down. I'm pretty sure you guys put the shit tequila in there. The fries were undercooked this time around, and my dad is making a complete ass of himself is screaming in my head, but of course I smile politely and say, "It's fine, but I should probably switch over to a Diet Coke after this."

"Diet Coke? What a joke! My daughter can't gain weight because she never treats herself. She's been like this since she was ten. Don't know where she gets it from," my dad laughs and, not so subtly, places his hand on her arm and lets it linger.

"Hey, there's no shame in ordering a Diet Coke! What do you think I drink all shift?" Mercedes smiles at me and politely moves my dad's hand off of her.

Well, since I didn't successfully vanish into thin air after that embarrassing chain of events, I have decided to excuse myself to the bathroom. Smart move, too, because I have been so distracted today that I have to pee like I'm holding in Niagara Falls. While I'm on the toilet, I hear two women walk in. One of them is clearly our waitress, minus the fake voice she coos to my father.

"That's brutal. The creep hasn't been around for a while. I was kind of hoping he'd croaked by now. Don't worry—I'll hold up my end of the bargain and clean the bathrooms tonight," the other server says, and I watch

36

through the slit between the door and the stall as she puts
on a fresh layer of makeup.

"Yeah, I feel bad for his daughter. She has to live
with the guy," Mercedes confides.

"Oh my God—she still lives with him?! I would've
tailed it out of that house on my seventeenth birthday. He
would've been in the rearview mirror and I would've been
halfway across the country." The other waitress almost
gets me to laugh out loud, but I stop myself. I don't want
anyone to know I'm here.

"Yeah, the worst part about Mr. Handsy is that he
acts like he's helping *her* out in their living situation, but
it's obvious that she's making sure he doesn't break a hip
or something."

"Sad. Anyway, have you had a chance to check out
that book that Josh lent me?" the other waitress asks.

"You and my boyfriend are really starting this
book club, huh?" Mercedes laughs. "Nerds. Both of you."

"No, no, no, it's not like that. I swear it'll change
your life. It had me reevaluate all of my life decisions.
Even working here! Which is why I put my two weeks in
today." She beams.

"You didn't?!" Mercedes gasps. "You fuckin' slut.
You can't leave me! What, are you and Josh going to go
join a cult or something?"

"No way." her voice lowers, and it's actually hard
for me to make out what she's saying. I find myself

inadvertently leaning forward to catch a conversation I'm not even a part of. "Remember years back when I hooked up with Coach Anderson's fiancée?"

"Of course, ho. I would've done it had you not beat me to it." Both of these girls are far more scandalous than I would ever be . . . even if I were models like them.

"Well, I was only sixteen at the time and I filmed us. I'm going to get a paycheck out of this. He's obviously got money. Might as well get paid for my 'pain and suffering.'" If Mercedes, or whatever her real name is, didn't gasp at the same time I did, they would've definitely heard me.

There's silence before the first waitress cackles at her reaction. She then excuses herself and tells her that she'll see her out there.

I don't know if she was serious or if this was their sense of humor, but something tells me that she wasn't joking because Mercedes even takes a moment to compose herself. When she looks up at the mirror and notices my feet under the stall, she turns around and talks directly to me through the door.

"Make sure your dad tips better this time around."

CHAPTER FOUR

The rest of the week at work is relatively normal. I guess I have to use that term loosely, because how often can someone say they've caught their boss stealing from their company and watched their nonreading dad completely engrossed in a book? While those events alone would've made for a *Twilight Zone* episode, it's actually been nice having him buried in a book for the past few days. He hasn't had SportsCenter on and actually waves me off when I offer to either cook or heat up those pizza slices. I'm not complaining. I would much rather knit in silence.

I look up from my work computer and see Trey and Jackie talking by her desk. She's laughing at whatever dumb joke he's said, but what's more surprising is that he has his arm around her waist and dangerously close to her ass. I can't say that I'm surprised that his marriage is falling to shambles or even that she would be the rebound, but doing all of this so blatantly at work surprises me.

When my gaze wanders from his hand, I look up at him and we lock eyes. I feel like a deer caught in headlights and put my head down. I go back to crunching numbers, but when I look up again I nearly choke on my gum as Trey begins to approach my office. This is just great. Why do I keep finding myself in these situations?

He opens the door to my office and gently knocks on the outside. It sort of defeats the purpose if you've already come in, right?

"Bella," he addresses me with a nickname I've always hated but have never told anyone to stop using, "how's it going?"

I shrug my shoulders and evade his stare as much as possible as I begin retyping the same numbers into my docket over and over, just so it gives off the illusion that I'm busier than I am. Either he doesn't take the hint or doesn't care. He closes the door behind him, sits across from my desk, and pulls up a chair that has collected so much dust that I think he'll have to go across the street to the cleaners after he sits down in it.

"Jackie and I—" he begins.

"I don't care and won't say anything, if that's what you're wondering. It's none of my business, and it's not like I have anyone to tell anyway." Trey is taken aback at my quick response, but after he regains composure, he can't help but laugh. An actual genuine laugh too.

"You know . . . that's the most words I think I have ever heard you speak in the whole five years I have worked here." He chuckles and shakes his head. "Good on you for being a real one, though. I appreciate that. Do you want to hear something funny?"

Not really. I am beyond my comfort zone right now and want nothing more than for him to just leave my office and let me be. But of course I don't speak up and look up to meet his eyes.

"I was prepared to come in here and try to gaslight you into thinking you saw something that you didn't, but that's not the kind of advice I've been given recently. If anything, why would I want to hide the real me?" Even though he's talking to me, I can tell that he's more talking to himself at this point. "You know, we spend days putting on these masks to everyone: our coworkers, our personal trainers, even our families."

Why is he still here? I'm not that interesting and I don't care who Trey fucks and what he does at the office. I just want to go back to my job and maybe watch some stupid cat videos. It's a huge disadvantage about being an introvert, though—people misconstrue silence as listening. You'd be surprised how many people just want to hear themselves talk and automatically take a liking to you because you hear whatever it is they have to ramble about.

"But it's not our real selves, is it?" He's been talking so much that I haven't realized how close he's gotten to me, and I am frozen in terror.

Now don't get me wrong . . . a lot of people wouldn't kick Trey Brunson out of bed. He's athletic for his thirties, soft mocha skin, and has a heck of a taste in fashion, but anyone I don't know who gets this close into

41

my personal space instantly loses points. He places both of his hands on my shoulders. Oh no—is he going to kiss me?! He's truly lost it.

"You should borrow my book." His face lights up as he looks down at me.

"What?" The word stumbles out of my mouth, and before I can ask him to elaborate, he takes his hands off my shoulders and starts pacing my room like he's discovered the greatest revelation.

"Of course! How can I be so closed-minded? Bella, you would love this book!" Okay so he doesn't want to make a pass at me.

"I hate that name," I mutter under my breath, thinking he doesn't hear me, but he does.

"You don't like being called Bella?" He mulls this over in his mind and a smile creeps onto his face. "Of course you don't! And that's what this book is all about! God, this must be a sign."

"The book is about me not wanting to be called by a common nickname?" He shakes his head and leaves my office with no further words. Okay, yeah, this week has been batshit crazy. I'm about to close the door to my office when he comes back in with a book in his hand. Not just any book. A copy I've seen in my own house. He thrusts it at me.

"Bella—er, I mean, Isabelle—you need this! If you don't like people calling you that, this book invites you to

tell me and the rest of the world 'to hell with that name.'"
He laughs which, oddly enough, is contagious and gets me
to join in on the laughter.

The laughter dies and the two of us look at one
another in silence.

"Trey. This is really nice of you, but—" I begin.

"Oh no, don't worry about it. My wife has a copy
and I'm just going to take hers tonight. She can fight for
the house and kids, but she's not getting the book." He
laughs again, but this time alone.

"No, you don't understand. I am dyslexic." Trey
tilts his head like I just told him I was from another planet.
I continue before he speaks again, "And my father has a
copy."

"That's not good." His energy has dissipated, and
he genuinely seems upset that I can't read his copy.
"Maybe the author has it on Audible or there's an audio
version of it. Oh! What about having your dad read it to
you after he's done?"

I could not think of a worse idea in my entire life,
but he seems oddly fixated on me checking this book out,
so I humor him. "You know, I would like that. It could
probably give us a chance to connect better."

You'd think I just told him he won the lottery
because he balls up his fist and holds it out to me. What
am I supposed to do here? Bump it? I awkwardly ball up
my fist and bump his.

"Your life is about to change, Isabella, and I am beyond happy for you." Trey leaves my office whistling but doesn't get far. He rushes back in and takes back his book out of my hands. "Sorry, but I'm still only halfway through it."

It doesn't bother me. It's his book after all.

Thankfully, the rest of the day is pretty uneventful. Even Tyreke seems to be less anxious when passing me in the hall. I am on the highway listening to the light hum of my engine when I look up at a digital billboard. I can't really decipher the words, but when it flashes to the book, I recognize it right away. Okay. Seriously, what the hell is up with this self-help book? I'm still old enough to remember when *The Secret* gained traction, but it was nowhere near the phenomenon that this book has been.

I begin wondering if it's the author. Maybe he or she is already rich and famous. People love copying what famous people do. Or I'm sure another rational explanation is that the author is from the area. I don't watch the news much, but I know how much communities love seeing their locals become celebrities. There has to be some sort of allure to this whole shtick.

I don't mean to be a cynic, but I have watched enough self-help seminars and did listen to the audiobook of *The Secret* to know that the overall message is as simple as what Nike's slogan is: Just Do It. If that's the overall essence of the book, then I can be a millionaire by just going around telling everyone those three words.

Even as I listen to myself, I can't help but notice how jaded I've become over the years. I do tend to judge others quickly and to be more pessimistic about things when people ask for my opinion. I used to not be like this. At least not until my best friend passed away.

And, sure, I'm not embarrassed to say that person was my own mother. She was the smartest, wittiest person I've ever known. She even made Dad more bearable than he actually is. I wouldn't say the three of us were a perfect family, but at least she made me proud of where I came from and didn't lecture me like my teachers did when I told her that I wanted to study finance.

"Every employer needs someone to look at the books. There's no shame in that, Sweet T." Mom claims she always knew what the T stood for, but I think she just made it up. It was an odd nickname, but almost like an inside joke between the two of us. I'm not so obsessed with going through life where I would think, "What would Mom do?" but I do find myself frequently asking myself how she'd react in a similar situation.

The rest of the shift was pretty uneventful, and I was excited to go home when all of my work was done— even more eager than the previous days, which is saying something.

The traffic light is red and, as I stop, I close my eyes to think about what Mom would do in this situation. It comes to me when I open them, before the vehicles behind me get impatient, and continue to drive. It does put me way far out of my comfort zone, but the answer seems so obvious: I have to read the book.

That's what Mom would do. She could be as skeptical and logical as she wanted, but she would never put something down without at least trying it. I know what you're thinking—how can someone who cannot read get through a book? The last book I read was in my second year of junior high: *Lord of the Flies*. It felt like torture and took forever, but every day I would rearrange the words in my head until it made sense. It didn't hurt that I actually cared about Piggy too. Kids can be so cruel, and the ending was depressing, but it was a mirror of the true nature of not just children, but mankind.

I was able to enjoy this literature even if it was painstakingly hard to get through it. After reading it I even had a fun discussion with Mom about what the author meant through his subtexts and what I would do if I were one of the boys who was stranded on the island.

Most people would like to think the world is just one big fairy tale, but I appreciate authors who tell it how it is: a cruel and relentless place.

My dad is not reading, which is a first for the week. It alarms me that I don't see him at all. I call his name throughout the house. A small panic starts to rise in me, and I take out my phone and dial nine and one before I look outside to see the bench press bar going up and down. Dad's working out?

I step outside and notice my dad huffing and puffing as he uses the bench press. "Easy there, Jack Lalanne," I holler to my dad after he finishes his reps.

"Har har, very funny, Sweet T." My heart flutters a bit. I secretly love being called that because it does remind me of a time when Mom was still alive. "Hey, can you be a dear and fetch me a lemonade?"

"Not to be a Debbie Downer, but are you sure you want me to get one? You're putting in all that work to gain that weight back in one drink." For a second I think my negative tone will burst his bubble, but to my surprise he only smiles and sits up.

"That's where you're wrong, Izzy. I have been working out all day. I don't want to watch the Spurs any more—" he begins. This statement alone gets a reaction out of me.

"No Spurs? Who are you and what have you done with my dad?" I laugh.

"I mean it, dear. I'm done wallowing in my own pity." He grunts as he finishes his last set. He nods over to his oxygen tank. Jesus, it's across the yard and practically baking in the sun.

"Dad, those aren't cheap." I turn to go pick it up, but to my surprise, he has nimbly walked over to me and gently grabs my wrist. I jump.

"I don't think I'll be needing that too much anymore." My father's words are crazy, but as I look deep into his eyes, I only see clarity. "It's been holding me back for too long, and before long I'm going to go back to work."

I try to stifle a laugh, but I cannot suppress it and it sort of slips out. I worry that I'm going to dampen my father's sudden upbeat mood. He doesn't flinch, though. In fact, he has one of those smug expressions. I don't know what's worse: my dad who was misogynistic yet leaning on me for support, or this delusional man who is on the wrong side of sixty but all of a sudden is acting like he's as healthy as a horse and has his whole life in front of him.

"I'd probably laugh at myself too," he continues as if reading my thoughts. "But I forgive you and even got you something while you were at work."

My father leads me to the spare bedroom where there's a tape recorder on the bed. I didn't even know they still made these. I think the last time I saw this one was when I was trying to play back my cello sessions in junior high. My dad's face is ecstatic as he motions for me to sit down in the room. The room itself used to be everyone's office space until Mom passed and my father and I thought it'd be a better idea to convert it into a bedroom.

Some of the furniture was too nice to get rid of, including the office chair that reclines back and even has a massage feature. I may or may not have passed out in this room in my early college years when I was studying for finals. I sit down in the chair and watch as my dad hits rewind on the tape recorder. It still has those buzzing sounds you can hear when a device is being sifted through. I begin to wonder if we could get any value out of this relic.

"You have gone far too long in this world living a lie." Dad starts the recording, and I hear his voice coming through the tape recorder. There's some static and my father was never the best at reading me bedtime stories, but otherwise his voice is crystal clear. Dad hits pause and looks up at me.

"Babe, this is going to change your life." He seems proud of himself and suddenly his words start gushing out. "I thought about how you've been miserable for a while now."

"I never said I was miserable!" I begin to protest.

"Izzy. You are going to be forty in five years and you live with your old man. You don't have any friends, and the last guy you went on a date with was that awkward neighbor from India." Wow. There's a lot to unpack there. From the fact that I have been taking care of this old man for the past ten years to the fact that Omar's family was from Pakistan. And to top things off, fuck you, Dad. I didn't come here looking for a roast. My father instantly reads all of this on my face.

I never have been much of a poker player.

"Izzy, I'm not trying to pick on you . . . I'm trying to help you."

"Right." I try not to sob, but my voice cracks as I retort, "Could've fooled me."

My dad has lost a bit of his momentum as he stops his pitch and collects his thoughts. He chooses his next words carefully. It's not unlike when he and Mom were in a fight and he already knew he was in a losing position. "I only meant to say that I feel like you have been missing something in your life. I didn't realize how much of a hole I myself had until I read this book."

"*Your True Colors*." I say the title and his eyes focus. His eyes meet mine, and there is a glimmer of hope in them.

"You know it?" he eagerly asks.

"Dad, everyone cannot seem to stop talking about it. Of course I know it." I shake my head.

"Trust me, I thought it was bullshit too. I mean, c'mon, some pansy-ass book is going to tell me how to live my life? Give me a fuckin' break." For the first time today, I am listening to my real dad speak and not this book fanatic. "But I watched this recent interview with Tim Duncan—"

Oh great. I don't know how your sports knowledge is, but Tim Duncan was a basketball player who won the Spurs five championships back in the early 2000s. He wasn't as flashy as Kobe, Michael Jordan, or even Lebron, but he bought into a system that made him become one of the all-time greats and, more importantly, brought my father joy.

And although it was great getting ice cream whenever they won and he performed his best fatherly duties when he was riding high off of a Spurs win, when the dust settled he became too arrogant and thought he knew the most about basketball. So much so that he would gamble on a lot of games, which at first was great because it seemed like he knew what he was doing. But as with every addicted gambler, he never knew when to walk away until it was too late.

I thank God my mom opened that bank account in our names, and when Dad became incapable of working, I was relieved he signed over the house in my name before the debt collectors could even attach my name to the horrible messes he made. The last thing I want to hear about is a basketball star and whatever influence he's had on my old man.

"He's got that new show on HBO about his workshop. You know, the one where he restores all these classic cars? They had this episode where he had a competition with some of the best car restorers in the world and guess what? He smoked them all! A part of the credit he said was from some book he picked up through a friend." Great. His eyes are glimmering like when the Spurs won those damn championships. You think he had those same eyes when I walked at my college graduation?

"So, if I start listening to this book, I can become the best car restorer west of the Mississippi?" I try not to patronize my dad, I really don't mean to, but he's drunk so much of the Kool-Aid that it sort of just slips out.

"Isabelle," he seethes, obviously losing patience, "that book helps us all unlock the best versions of ourselves, and I know you're smart enough to know that's what I'm telling you."

I can feel his eyes bore into me, and I know that I don't really have a choice but to listen to this damn thing. Besides, Trey would also be enamored that I joined the book club. I suppose there's no harm in giving it a listen.

CHAPTER FIVE

I'm only thirty minutes into it and I want to rip off my ears. Is there something that I'm obviously missing? I can't imagine how this self-help book has sold so many copies and has duped my dad and Trey. Then again, they aren't the sharpest tools in the shed. Maybe that's where it gets its traction—with all of the simpleminded folks.

I have to hit pause on the tape recorder as I look for more answers. I pull out my phone and talk into the search engine: "Siri, give me an audio sample of the book *Your True Colors.*"

"I'm sorry," Siri says, "there are currently no audiobooks or samples of *Your True Colors* by Rex Sutter." That's odd. Wouldn't he want to corner the market with as much publicity as possible? Maybe it's too new for that. "Would you like me to order you a copy of *Your True—*"

"Siri, what year was *Your True Colors* released?"

"*Your True Colors* by Rex Sutter was released in June of 2021." Nearly five years since its release and it still doesn't have an audio version. Talk about an untapped market. I put down my phone and turn on our desktop computer. What's nice about this computer setup is that it still has my microphone attached and is user-friendly for people with dyslexia. I turn over the mic to make sure the batteries still work and, thankfully enough, we're back in business.

I search who Rex Sutter is. Images are limited, and his background is straight-up weird. He is a Canadian from a remote village. Except "village" is an overstatement. They lost their title by not having enough of a population, and it is more commonly referred to as a commune. I think most people just assumed he was from a town called LaScie, which isn't even that much bigger, in Newfoundland. But thanks to Google reverse images, I notice that the vast majority of photos taken of him were in the even smaller village known as Black Wolf Creek.

How ironic is that? He's got the world as his oyster yet may not even have had internet or plumbing until his teenage years. Okay, there I go being judgmental again. Maybe his book can save me from myself, but I am not listening to my dad speak for God only knows how many hours. So this guy grew up on a farm with no one around. Maybe that was the real secret in life and where the rest of us have failed so badly. He didn't have to put up with other people's bullshit so he had enough time and space to gather his thoughts.

He had an odd upbringing, and even more of a mystery surrounds what was happening during his formative years. I thought I was a ghost, but this guy is pretty good at keeping a low profile. Well, outside of having a best-selling book, this guy has no Instagram or LinkedIn. Even older social media platforms like X and Facebook have only fan-made accounts. Like every millennial, I have to check out what the hermits on the internet are saying on Reddit.

There are threads upon threads of people worshipping this guy's work. Of course there are a few haters here and there, but man, are they outnumbered by his worshippers. A lot of comments like, "You just didn't get it," or "If your too dumb to understand, that's okay, man." And of course I'm cringing at the people who call others dumb but still cannot tell the difference between "your" and "you're."

Reddit is one of the most toxic places on the internet, but I actually praise it for being diverse in its hate. There are usually groups or subgroups dedicated to disliking a product as much as there are ones raving about it. You could get your hate from any form of media: Harry Potter, Marvel, Disney—you name it, but for some reason there's not much bad talk about *Your True Colors*.

What kind of rabbit hole am I plunging into? I came here to see where I could get an audio version of this book and am now playing rookie detective on a famous author while I delve into online communities to find more people who hate this book.

But do I? Do I honestly hate it? How can I dislike something that I haven't even read completely yet? Jesus, I haven't even gotten through a chapter of this book and I already see it shaping me. Looking at myself inwardly. I don't want to be so cynical and assume the worst, but at the same time you've gotta admit that it's fishy. I'm not saying my dad turned into Saint Peter, but he's definitely been more pleasant these last couple of days than the previous ten years. And if Trey had not read that book, I think our longest conversation would have been about the weather.

I'm scrolling through the comments, completely disconnected and unaware I'm looking for key words, until I see the word "sicudie," which I can instantly rearrange into "suicide." I pull up the comment, highlight the paragraph, and let the computer speak to me.

"You guys are reading the gospel of the devil and I'm not even a religious man. Your stupid book killed my brother." The words send a chill down my spine. "He started reading it and he was normally a soft-spoken guy. He would always take the high road and never really confronted anyone. His easygoing personality got him a great career and a nice life."

I highlight the next paragraph and let the story continue. "He starts reading it and talking all this shit to our mom, saying how she only married my dad for his money, then he turns his attention onto me and basically says that outside of football, I would be nothing. That I'd be lucky to get a job as a greeter at a Walmart. I'm not saying I'm the smartest guy, but I worked hard to get my degree because of my sports scholarship. He stormed out of our family dinner, and at the time, we were too pissed off to check in on him.

"Fast-forward to two months later, and I find out that he broke into his boss's house and assaulted the man's wife. He graped her." My heart sinks when I hear this because I know the user couldn't type the actual word. "Well, lucky little brother found out the hard way what gun owners do when you break into their house to fuck around and find out.

"I cry to you guys as I type this and I know a lot of you are just going to call this post 'fake' or that I'm starving for attention, but that book changed him. He wasn't like that, and I can promise you that those were *not* his true colors.

"After his death, my parents couldn't bear to go through his things, so me and my wife went through his belongings. That stupid goddamn book. I know in my heart that that was the root of this all. He had multiple copies, and I could see that he would circle key words and highlight certain areas.

"His password for his computer hasn't changed since high school so I was able to pull up his own 'writings.' It was more of a manifesto than anything else and had this crazy talk about taking revenge on people who have wronged him. Within these pages he had vivid insights and often had internal battles when he thought about me. He loved me and would always be grateful for the times I stood up for him in our youth, but apparently he had huge crushes on some of the women I would hook up with."

My eyes dart to the comments below, and I can't help but see the Rex supporters absolutely rail this guy. "It sounds like your brother was a psychopath. He could've read James Patterson books and sympathized with the killers. Stop trying to make a connection between the two."

Another comment: "So the book unlocked what he truly was: a bad human being. Sometimes the mirror is hard to look at."

One of the top comments got the original poster to respond. "Even if this story is true, you can't even link YTC to this nutcase."

The original poster responded with, "That's where you're wrong! I found exact verbiage used in our guy's precious manual that was in my brother's manifesto. Had my brother never picked up that book, he'd still be alive. You all are sick ducks." You get used to seeing language edited so it won't be taken down.

I look up at the clock and notice that it's almost two in the morning. Jesus. How long have I been online? I still have work tomorrow. I couldn't tell you why, but I screenshot the original user's name and turn off the computer.

I get dressed in my pajamas and go to the kitchen to get a glass of water before going to bed. My dad's lights are off, and I can hear him gently snore. The house is silent, and I pour a glass while deep in thought. When I make my way back into my room, I look down at the table where my dad's copy of *Your True Colors* sits. I pick it up and throw it in the trash.

CHAPTER SIX

Have you ever been so consumed with your thoughts that you are on autopilot? You don't remember choosing your clothes for work? You can't say how long you took in the shower or whether you brushed your teeth or not. You drive to work and are so lost in your thoughts that you don't realize it's Saturday until you see an empty parking lot. A more aware version of me would've easily turned back around when I noticed the lack of traffic in the morning, but obviously, I'm not here mentally.

I groan and let my head fall onto my horn, and it goes off. Who cares who hears? It's not like anyone is at work anyway. I look up and adjust my glasses. Is that Jackie?

Coming out of the building is Jackie with Trey following not far behind. I tilt my head at the two and it's obvious that Jackie is missing her bra.

What is this? Our workplace has turned into a cesspool of God knows whose fluids stained into our desks or wherever these two rabbits came from. Trey looks up and sees me, and he merrily smiles and waves. Great. Just fucking great.

Before I can start the car engine, he's pulled Jackie along with him, and he taps obnoxiously on my window. Please just leave me alone.

"Hey, Trey. Jackie." My window is cracked slightly, but Trey doesn't seem to mind.

"Catching up on some accounts over the weekend. I needed the backup." He slaps Jackie's ass as she giggles and yelps in pleasure. Gross. I feel like I'm doing an obvious job at showing my discomfort, but it doesn't seem to faze them.

"You're missing your bra," I say to Jackie. She looks down and stifles a laugh.

"I should probably go back and get that!" Her laugh is hideous and sounds to me like nails on a chalkboard. "You're the best, Bella."

"It's Isabelle!" I snap, my patience finally wearing thin. Jackie stops laughing and looks at me, offended. I turn to Trey, and instead of being offended, he looks . . . proud?

"That's what's up, Isabelle! You're reading that book, huh? You don't like it when people call you whatever they want, and you're going to do something about it." I don't correct Trey and tell him that I think the book is complete horseshit, but Jackie turns her attention to him.

"Just because she's as big of a nerd as you, it doesn't give her the right to talk to me like that!" Jackie punches Trey in the arm.

"It's not like that, baby. When you read it, you'll really appreciate what Isabelle is doing right now. I mean, c'mon, would you like people calling you Margaret?" he teases her, but all the color drains from her face.

"Don't use my first name out loud," Jackie, or possibly Margaret, hisses at him.

"You're right, my bad! But we've got a real one in our presence. Isabelle here has known about us for some time and has not once gone to HR. I wonder what other secrets she holds." Trey winks at me.

I cringe. Maybe my life was better alone. I forgot why I stopped talking to people in general. I'm about to start up my car when Jackie looks at me. Like, actually looks at me for the first time.

"What are you up to today, Isabelle?" I ignore her enunciating my name as if it's royal.

Lie. Tell her you're volunteering or have to go to church even though you haven't done that in twenty years. You have to work a side hustle. Anything! "I'm not doing anything today."

Jackie looks me up and down and sighs out loud. "I can help you."

"Help me?" Did I miss something in the conversation?

"Oh no way! Are you going to *She's All That* her?!" Trey exclaims as he looks at Jackie, who nods in agreement.

"She's all what?" I struggle to keep up.

"I'm going to give you a makeover. On the house. Trey is right. We do sorta owe you one." Jackie takes out her phone and begins adding my name to her contacts.

I am frozen in place and am once again on autopilot. I can't tell you why I don't fuss over this, or why I give her my actual phone number and agree to be at her roommate's beauty salon later this afternoon. Trey keeps insisting that we take before and after pictures for the Gram. Outside of knitting or listening through the walls in the house to Dad's sports talk radio, what else *was* I going to do today? Play detective on an author who's selling a bunch of books? No, I think I've given him too much attention already.

Jackie's roommate works for a very high-end chain of salons. You would have to be living under a rock to not know about Zesty's. They usually only have shops located in the richer parts of town, so it doesn't surprise me that I go to the more upscale mall. I try to protest to the staff about having a valet park my car, but they insist that they only work off tips. Yeah, but then I feel guilty for not tipping you, or if I do, you'll judge how little I give you, but the young man is persistent and I find myself handing over my keys.

Denise is Jackie's roommate, and she seems nice enough. Nice in one of those harmless ways where she feels the need to talk your ear off without letting you get one word in. I couldn't even fathom a conversation between her and Jackie. I've only been in the seat for ten minutes and she's already told me about her childhood, her favorite places to eat in Provo, Utah, and how many reality shows she watches weekly. I occasionally grunt in agreement, because my face is covered or the water is running too high.

I'm not being waterboarded, but it sure feels like a torture technique as I fight back tears while Denise forcefully pulls at the knots in my hair. I never really thought of my hair as a bird's nest, but now I cannot unsee it after we first looked in the mirror and Jackie made the remark. Which, speaking of my new hairstylist's roommate, she's gone.

Trey was already whispering in her ear while occasionally nibbling at the corner of her earlobe. If this were me a week ago, I would've awkwardly looked in any other direction. Now I almost view it as a game and continued to stare. They either didn't feel my eyes on them or just simply don't care. Regardless, it must've been when my head was tilted back and Denise was scrubbing the shampoo into my hair that they made their exit. I better not be stuck with the bill.

I'll admit that when Denise starts to massage my temples, it loosens me up entirely, and I feel my body go slack. Denise actually stops her conversation about different breeds of pugs and nods her head in approval. "I can already see you de-aging. The importance of creating smooth skin is having healthy habits like this. It helps your cells repopulate."

Even though it all sounds like cosmetology bullshit, I can't argue how much lighter I feel and allow her to continue massaging the sides of my head and make her way down my neck. I don't think I've been touched intimately since my mother was in my life. Fresh tears start to form in the corner of my eye, and I barely whisper the words "thank you."

I instantly regret it and look up through blurry eyes, imagining I'll see a very judgmental Denise, but am surprised to see her gently grab a tissue and dab at the corner of my eyes. I feel like she's shifted into a completely different person because she starts to speak to me in a different tone. It's as if this work voice is a front that she continues to wear in front of her roommate.

"Your body is rigid. You seem like a guarded person and for good reason. I'm going to help you look better, and I'm sorry the world has been so cruel, even if they didn't know they were ignoring you. I used to be the biggest tomboy and thought I didn't care what people thought about me, but after some light makeup and a girlish haircut, the world changed overnight."

My eyes meet hers and I refuse to talk. I want to hear more of what this stranger has to say.

"Whether you know it or not, your looks have been a stance of rebellion, and I don't blame you. Why should we cross our legs and be dolls to meet impossible standards for this world?" For the first time in my life, I think I like someone who isn't my mother.

"Then why do you do this? Contribute to the impossible standards?" My voice is steady, and I don't dart my eyes away like I would normally do when speaking with someone.

"Sweetie, I may be self-aware, but I'm not stupid. I recently dated a guy who is a lawyer, and I make more than him." Despite myself, I laugh at this. I know she wasn't joking, but that's just objectively hilarious. She joins in on the laughter and her old phony voice returns. "Okay, now let's get a foundation that matches that beautiful pearl skin along with a really kick-ass eyeliner that complements your cheeks."

Who needs that self-help book when you have this kind of human interaction? Denise could be a great therapist if she ever decided to switch careers, but it looks like she's sort of discovered the path to success within these walls of this superficial store. I am about to look into the mirror and see the transformation but look over at the cash register.

A woman is being rung up, and while she's waiting she reads from the book. What is everyone's obsession?

"Can I ask you something?" I probe.

"Don't worry about the bill," she waves her hand dismissively. "Jackie was only going to cover half of it, but honestly it was sort of a dick move that she ditched you here." Jesus, I almost forgot about the bill. This is a high-end place, and even if Jackie covered half, it can't be less than a couple of hundred more dollars. It's not like I don't have the money, but supporting my dad and myself is not easy.

"Oh my goodness, thank you, but no it wasn't that . . ." I trail off and try not to stare at the woman at the register, but I'm truly at a loss for words about how this book is getting most people's attention. "Have you read *Your True Colors*?" I actually catch Denise rolling her eyes before she turns to me. Her demeanor toward me changes and is, quite frankly, a bit rude.

"Listen, I know that that book has probably helped you through some hard times, but I'm not interested in reading—" she begins, but I cut her off.

"You don't buy it either?" And like that, old Denise is back. Like the real Denise I met just moments ago. She leans in closer so her coworkers cannot hear her.

"You're not one of them?" If this were middle school, it would be like us passing notes in class, so I find it a bit humorous that she feels the need to talk in a low tone.

"One of them? You act like it's some sort of cult—" I talk in a normal voice, but she shushes me right away and talks in an even lower tone.

"Lower your voice. My boss is a huge fan," she says, nudging behind her where another woman is taking care of a customer and doesn't seem to have heard our conversation.

"Sorry," I muster. I would hate to get her fired for my big mouth.

"You're good." Denise loosens up a bit but still seems on guard. "Why would you ask me about that nonsense?"

"I don't know. You had really good advice and seemed worldly. People have been opening up to me more than usual lately, and that was a common factor."

"The book?" she inquires.

"Yeah. No matter which direction I turn, I cannot seem to get away from it." She watches as I speak and seems to analyze every word.

"This is probably out of line, but can I get your number?" This catches me so off guard. When's the last time someone needed my number? I awkwardly reach into my jeans and pull out my phone, where I allow her to put in her phone number and have her text herself. "I guess I should've asked you this, but . . . you've read it, right?"

I know I shouldn't lie. This could be the first friend I have had in a long time, and it's probably not the best to start a friendship off with lies. I nod my head. Her eyes dart back and forth.

"Good. Listen, I can't talk much about this here, but I would like to meet up and have a sort of anti–book club on the situation." What situation is she even talking about?!

I just nod as if I know exactly what she's referring to and let her turn the chair around so I can look at this new stranger in the mirror. For the second time that day, I cry. Who is that beautiful person, and where did Isabelle go?

CHAPTER SEVEN

I was hoping to avoid this, but I can't hold it off any longer. It's time I start reading this book. Would you rather cut off your arm or leg? That's the decision I'm left facing. On one hand I can have my dad finish his little voice acting career and try my hardest to listen to him stumble over his words, or I can work my way through it like I have done with so few books in my life. Naturally, I choose the second option.

I have been up all night and barely gotten through one chapter out of fifty, and it's been excruciating, but not without progress. I can finally understand the allure. Without going into too much detail, the book does a good job of isolating you from this reality and connecting with you as if you are speaking with a long-lost friend. I can't describe it, but it has a way of making you feel like this was a love letter written only for your eyes. If I weren't rereading every second, I could see how anyone could get lost in its charm. Yet, there's something else that's nagging at me.

While looking at the structure of some sentences, it seems rather odd that the author put it in those words. It's not like a Victorian era reading, but it's almost like the author is purposely pausing in areas that are not complete thoughts, leaving the reader some room to fill in the blanks.

That in itself is weird. If everyone is filling in the blanks, then essentially everyone is reading different versions of the same book. I also notice how frequently certain expressions are used. Phrases like "I hear what you're saying," and "you are valid to have your thoughts," or even "you are seen" are scattered throughout the beginning pages, and I wonder if I have fallen victim to its design.

And also I cannot get over the blatant use of the words "primal" and "id." It's not until I decide to go back and reread it that I realize that the words were spelled correctly the first time around in my twisted brain. What's odd is Rex did this on purpose, or at least I think he did. He renamed them as "mipral" and "di." He uses these made-up words as ideas he's formulated. They're anagrams. Every Scrabble player's dream, but thanks to my disorder I just automatically put the letters back in their correct place.

But why would he feel the need to hide the words "primal" and "id"? Isn't "id" supposed to be short for "identity"? Or is id referring to something else?

Knock, knock, knock.

I jump. My dad is standing there, and he wasn't loud, but it still catches me off guard. That and the fact that there's a woman who's about twenty-five years younger than him around his waist.

"Dad?" I look at her, and either she just got out of a club, or she is most definitely an escort. What the actual fuck?!

"You're reading! That's great! I told you that you should be engrossed in *Your True Colors*. It's going to be the best decision you've ever made." My dad abandons the escort and enters my room. I feel like it's unclean now.

"Dad! Who is that?" I look past him to the escort, who doesn't look phased. She has droopy eyes, and it appears that she's high on something. My dad looks over his shoulder at the woman and waves his hand like it's nothing. I don't think I've ever raised my voice to my dad, but I don't hold back. "Dad," I say through gritted teeth, "could we have a word in the living room?"

In a normal world, I could imagine my father being reverted back to his childhood self, shoulders sagging and getting an earful from his daughter to the same beat that a mom would scold her teenage son, but we left reality behind a while back.

My dad doesn't look rattled. He doesn't even look annoyed. He allows me to talk about the dangers of bringing a clearly unlawful service into this house and how there could be even more trouble that follows, whether that be this woman's pimp, paraphernalia, or even illegal firearms she has in her purse. "I don't even want to know how much you're paying her. You think we have the money for that?"

"I think five hundred a night is pretty reasonable." My eyes bulge out of my head at his nonchalant tone, and I try to think of where on earth he found five hundred dollars. I'm not the type of person to squirrel away money within the house. Maybe it's his allowance, but even then, he'd have to put away months of it at a time without touching it.

This conversation is steering off topic, and I should be focused on the immorality of this whole fiasco, but I find myself going back to the finances. What can I say? I've always been good with numbers. "Where did you get that, Dad?"

"Jaylen Brown is a great second option, but with Tatum out he's not scoring over thirty tonight. Factor that in with Curry becoming more of a facilitator in what's likely his last year in the league, and it's a parlay you just cannot pass up." My heart sinks. He's gambling again. Is he for real? The twelve-step program we put him through. The times he looked at me and Mom dead in the eyes and promised he wouldn't do it again.

"You promised." My voice cracks. What I need more than anything is for my father to shush me before I let the waterworks loose. For him to take me in his arms and coddle me and tell me that it'll never happen again and that he'll send the prostitute home and count his losses with his winnings. But of course none of that happens. He doubles down.

"You'll be proud of me." He practically ignores everything I have been saying tonight. "I made a simple fifty-dollar bet with Eddie on the first game. Today was the NBA tip-off with seven games tonight. Not only did I win the fifty, but I turned it around and put it all on a four-leg parlay. Paid out in hard cash. Went to Lester's Shack since it's all under the table . . ." My head was already spinning, but the mention of Lester's snaps me back to reality.

Lester's Shack is the dirtiest bar in the city. It's also a not-so-secret place where people place bets. Dad made a lot of enemies there, and I'll never forget the soccer game I had in junior high where two bikers came to the sidelines and not-so-subtly broke my dad's arm right there on the sidelines where everyone could see.

Children cried and some of the parents started to panic, but after one biker held him and the other one did the deed, they were gone surprisingly quickly. Covered from head to toe in tattoos, it was not hard to make them out when the police came for a report, but my father seemed adamant about not filing charges and looking for them.

Mom was so calm and collected, you would think she was the one who orchestrated everything, but she did take matters into her own hands. Later that very night, she withdrew the debt that our dad had collected. She dragged him to the bar by his broken arm and put a self-ban on him from that place. Despite how much pain my father was in, the humiliation was worse. The scummy people who worked there almost looked at it like a mom punishing a little kid. Worse, they called my mother a lot of derogatory words before she left, but the owner looked my mom dead in the eyes and promised her that our dad wouldn't be allowed to step foot in that place ever again.

This is what I was told secondhand.

Of course neither of my parents told me that story, and had Sarah's mom not been a bartender working that night, I would've never believed it. Years later, Sarah would later tell me what really went down. Because she was sweet, at the time she just said that Mom and Dad went into the place, paid their dues, and my father said he wanted nothing more to do with it. What a joke. Even at thirteen, I knew that my classmate Sarah was full of shit, but I chose to live in oblivion until we were juniors in high school.

"New management." My father smiles proudly. I look at him, confused, before my father speaks up again. "I'm no longer banned from the place. Which is just as well. Bygones be bygones."

"You're not going back there." I put my foot down, but he continues to act like a toddler.

75

"I don't think you can make me do anything. What are you going to do? Kick me out?" My dad laughs at the idea, but I actually feel feisty enough to open up this can of worms.

"Legally, I can." We both know damn well the house is only in my name.

"Yeah, I suppose you could." He shrugs. "But I've established residency here for a while and can easily pull squatter's right."

"What?" I am honestly in the dark on this one.

"Oh yeah, look it up. You can call the cops, asking them to make me leave, but I have been living here for longer than a couple of weeks and even have mail delivered here. You can't just kick me out without going through the legal proceedings first, so yeah, I'll wait. That is, if you go through with it."

He's so smug right now that I feel like punching my own father in the face. Where is all of this primal rage coming from? I'm the biggest pushover on the entire planet, and now here I am questioning whether or not I need to kick my own father out of my house or get violent with him.

I take out my phone, and my father looks amused. "Maybe I can't kick you out, but you're obviously doing illegal activities in this house that I don't want to be an accomplice to, so yeah, I'm sure the police would be interested in the prostitute that's in your room."

76

Finally, the color drains from his face as he realizes that he is not invincible. He grabs my phone before I can even think.

"Dad, what the fuck?!"

He's about to throw it on the ground and shatter it when he stops himself. There's rage in his eyes, but when he looks deep into my soul, he can see the frightened little girl he calls daughter. And only for a moment, I see the father who raised me. It feels like a nanosecond. It's only a glimpse of the old him, but I do see it in there.

"You'll get it back when I'm done." And like that, he leaves my room with my phone.

CHAPTER EIGHT

It's not until five in the morning that she leaves. I sleep in the computer room because it's further away from their room, and I put on music loud enough that drowns out most of their session. This isn't to say that I didn't hear the occasional grunt and/or fake orgasm. I've dealt with bad parenting from him throughout my life, but this takes the cake, and I don't think it's something he can ever come back from.

Not even half an hour after he left my room, I was on the computer looking up squatter's right laws and deciding to follow through with the paperwork. It may take months for everything to go through and maybe some court battles, but I can no longer live under the same roof as that man and will be damned if I am the one who gets kicked out of my own house.

I look back at my initial reactions, though, and scold myself for treating her like the plague. She was obviously strung out on something and had made some horrible decisions in life to be sleeping with someone who is nearly triple her age. My father has always been an opportunist, but this was at the expense of someone else's dignity and at her lowest point in life. That's horrible enough, but I do wonder how much of that was my dad and how much of it was the book.

Now don't get me wrong—I do think people should be held responsible for their actions, but at what point was Dad just being duped into all of this? I know it was only brief, but I did see my old father in those eyes, and I can say with conviction that he still lives there.

Right now, this is an internal struggle that I have because I know what I would tell someone if they were in my shoes. Essentially, to tell their father to go fuck himself and be on their way. But it's so much harder when you're in that actual position. For better or for worse, this is the only family that you have left, and no one is perfect. And it's not like that my father has always been the biggest piece of shit. When things go his way, he has made some nice gestures. Even if it was all self-serving. What was he going to gain out of this? The side of me that wants to sever all ties with Dad asks the hard-hitting questions: Do you really love him, or are you starving for attention? That light massage around my temples proved that. Are you so deprived of human interaction that you'll accept anything at this point?

Ever since that book has entered my life, I have been in such deep introspection that I feel myself unlocking things in me that I would have never given a second thought to before. I am the quiet kid who no one notices and who leads the most boring life. And yet here I am getting philosophical with my life choices and what I should or should not be feeling.

My neck hurts from sleeping on it awkwardly, and I decide it's time I crash in my own bed. At least the sex worker is gone and I don't have to worry about hearing anything from my old man. He's always been a heavy snorer, and he's passed out in his room. I wander back into my bedroom and notice that my phone is on the bed.

At least it's not shattered. I pick it up, and even though it's low on battery life, I notice how I have a barrage of texts. Damn. That's never happened before. It's from Denise. She was excited to meet another person who was not sold on the bullshit that Rex Sutter sells. She tells me that she wants to meet up at a late-night diner after her shift tomorrow, which would now be today. She says she wants to introduce me to a friend who has been keeping tabs on this phenomenon. There was a long period where she didn't text, and the final one was a simple "hello?" and I assume she must've blocked my number after that because who wouldn't? It seemed like I thought she was a crazy person.

That's just great, Dad. Scare off the first friend I've had in years because you wanted to get laid. I text back that my phone died and it is now just charging, and I am surprised to see the text go through. Even more surprising, I see the bubbles indicating her texting back. She seems in good spirits and asks if I'm able to make it tonight. Of course I'm going to go. She's ecstatic and sends me some quirky emoji. I send a thumbs-up. My goodness, Isabelle, even in texts you're awkward.

My eyes are heavy and it's still a full day and early evening until we meet up. That pillow on my bed looks like the best thing anyone could offer me right now. I lie down and drift off and begin to have dreams about the past.

*   *   *

I pull into the driveway, and the minivan is open with Mom hauling her luggage. I left sixth period early so I could catch her, and I am glad that I did. My dad is smoking on the balcony and not lifting a finger to help her. On brand.

Mom looks up and smiles at me as she waves her hand and then retreats back inside to grab more luggage. I park off to the side of the house to make sure they have room to leave when they drop her off at the airport. Hopefully I can convince them to let me tag along. I don't see why not—my homework is done for the week.

"Hey Izzy, you didn't just ditch school to come see me take off, did you?" Mom teases as I see her hauling two full suitcases. I help her with one of them.

"I'm two weeks ahead of the other kids in history."

"Of course you are." Mom smiles, and the two of us go out to the minivan and load the luggage in the back. My face falls a bit as I look at the fifth bag we've loaded. Mom catches all of this and

81

gently rubs my back. "This trip is going to be a longer one. I agreed to a three-month stint."

I feel the air in my lungs escape as if I were just sucker punched in the gut. Three months?! I can't stay here with Dad for that long. I understand Doctors Without Borders needs as much volunteer work as they can get, but what about her job here? Mom senses the question and gently grabs my hand to lead me inside.

"I quit the hospital yesterday. The three of us will be insured through COBRA while I'm gone. I've been there long enough to know that there's a good chance they will still be hiring when I get back. This isn't to say that I'm even going to go back to Heartwood. The pay is great, but I've never seen a more dysfunctional organization in my life. Those people on the top . . . it's as if they just don't care." While Mom has the most soothing voice anyone could melt into, my father is either not charmed by it or too upset.

"Listen to your mom. This was a wonderful opportunity that she couldn't pass up." His voice is robotic and less than sincere. My mom doesn't skip a beat, though, and speaks as if on cue.

"I also feel this is a great opportunity for you to get some work after school. Summer is coming up shortly, and last summer all you did was stay cooped up in your room after I repeatedly tried to get you to go find some friends." What is this? Pick on Isabelle Day?

"I thought you said I didn't have to work as long as the grades were up." The anxiety seeps through as I realize that if I were to get a job, I would have to interact with more people.

My mom lifts an eyebrow and sighs as she thinks of how to approach me. "Isabelle, you can't look at this as a punishment. Had

I not been so busy at work, I would've socialized you more during your formative years."

That's just great. I feel like I'm being compared to a dog right now. Where is all of this coming from? I leave school early to see my mom before her big trip, and now I'm being told she is going to be gone for longer than two weeks, and that I'm to get a job. She'll be gone, though, so maybe I shouldn't fight this too hard.

"Your father is going to make sure that you have a job, and I already got you an interview with the accounting firm that Stacey works for." She can see me trying to place who Stacey is, and my mom's face doesn't falter. "Sweet T—that's Jessica's mom. Your old babysitter. Why don't you drop off your backpack and freshen up before we go to the airport?"

I don't hide my disappointment. I know that she's used to my sulking, and I try to make it evident as I go into my room. I drop my backpack on the bed, grab one of my pillows, and scream as loud as I can into it. I feel tears well up in my eyes but refuse to let them come out. I round the corner and am about to rejoin them in the living room when I hear my dad speaking.

"Her first paycheck won't come for at least three weeks." My dad sounds irritated.

"I've made sure we're caught up on the bills. It's not about the money. She can't just stay in her room all day. Believe it or not, Tanner, she doesn't share your enthusiasm about basketball."

"What do you want me to do about it? I can't help it that she's antisocial."

"I'm not asking you to do anything except make sure she stays at the job I just got her. Jesus, sometimes it's like I have two kids and no other parent in the house." Mom's normal "nice tone" is being challenged right now. She sighs audibly, and even though I don't see her, I know she's put on her pleasant mask again. *"Let's not do this before I fly out. It's still three hours until my flight departs. If we're quick we can still catch happy hour over at Applebee's."* I step out from around the corner and either my mom knew I was listening or had a hunch. She winks at me. *"Ready, Izzy?"*

I wake up.

CHAPTER NINE

I don't know what time it is, but I can see it's dark outside. I groan as I get up from my bed, still dressed in the same clothes from yesterday. It probably would've been a good idea to charge my phone before my nap, but of course I didn't do that, and now it's at fourteen percent. Not ideal, but I still have time to get some juice before meeting Denise.

Except I really don't. She wanted to meet at eight tonight, and it's already six forty-five. Fuck. I'm not even dressed. She can't see me in the same clothes I was in yesterday. The meeting spot is halfway across town and I probably shouldn't be late, but at this point, what choice do I have?

I find a quick change of clothes and rush to the bathroom, where I collide with my dad.

"Whoa, easy there, slugger." He seems in good spirits, as if the last twenty-four hours haven't traumatized me one bit.

"Dad, I'm running late and really can't do this right now." I go into the bathroom and before I close the door, my dad holds my wrist.

"When you were sleeping, I checked in on you and was reminded that you're reading it as well. I know you seem mad now and probably think I'm the worst man in the world, but I promise you that it'll all make sense when you finish it." Even though he sounds like some born-again Christian, I do see sincerity in his facial features, and what is that—actual tears?

"I wasn't the best father," he continues, "but I am beginning to see the parts of me that needed work. Including being there for you."

I should slam the door in his face and tell him that he was never there for me as a kid and that he only attended my recitals because Mom dragged him there. Dads don't bring prostitutes to their home and force their daughters out of their room or pawn off their favorite instrument to help pay gambling debts. But I do none of this and don't even recognize my voice as I comfort him. "Dad, I want to revisit this conversation. I really do, but right now I need to get ready to meet a friend."

My dad sniffles a little but nods his head and allows me to shower. I'm lost deep in thought when I hear the door to the bathroom open again, just to shut quickly. I peek my head out of the curtain and see a couple of hundred-dollar bills next to my clothes. The note reads "fun Have tonight." When was the last time he gave me money? Has he ever done that?

86

I don't put the product in my hair that Denise recommended or apply the makeup that she included with my session. I probably look like an ungrateful, privileged customer, but I'm more concerned with getting there on time as I race twenty miles over the speed limit. Siri guides me to the late-night diner. I arrive fifteen minutes late. My phone has been charging in the car and is now only at thirty percent, which I suppose is better than nothing.

The lot is deserted as it only has about five cars altogether, but how many of those are the staff's cars? Is she even here? Maybe after ten minutes she thought I was full of shit and bounced. I wouldn't blame her; I'm not the best at driving and texting at the same time, so I couldn't even give her the courtesy that I'd be late. I think about turning around even if it means having an awkward conversation with my dad, but I should at least see if she's still here.

When I walk in, the place is a ghost town. I am about to turn around when I see Denise wave me over, a shorter Asian guy sitting with her. She looks drastically different than she did at the salon. Her makeup is off, and she instead wears this look of confidence that suits her better than the phony valley girl persona she has at work. I approach the two and Denise nods and pulls out a chair next to her to.

"I know . . . it seems like a really odd place to meet, but Kai's brother works here and we can use their

87

Wi-Fi and get on an anonymous VPN. Oh! Sorry, this is Kai." Kai's eyes bore into mine, and neither of us says anything. I hold out my hand, he takes my hand, and we shake.

Kai looks far more intimidating up close. He has a full head of hair that is styled really nicely. It has to be from Denise—otherwise I think I would be jealous his hair is that wild. He has thin-rimmed glasses that do nothing to hide the intensity in his eyes. There's an aura about him too. I wouldn't put him over 5'5", but if I ever encountered him with ill intentions, he'd be the last guy I would want to start a fight with.

Denise either doesn't notice the discomfort and/or disdain that Kai has for me or chooses not to pay attention to it. She whips out a small notebook where she has passages written down with key phrases circled and hands it over to me. I don't disclose how hard it is for me to read these words in a coherent order, but I am polite and look at the images that go along with them.

It's detailed. There is an actual timeline where she has written key dates that go back to the late nineties or maybe before. I can't read if 9916 is 1996 or 1969 and am too embarrassed to ask. But I have to assume that it's the nineties or otherwise there's this big blank, because most of the other dates have twos in them, which is at least past the twentieth century.

The book came out less than five years ago? Why focus on . . .

"That's his birth date." Denise follows my eyes and my face instantly reddens.

"The author's." I feel the need to piece the puzzle together quicker than I anticipated because I don't have the guts to tell her that I haven't even read the book front to back yet.

"Tentative date," Kai adds while shooting Denise a glance. Denise doesn't waver and continues.

"Rex Sutter isn't even his real name. And from what I gather, he's not based in the small town of LaScie—" Denise begins, but I interrupt, because I, too, have gone down the rabbit hole.

"People assume because that's the biggest town nearby, but he's actually from a lot smaller of a village." Denise sits back, impressed. I continue, "He grew up in a village called Black Wolf Creek."

Was that a look of approval from Kai? It's hard to decipher, because even though I've known him for a whole five minutes, he seems like a person who keeps his cards close to his chest.

"That was one of the potential villages we were looking at, but it didn't check out." His tone is not as abrasive as I thought it was going to be, but I am still wondering how I got this one wrong.

"It could be, though." Denise bats for me, and I wonder why any of this matters. She turns to me and wants me to continue. "How did you come up with that?"

"I've only been able to find five images of him online. And I was able to reverse image search some of them. Three of them were taken less than five miles from the commune."

"Commune?" Denise asks.

"They lost their status as a village back in 2005." Thank God I actually did some more research while restless last night. I found myself looking up a little bit more information on Black Wolf Creek. Still, there wasn't much to go off of. Their residents either keep a very low profile or are more reclusive than I am.

"It's possible that he would visit the area. Small-town folk have to venture out to have fun too," Kai suggests. I could see the wheels in his head turning as he thinks about everything.

"His name is Cain Skaggs." Denise pulls up more images of Cain for me to see.

"Why the pseudonym?" I ask.

"That's the million-dollar question," Kai says. He pulls up his laptop and turns it so I can see what is on the screen. "Cain Skaggs has done mission work throughout the world prior to being a self-help author. Paraguay, Congo, Syria . . . a lot of the developing nations; you name it—he's been there."

"He grew up in a strict religious household—a sect of Mormonism that was even more extreme than the laws they have, and they were banished," Denise informs me.

"Polygamist?" I ask, though I'll be ashamed to admit that's really the extent I know about the corruption of the LDS religion. With as much time as I have spent alone, I scold myself for not becoming more worldly and getting to know more about other cultures.

"Among other things," Kai half smiles to himself.

"Yes, polygamy was already a heated issue that most of the church has condemned, but there were other things that sort of . . . how do I put this? Clash with the ten commandments." Denise explains this, and I cannot get over how educated she actually is. It's sad to think that she makes more money acting like a bimbo than being her natural self.

"I haven't seen any biblical teachings in *Your True Colors*." Shit, I should really close my mouth. I can't speak on a topic I know nothing about. Reading one chapter doesn't make me know the whole book, but to my surprise, they are impressed again.

"Right, Isabelle?! There's nothing of that within the book. You'd think there would be subliminal messages about walking the righteous path or even the mentioning of God's firstborn son, but we don't see that, do we?" Denise says.

"But there is subliminal messaging, though. Maybe I'm looking at it wrong." Why do I feel so comfortable talking?! I really need to quit while I'm ahead and go back to listening.

"What do you mean, Isabelle?" Kai inquires.

"It's nothing. Really. Maybe I am just looking at it differently." I try to brush it off and lean forward to his computer, but Denise gently touches my arm as if the two of them want me to elaborate. I am extremely self-conscious and don't want to appear dumb to them. I wait, but it seems like they're genuinely interested in what I have to say. Finally, I crack.

"The book is full of anagrams." Kai watches me closely as I continue, "The words 'di' and 'mipral.'" I wait for the two of them to decipher them, which doesn't take long.

"'Id' and 'primal.'" Kai's wheels are again turning in his head. "Whoa."

"Those words that Rex said he made up for his exercises. Oh my goodness, Isabelle, I knew there was a reason we crossed paths." Denise takes back her notebook rather harshly and starts to scribble these words.

"How did you figure this out?" Kai genuinely wants to know, but I don't know these two well enough to tell them it's because I am a freak of nature who doesn't know how to read. I shrug my shoulders, but thankfully they don't press further.

"I bet there are more subliminal messages scattered throughout the whole book," Denise talks to us both but mainly looks at Kai. He nods and takes back his laptop as the two of them write and type. I sit there, awkward, not knowing what to do, but I will say that I feel optimistic about how tonight has been going.

I somehow disarmed Kai's defenses, and Denise feels that it was destiny that the two of us met one another. Even if they may be a little kooky and wear tin foil hats, they are the first friends that I have had in a very long time. Who knows? Maybe after our little Scooby-Doo research, we could do normal things with one another. Go to the movies, see local concerts, check out new restaurants. I find myself daydreaming about this and don't notice that Denise has been talking to me.

"Well, what do you think?" Shit, what was she saying? I think it was about going somewhere. I'm like a deer in the headlights, so I just nod my head. She squeals in approval and hugs me. "That's amazing, Isabelle. I knew I was right about you. I'll let you know tomorrow when the tickets are bought."

Tickets? Like my father would say, "Jesus, Isabelle." What did I just sign myself up for?

CHAPTER TEN

I'm supposed to be working on next week's numbers, but I find myself looking into Cain Skaggs. Wouldn't it be funny if he had a brother named Abel? No such luck, though. I also feel like I need to do a better job of looking into this religion in general, but I find it hard to locate it due to most of its followers not even using the internet. Get with the times, people.

Maybe this is a strange coincidence, but because I have a hunch about something, I'm going to look into it further. Those who have come in contact with Cain actually abandoned social media after meeting him. I found a couple who used to be social butterflies and would constantly be posting about their lives, until they found the righteous path with Cain and left their superficial lives behind. I'll admit that I can see the allure of not having a digital footprint of everywhere you go. I personally only created social media accounts so I could see what my coworkers were doing. I'm nosy—always have been. I just use my middle name and my mother's maiden name.

Most social media accounts are completely anonymous, but I found out the hard way years ago that there are open profiles, and Snapchat notifies their users when someone views their profile. I overheard my coworkers in the break room ask who Claire Nuciforo was, and my heart nearly lodged up into my throat.

Now I have to be much more cunning when looking through things, even though I know I was just an afterthought to them. But these people that Cain had met were not like me. They actually had lives, and one of the siblings of a newfound member of his church kept all of the photos he had on his Instagram before he deleted them. They were breathtaking photos. I don't blame the sister for being so upset—her brother led quite the adventurous life and had the most handsome smile. It really can't be that much of a sin to let loose, can it?

There's another knock on my door, but either I've grown accustomed to people sneaking up on me or I just am not getting as rattled anymore. Tyreke is peeking his head into my office.

"Good job on those numbers last week! Have you found any more . . . discrepancies?" I squint my eyes at him. My goodness. This again? That seemed like another lifetime.

"Nope. Nothing on my end." I shake my head, which seems to be exactly what he wants to see and hear.

"That's great! You know, Isabella . . . I think an overdue raise is in your future." My name is not Isabella, it's Isabelle, and I already made it clear that I don't want to get involved with whatever shady shit this guy is doing, but I desperately want to get back to my research, so I humor him.

"I know you'll compensate me appropriately." At this statement, Tyreke lets out a thunderous boom of a laugh.

"You've been reading *Colors*, haven't you?" He laughs. My goodness. This book is like a pandemic. I fake a smile and let out a little noise. He nods his head as if there is an understanding. "It changed my life for the better too. Good things are coming for us, Isabella, I just know it."

He leaves my office on a good note, I guess. In normal circumstances, I wouldn't have played hardball and would've loved to anonymously go to the HR people and just completely remove myself from the sticky situation I found myself in, but now I have really gone off the deep end as a junior detective. My work is still better than the majority of the clowns out there in the office, but I haven't been myself, and it'll most likely show if I don't put my head back into the game. And I am definitely going to . . . when Denise isn't staring at me through the window. What on earth is she doing here?

I stand up and start walking toward her when Jackie screams for her roommate and rushes over to hug her. Denise's body is stiff and she moves past her: "I'm not here for you."

Jackie is stunned and doesn't know how to react when Denise marches over to me. "Why haven't you answered your phone?"

I'm confused. My phone? I pull it out, and my heart sinks when I see that I have eight missed calls from her and over twenty texts. I'm as speechless as Jackie. "Hey Denise, long time, no see," Trey chimes in as he obliviously walks past us.

I take Denise's arm, lead her into the room, and shut the door. Trey attempts to be playful with Jackie, but she pouts as she points in our direction. I would probably enjoy this turn of events if I weren't in so much trouble. Denise's tone and attitude don't seem like she wants my attention in a good way.

"Was that all bullshit for you last night? You just humor me and Kai? You probably think we're just some lunatics on some personal vendetta, but it's more than that—"

"Denise," I interrupt and try to get in before she bulldozes right over me, "I wasn't avoiding you. I'm at work, just like I wouldn't expect you to stop working with a client."

"Oh cut the shit, Isabelle. You told me yesterday you were okay if I bought the tickets. The flight leaves in two hours." My heart drops, and I feel like all the air has escaped my lungs. Flight? Was that what the tickets were for? She reads my body language. "Isabelle. We're going to

97

Newfoundland today. You agreed to this yesterday." I try to recover.

"I thought you were joking." my voice sounds like the old meek Isabelle everyone knows.

"Did it seem like we were joking yesterday?!" Denise is so loud that people outside our office stop what they're doing and look in our direction, but she pays no attention. "Listen, don't come, fine. But it'll be over my dead body before I let my brother's death be because of this cult."

Denise storms out and, for a moment, I cannot gather my thoughts. My body is about ten steps behind my mind, and by the time she is outside our office door, my legs react and start chasing after her.

"Denise! Wait up!!" Despite eating healthy and occasionally going on lengthy walks, I am finding out the hard way that I am out of shape and really should exercise more. "Denise!"

I'm able to catch up and place a hand on her shoulder. To my surprise, she stops and turns around, annoyed. "Kai is waiting at the airport and told me you'd flake, but I had to be sure."

"I'm coming, really." Why on earth would I agree to any of this?! I still have a job to do and it's only Monday. I can't just walk out like that and possibly go on a wild goose chase.

"You're thinking of excuses right now. It's all over your face." Am I that much of an open book? Shit. I feel like no matter what I say, she'll just roll her eyes and walk away. I pull the only ace I have left up my sleeve.

I reach into my pocket and take out my phone. I open her unread messages and hit the play button on them. The phone starts reading her first text.

"What are you doing?" she asks as she looks oddly at my phone. I stop playing the first message and go to the next one and play it, then the third, then the fourth. She's confused and looks up at me.

"I can't read," I confess. "I'm dyslexic."

I can see her reading my face, and she can tell that I'm not lying. Her face scrunches up as she thinks back to last night and basically all the interactions we've had.

"But all the things you found out . . ."

"Okay, I guess I can read, but it's really hard. Like harder than most people. The words rearrange in my brain and it's hell trying to piece it back together." I can tell that Denise is thinking about this and nods like it all makes sense.

"This is why you're not under his spell." Denise could be on to something, and I'll admit that it's been a weird ride, but I'm not sold that it's not just all great writing.

"From what I've gathered, Rex or Cain or whatever his name is, is an actual good writer. I'll admit

99

that when I was trying to read it, I noticed how he does a great job of disarming you and making you feel like you're special, but I don't know if he's a cult leader."

"He is. And he's dangerous." Denise finally calms down and has cooled off enough to speak to me rationally again. "And we're going after him. If you don't want to come, I understand. Don't worry about paying for the plane ticket."

Denise turns around and walks away. I close my eyes and exhale. I'm going to regret this, I know it. "Denise, wait up. I'm coming."

CHAPTER ELEVEN

Kai is surprised to see me. I'm wondering if they put money on it, because I see a brief look of disappointment before he shakes my hand. What's this asshole's deal? Just because he's attractive doesn't give him the right to constantly make me work for his approval. I've dealt with my dad for over thirty years and don't need another jerk like that in my life.

The TSA is surprisingly quick and we arrive less than ten minutes before they began boarding passengers. Kai and Denise begin talking about the itinerary, but I find myself focused on the aircraft we're about to board. It's a safe design and has had no safety issues within its past twenty-five years in circulation. The pilots also have over twenty-eight years of experience between the two of them.

While the two of us are in the back of an Uber, I was glued to my phone and nearly whispering every question before fully embracing my dyslexia and talking loudly with my phone, asking it a hundred questions and trying to validate the safety of this trip.

Denise wasn't shy when noticing my extensive research and put two and two together. "Not the best

101

flyer?" she asked. I shook my head and didn't want to go into details about how horrific my mom's plane crash had been. I was already getting sympathetic looks due to my impairment; I didn't want to be a complete pity party. "Reach back there and grab my backpack." I did as she said, and when she told me to open her front pocket, there were breath mints.

"Does it really smell that bad?" I asked as I blew into my hand to check my breath.

"They're Valium. It should help you relax on the plane ride. Security has never confiscated it. My brother was a terrible flyer too." The old me would've dismissed them, but there were a lot of butterflies in my stomach and we hadn't even reached the airport yet.

She gently holds my wrist, pulls me away from Kai, and whispers to me, "You've got this." I muster up a smile and board the aircraft. "Don't worry. I don't think the pilots will be reading *Your True Colors* while flying." I can tell she instantly regrets her dark humor joke, but I surprise her by smiling and then gently laughing.

We both laugh. Kai walks up to us and looks at the two of us. Denise waves him off while secretly winking at me, "Don't worry about it. Let's go find this second coming of Jesus."

The flight attendants are nice enough, and I feel that Denise must've tipped them off about my hesitancy, because they bring me a water bottle and some crackers before everyone is even finished sitting down. Denise reaches above us and points her AC knob toward me so I get double the air. I know that I should open my mouth and protest, toughing it out and downplaying my hesitancy, but I welcome every little gesture. Each kind act helps soothe me a little more. For good measure, I take out two Valium and gulp them down.

I close my eyes and tune out the background talking of the other passengers. My body is stiff as the aircraft takes off from the tarmac, and the ascent is more horrific than any roller coaster I've ever been on, but soon I feel the effects of the drugs. I become more serene and allow myself to succumb to sleep.

*   *   *

That's odd. I am off work early and should see my dad watching some playoff game. Even though he's not gambling anymore, he's still addicted to the sport . . . even if the Spurs are no longer relevant. Instead he has CNN on and occasionally flips back and forth between that and FOX. He's never been a political kind of guy, but my stomach drops as I see coverage from both stations: a commercial American aircraft exploded miles after leaving Colombia.

Dad turns around and sees me, but I don't register his expression as I rush to the bathroom and vomit today's lunch and breakfast from earlier this morning. I lift my head out of the toilet and see my dad kneel down to join me at eye level: "It was her flight."

"No. No, no, no, no, no . . ." I begin to fight back tears and my dad reaches out to hold me, but I lash out at him and scream. I punch him on the side of his head, then another fist nicks his jaw. More fists fly, but he puts a bear grip over me and my entire body loosens. I cry hysterically and cannot stop. Dad, who is not the most affectionate of men, says nothing, but he doesn't need to.

Weeks later there is a service for Mom. A lot of the people in the community came out and offered their condolences and side dishes. It doesn't matter. They'll go to waste. I have stopped eating, and even dad has shed a good twenty pounds. I stopped going to work after the bereavement days were issued. My former babysitter's mom came over to the house numerous times trying to get me to answer, but my father and I let the bell ring. At one point we lock eyes through the window and no words need to be exchanged. She only stops by the house one more time and slips my final paycheck through the slit of the front door.

Dad recovers quicker than I do, and I genuinely don't resent him for that. I will never recover. I am broken forever and have lost my only friend. He is in a state of panic when he realizes the account he and my mom shared is getting low. I already met with the lawyer, and he isn't even aware that I am the primary homeowner now and that there was a life insurance policy that will pay the bills on this place long after the day I die.

I don't tell him all of this yet, because I just don't want to talk to him or anyone really. I know that my bedroom smells. I know that I eat once a week and hardly even do anything else than feel sorry for myself, but my dad braves his nostrils and enters my room. I can see the disgust in his face that he tries so desperately to hide.

"I know you don't care, but I have three leads on jobs, and I'll make a deal with Eddie or the sharks at the dive bar to get us a loan." I didn't know anything would bring me back to reality, but the thought of my dad going back to gambling after beating it and Mom laying down the law . . . I finally awakened.

I get up, and it feels odd using my vocal muscles. How long has it been? Two, three months? I tell him everything. The mortgage and the account she and I set up (of course leaving out details of how much is truly in there). He listens with fascination and then looks betrayed. Beyond betrayed. I have seen him break my heart and Mom's countless times, but this is the first time I have seen him on the receiving end. Good. Maybe if you had fought harder for her, she never would've left.

"Give me the money to pay for the mortgage payment," he finally says.

"Why? It's in my name." Even though I know the answer already, he begins to rant.

"Why?! Maybe because we've been getting mail for the past three weeks threatening foreclosure." He begins to mutter to himself, "Jesus Christ, Sydney, you put our bills in the hands of a child." I

105

am expressionless as I look at him. "Just give me the money, Isabelle. I know which bank we went to."

"Let me put on some shoes. I'll go down there." Is this really happening? I thought I was never going to leave these four walls, but then again, if I don't pay, then some suit will eventually remove me from this house.

"You're not going anywhere like that." I look up at him, a bit confused. "Izzy, I love you, but you smell worse than a skunk's asshole."

Beat.

It definitely wasn't voluntary, but I find myself laughing. My father drops his stern expression and joins in on the laughter. The two of us are wheezing and leaning on one another for support. I decide to shower.

Later that month I convinced my father to apply for jobs anyway. I never would tell him how much was in the account but made it seem like we were not going to make it past a year on what Mom left us. He bought it for a while, but after year five he was hardly contributing to the bills and seemed to wise up. My dad would find himself getting fired from multiple jobs and even asking for money.

Somehow he knew we were sitting on a lot, but I didn't want his gambling habits to return, so I had to buy into a charade and apply for a job myself. Despite not having a college degree yet, I was always damn good with numbers and took a flyer on a start-up company. They seemed nice enough and even worked around my school schedule as I accepted a scholarship through one of my mom's colleagues.

I acted grateful for getting the job and even cashed my first paycheck in front of my dad, telling him we were basically on fumes. I don't know if he bought it, but even if he didn't, I think he was impressed with me for going through with getting a job.

In hindsight he never bought that we were broke, and I think he always knew I didn't need to work, but he knew it would help socialize me and give me purpose if I went out there and got out of the house and into a routine. I am also realizing, now, hundreds of miles away from home and high in the air, that my dad hardly ever hit me up for money. Sure, he had to live and eat, but he didn't necessarily treat me like a cash cow.

Tanner Dunham may be a chauvinistic, deadbeat asshole, but he is still my father.

CHAPTER TWELVE

I open my eyes groggily as my body shakes left and right. When they're fully open, I look around the plane to see nearly everyone gone. The flight attendants are waiting patiently but are obviously annoyed. Kai is at the front of the plane with his backpack, sighing visibly and looking down at his watch. Denise looks at me and asks if I can stand up. I groan and get up.

"What'd you give me? That knocked me out."

"Shhhhh." She shoots me a menacing look, "Maybe keep the drugs on the down-low? You know it's a felony to bring it on a plane, right?" she hisses through her teeth.

I nod and apologize to the staff as I rush out of the cabin of the plane and trail Kai and Denise as they talk about the rental car and the next steps of their game plan. I feel like a third wheel, obviously not knowing how I can contribute even if I wanted to join in on the conversation.

We weave through the airport until we find ourselves waiting for a rental car. There's a small man behind the counter with an old-school phone in front of his customer. The two of them are obviously waiting to get through to customer service. The customer looks like a construction worker type with little patience. I can practically feel the heat coming off his forehead.

Meanwhile, behind the counter, the employee doesn't seem to have a care in the world as he reads a copy of, you guessed it, everyone's favorite book. This doesn't bode well for the already livid customer.

"Young man, can you go fetch me your boss?" the blue-collar worker demands, but the employee doesn't lift his head from the book.

"Yeah, I'm not going to do that."

"And why the hell not?" The customer's voice rises. The employee sighs and puts his book down as he looks up at him.

"What do you want? You said that you wanted a refund on the ticket you got on the freeway, and I told you that I can't access that on my computer, so we're calling the department that can get you that info." The words sound reasonable enough, but the tone is undeniably condescending.

"We've been waiting for thirty minutes," the man retorts, and the employee laughs.

"First time?" He puts his nose back into the book, but the large man slams his hand down on the book to block him from viewing it.

"Go. Get. Your. Boss." Each word is more threatening than the last.

"Get your hand off of my book." The employee is no longer smirking and actually looks offended, which gives the customer some small satisfaction.

"And if I don't?" the man taunts.

The employee lifts the receiver of the phone and hangs up the phone call they are both waiting for. The customer stops smiling and grabs the man over the counter with both hands. The three of us are stunned, mouths open, not comprehending what we're watching.

"Should we call the cops?" I ask in a very low whisper, but I look over at Kai, who is actually smiling.

"Hold up. I kind of want to see where this goes." Kai doesn't take his eyes off of the situation.

The man clenches a fist and holds it close to the employee's face, who taunts him, "Go ahead, man, do it. I'd love to get this on camera." He nods over to the corner where, sure enough, a camera is rolling on this whole interaction.

The construction worker loosens his grip and lets the guy go. Reluctantly, he turns his back and huffs as he storms out. He's almost out the front door when he turns around and points a finger at the employee's face. "It's not right. Your company knows damn well I didn't speed, and I'm most likely going to lose my job over this."

I actually start to feel bad for the guy, but the employee doesn't. He gets out of his chair and approaches the man at the front door. Can the little man fight? Even if

110

he knew three different martial arts, I'd still put my money on the customer.

"Take this." He hands over the book that the construction worker was about to destroy moments ago. This completely takes the man off guard, who looks at the little man like he's crazy. Maybe because he is.

"I don't want your fucking book," he spits out at him, but the man doesn't accept the rejection as a choice. He shakes his head and puts the book in his hands.

"It'll help you. I've already read it twice and I promise you, man, it will help you." At first I think the construction worker will throw it in the garbage like I did a while back, but he accepts it. He looks confused, like he doesn't know why, but he takes it and leaves the office quietly. A woman behind us claps.

I jump because I didn't even know she was there. This plump woman, who is about twice my age, shakes the employee's hand. "Way to spread the word."

The small man shrugs his shoulders and modestly speaks. "I'm just glad he didn't get my manager. I've been making decent money skimming from the cash transactions while voiding their orders and just need a few grand more before getting fired from this place."

I turn to Denise, and our faces both say "can you believe this guy?" But when we get to the front counter, Kai leans forward to the man working the booth.

"Heard you earlier. If I give you a thousand dollars in cash, you'll check us out and not get our information because it'll just be a voided order?" I cannot believe Kai, but he's actually asking this.

"Dude, you heard I need at least two grand." He's offended but listening.

"Come on, man. This will be half your goal and then you can either be a grand shy and quit or keep riding your luck longer. Follow your mipral." Kai pulls at the right strings because the short man reaches inside his drawer and pulls out a set of keys.

"An extra five hundred and I'll wipe this camera's footage after you step foot off the property." Kai rolls his eyes but looks over at Denise. She nods and reaches into her purse. Am I currently an unwillingly accessory to grand theft auto? I've never felt more simultaneously nervous and alive in my whole life. The little man winks at me as we head out the door.

"We better hurry," Kai urges us as we speed walk to the parking lot where the cars are.

"He might change his mind?" I ask, hardly able to breathe.

"No. He'll hold up his bargain, but I've seen people who've read the book as much as him. Money isn't all he's been taking." Kai speeds up.

"More than money?" I don't follow, but his eyes wander purposely over my body and then to Denise's. My eyes widen. "You think he's . . ."

"Oh he has . . . and he hasn't been caught yet." Kai unlocks the car as we quickly load our things into the trunk. "I can see it in his eyes."

CHAPTER THIRTEEN

The three of us stop at a desolate gas station where Denise suggests we swap out the license plates. Kai agrees and scouts the area for cameras before reaching into his bag and taking out a screwdriver. When did these two become Bonnie and Clyde? We went from hunting a cult leader to being straight-up criminals. If it wasn't some big corporation and such a victimless crime, I'd be more concerned. But is that even true? Have you ever had it where you know in your deepest thoughts that this is all wrong, but now you don't want to be isolated from a group?

The gas station doesn't have cameras, but I look off in the distance and I can faintly see lights on in an older house. Outside of that lone home, it's a pretty desolate place. Nothing but trees for miles, and it's actually kind of genius switching out the plates with the Oldsmobile in the lot. Chances are, the owner won't even notice that it's not the correct plate unless they get pulled over.

After Kai switches the plates, he nudges us to hit the road again. While he was doing this, Denise prepaid for some gas. She was already done by the time we return to the car. I didn't even realize that I was subconsciously being the lookout. Should I feel honored or insulted? Regardless, this criminal activity has me nearly as speechless as the time in life when my mother passed away.

We're on the road and I take the back seat again. I have lost focus on the world around me and cannot even hear Denise call out my name until I snap out of it. I look at the water bottle she's offering me, along with a bag of chips, and I shake my head.

"You have to eat and drink. I haven't seen you consume anything all day," she insists. I am about to argue when I realize that it'll be simpler to go along with it. So I accept them.

"Thank you." I can hardly hear my voice. Denise doesn't take her eyes off me. She unbuckles her seatbelt and climbs over the front and parks herself right next to me.

"Do we scare you?" She doesn't try to lower her voice, and it doesn't feel far off from a kidnapping at this point, but since I am afraid of confrontation, I just shake my head and avoid eye contact.

"No, of course not," I say, but even I wouldn't buy that. Denise stares at me for what seems like eternity. She sighs and finally speaks.

"Kai and I can be a bit much. I get that. But we're just covering our tracks and trying to stop something really bad. You see that, don't you?" Denise doesn't sound too far off from my mom when she used to try to reason with me.

"Don't do that." Kai looks up from the road and glances at us through the rearview mirror.

"Do what?" I'm about to ask, but Denise beats me to the question and asks it.

"Don't try to convince her to think any certain way. Isn't that what we're trying to put a stop to?" Kai argues. "Isabelle. You've spoken a total of maybe ten words since we left. What's on your mind?"

No one ever asks me for my opinion, and there's a momentary blank. What do I even think about everything? I can say the first things that come to mind, but then they'd just be words that Denise wants to hear. Do I disagree with her, or do I want to put a stop to all of this madness? I think that I should say something soon because now they both look at me in anticipation.

"I've gone along with everything so far, but I guess my concerns are your methods." Denise is about to ask for further explanation, but as she does, Kai silences her. They wait for me to continue. "With how stealthy you two have been, I wouldn't put it past you both to find Cain and kill him."

I feel like all the air has been punched out of my body, because even though I had an inkling that this was their agenda, hearing it out loud makes it sound even more mad. Who does that? How is the justification of murder

116

right no matter how you spin it? They both think I'm done and are about to speak, but I find myself continuing.

"Okay. For shits and giggles let's just say we go through with it. Cain is dead. It wouldn't take long for his followers to find this out and then his book sales skyrocket even further." I am actually quite impressed with myself, like maybe these words are coming from the heart. It feels a lot like verbal diarrhea right now.

"Make him a martyr." Kai says as he mulls this over in his head.

"Precisely. We think his book is popular now? Imagine a new age religion being spawned from all of this. Wouldn't that do more damage?" My voice commanded the entire car and it felt good. Not just because what I said made sense, but because I spoke and people actually listened to me.

Denise is obviously upset about my point of view. I can tell no matter how much she tries to hide it in her face. However, she's not the type to not see other people's points of view. "What do you propose we do when we get to him, then?"

I scrunch my face, because even though I am on a roll, I really have no idea what I'm doing. Kai and Denise could very well be future killers, but at least they know who they are and have a plan that they are willing to execute. Kai seems to be interested in meeting me right now, but how can I introduce him to myself when I'm not even familiar with who I am?

"I don't know," I confess. There's a moment's silence before I speak up again. "But I do want to talk with him first."

Denise snorts and looks out the window. "The man's an obvious narcissist. I gathered that much through the book. He doesn't seem like the type to listen to an enlightened conversation."

"Mmmm, I wouldn't say that." Kai shrugs his shoulders as he continues to drive.

"You wouldn't?" Denise tilts her head in his direction.

"Manipulative, yes. Controlling, absolutely. But self-ego? No. I have read through it three times now and he seems quite the opposite. He's an echoist," Kai suggests.

I'm way too embarrassed to ask what that is. Fortunately, I don't have to. Denise leans forward and asks, "An echoist?"

"Sure. Someone who convinces others to fulfill their desires . . . even if it's at the expense of his own. In theory it sounds compassionate. Who wouldn't want to put others first and be selfless?" Kai strikes me as someone who most women would look past, but those women would be making a huge mistake. He's a knowledgeable person and speaks only when he has something smart to say.

I chew over his words in my head and begin to question if we are the bad guys. I have to ask: "If he's selfless and convincing others to fulfill their desires, then why are we trying to stop him?"

Our eyes lock in the rearview mirror. "Because most people's true desires are horrible and self-serving. All the narcissistic people in our society—this man is giving them an excuse to drop the charade and truly embrace what they desire. And what a lot of people desire is past the limits of religion and law."

CHAPTER FOURTEEN

It's pretty early and barely dusk, which is why I'm surprised the car pulls into a janky motel when we're less than three hours away from the area where Cain could be located. All of it sounds so crazy when you think about it: what if he's not even there? His book is a bestseller and for all we know, he could be sipping some margaritas in Spain.

"Why here?" I ask as we park the car. For the first time since meeting him, Kai doesn't seem annoyed and genuinely answers me.

"This was the only hotel that took cash transactions."

"Really, Kai? After that talk, we're still going the bandit route?" Great. Just great, Isabelle. Just when you were getting on his good side, you had to mock him. But he's not offended. In fact, he looks amused with me.

"If we get caught, you'll obviously be the first to crack. That's so cute that you actually still believe that my name is Kai."

I stop walking and look at him. The two of them stop and, after a moment, he starts laughing.

"I'm only kidding." I exhale the breath I was holding. "Or am I?"

He winks at me and walks past us. Is this flirting? As if right on cue, Denise rolls her eyes and elbows me while saying, "For Christ's sake, get a room you two."

"Maybe we will." Did I really just say that out loud and not just think it? My face instantly reddens, but Denise looks at me, amused, and laughs.

"Give one average girl a makeover and suddenly the real her comes out." I stutter as I try to tell her that I was just kidding, but she doesn't buy it or really care. "You asked earlier why I am a part of the cog of people's impossible beauty standards. This has been a part of it. Outside of the pay, it feels amazing making women feel better about themselves. When they leave that salon, they are a new person and have given themselves more self-respect. I know that looks are only skin-deep, but everyone should feel good about themselves."

Just like her work back at the salon when she was massaging my temples, she seems to know how to touch people in the right spots, even with her words. I find myself glad the world has gone insane and subscribed to *Your True Colors*. Without it, I would've never met these amazing people. We wait inside the lobby when Kai comes back and hands us our room key.

"I'll be down the hall. I was able to get the last room with two twin beds, so no one has to sleep on a couch. Rest up, bandits." He turns to go to his room and I find myself saddened he's leaving.

121

"Hold up," Denise says. "We're going to unpack, but I think we should meet up at that diner after we freshen up because Isabelle isn't even aware of our game plan. I think we keep forgetting she was a last-second addition."

"There's really not much to it." I try not to hide my disappointment, but he adds, "But, yeah, I am a little hungry and don't think it's a good idea to keep going off of fumes and junk food."

My stomach grumbles at the mention of food, which they both hear. This is not happening. For once, I would like the attention to go back to being off of me.

"Yeah, it looks like Isabelle could use some food as well. Meet us outside our room in thirty minutes."

While we're inside, we do what Denise said we would: we unpack and select new clothes (thankfully, I bought some at the airport, and Denise said I could borrow hers if I run out). Looking down at the three different outfits, I know that I overthink what to put on.

"Don't make this an issue." Denise gets out of the shower and looks at me, thinking about what to wear. I don't follow, so I let her continue. "This isn't a romantic getaway. Kai's eyes are still on the prize, but I don't want him distracted."

"I'm still about the mission," I protest as I dig into my purse and take out my copy of *Your True Colors*. While on the road, I was able to get through fifteen more pages and have highlighted what I believe are hidden phrases, potential anagrams, and overall clunky sentences that could mean something.

Denise grunts, obviously not completely sold, but nods for me to get in the shower. I don't argue further and get in. While the water runs I find myself, for once in my life, being upset at someone who's not my dad. Is it a crime to be attracted to someone now? I wasn't even going to go on this stupid trip, and now she's questioning my loyalty. "Someone's shark week started early."

I instantly cover my mouth like she's heard me. My mom didn't raise me to say such nasty things, even if it's behind their back. No, *especially* if it's behind their back. I find myself needing to remember that I wouldn't be here if it weren't for Denise.

As I rinse my hair with shampoo, I begin to think about it more, though. I've seen Denise with the full makeup and cosmetics, and she looks like any stereotypical future trophy wife. She doesn't know what it's like not having any male attention. Who's to say I can't flirt and follow through with the plan? She's jealous and obviously wants me to leave the picture. It even says in chapter three that you need to acknowledge when others are secretly waiting for you to fail.

The rhythm of me washing myself comes to a complete halt. What the hell was that? For a moment, it was like my mind was being hijacked by someone else and

123

filled with presumptive, hateful thoughts about my friends. What the actual fuck.

I get out of the shower and notice that Denise is gone. I open my phone and it says that the two of them are already walking to the diner. It's less than two miles away and I can pick them up if they haven't made it there already. Sure enough, the car keys are on the vanity. How long have I been lost in my thoughts? Whatever. I cannot think about that right now. I hurry up and choose the first outfit and leave the hotel room.

The two of them almost made it to the diner and they laugh when they see me pull up to them. I slow down the vehicle and roll down the windows. I feel the need to apologize profusely: "I am so sorry you guys—"

"Sorry, we don't get in cars with strangers," Denise cuts me off and teases me. Even with a quick glance I feel there's an unspoken forgiveness. Water under the bridge.

Good. She's the closest friend I have had since Mom, and I don't want to lose that over a boy . . . even if he's a handsome one. Ugh. How do men do that? They take ten minutes to get ready and look amazing without any effort.

Even though the diner is visible from where we are, the two of them get into the car. Denise in the front and Kai in the back. The diner looks a bit run-down, and there are only four other cars in the parking lot. Some teenagers vape near the entrance next to the NO SMOKING INSIDE sign. I assume the owner has made them go outside.

"Were you able to get your mom's credit card?" one of the blue-haired teens asks his friend.

"Yeah, but if we're going to get something, then it has to be big and arrive quickly. She'll cancel it pretty soon if it's on her radar." The other one inhales his vape.

"Didn't you pay attention to the fourth exercise? It says you shouldn't worry about ever getting caught as long as you are strategic about it." The other teen takes out the credit card and shows him.

I can hardly believe it. My dad is probably triple their age. How far does the demographic go for this book? Does it cater to everyone, regardless of age, gender, or ethnicity? If my head wasn't in the game before, it's back now. This book is dangerous and I'm glad we're going to try to do something about it.

It doesn't take us long to be seated, and the waitress looks completely haggard and run-down. I briefly catch a glimpse of her younger self when her face lights up at the sight of customers who are not local teenagers. Denise, of course, is charming and gets her to shed an additional ten years off her life. That's the effect she has on people, and I hope she never loses that. We need more people like that in this world.

We sit down, and I am desperate just to order right there and then when she asks for what we want to drink, but I wait patiently. While the two look over the menus, my stomach makes its presence known again, which consequently causes my face to redden. Denise could tease me more about it but ignores the opportunity and looks to Kai. "I was thinking the BLT? You?"

"Can't go wrong with a diner's cheeseburger. Hold the tomato and we'll call it a meal." He puts down his menu.

When the waitress comes back around, she takes our order and I end up getting the same thing as Kai. I feel like I can eat the whole cow but am curious how a cheeseburger tastes without tomatoes. Kai reveals his notebook and shows us the map he's drawn of the area. It's actually pretty good, even the little landmarks he's made: rapidly drawn churches, crops, and the town hall.

He explains how there is no vehicle access to the main road where the people in the commune live. It would be better for us to leave early so when we get there we can walk to the village. I ask how long it'll take for us to get there, and he estimates about four hours if we can speed walk. I don't show my hesitancy. Can I keep up?

The obvious question looms, and I know that Denise wants me to ask it, so I do: "Won't people see us coming?"

126

Denise takes out her duffle bag and tosses me fake press passes. She reveals a camera, lights, even microphones. They look professional, and I inspect them.

"We've been corresponding with one of the members of the commune. Great job by pointing us in the Black Wolf Creek direction. Turns out I was able to track down one of their members and told them that we were wanting to record a documentary on the white Haida ermine," Kai explains to me.

Denise can sense that I haven't followed, and she spells it out for me: "It's a rare rodent in the Canadian wilderness. We got access to be on their commune because of research purposes." She nods over to Kai. "For this trip, that's Kyle, and I'm Danielle."

"What's my code name?" I ask.

"We didn't include your name in the email. We will explain that you're one of our interns. So, we can call you whatever you want," Denise suggests.

"Sydney. I want to be called Sydney," I quickly tell them.

CHAPTER FIFTEEN

The two of them go over further points, like where we're going to park the car (obviously somewhere where it cannot be towed), and Kai shows me multiple images of landmarks and buildings that were in the background of the pictures of Cain. Although we do not know where they are located exactly, we're going to keep an eye out for them.

As an exercise throughout the evening, we refer to each other by our new names. I slip up a few times, but rather than scolding me, Kai ignores me as if I hadn't talked to him. It works quite well. It took me this long to get his attention and I'm not prepared to lose it again.

The food is great, but that's probably only because we were all starving. I insist on paying, but Denise doesn't allow it. She assures me that it isn't out of generosity but rather that she is just covering our tracks by not leaving a digital footprint. I haven't watched many thrillers in my life, but this all still seems surreal. Am I really tracking down a cult leader while breaking a dozen laws? For once, I feel like I am living the most interesting life compared to all my coworkers.

Throughout the years, I would hear about Santiago's vacations in other countries or how Jackie's sister was a cheerleader for the Dallas Cowboys and would sometimes travel with the team and attend celebrity-filled parties. Even Tyreke has been featured on the local news numerous times for the nonprofit organizations he created . . . wait a second? The same boss who was embezzling funds from our company? I laugh out loud.

"What's so funny?" Kai looks at me as we wait for the bill; I hadn't realized how long I have been lost in my thoughts.

"Nothing. Something I realized at work." I am only now realizing that I gave my boss some excuse about a fake family emergency and how I'd be gone for this week. Even though they haven't called and checked in, will this take longer? How much time do I need to give myself? "What do you do back in Texas?"

Kai genuinely smiles and exhales. "Would it be crazy if I told you that I don't actually live in Texas?" I look at Denise, and she nods her head. He continues, "Denise and I met on a forum about *Your True Colors* and have been conversing online for the last couple of months. There are two more of us who were supposed to rendezvous back in Austin, but they chickened out."

"Our home was the meeting location? What if it ended up being somewhere else?" I realize it was a dumb question as it left my mouth, but Denise is gentle.

129

"Then I would've probably left before meeting you. It must've been fate to have you join us, and you're already more reliable than those clowns we met online."

Kai snorts. "I have a strong feeling that one of them was just a fourteen-year-old boy who thought he was more edgy than he really was."

I am not a believer in God or the afterlife. If there were a maker and he or she would be so cruel to take away the one best friend I had when I have done nothing wrong in life, then that maker has a sick sense of humor and could've focused on bigger problems in the world. Fate? It's a term I don't think I can get on board with, but I am grateful for the hand I've been dealt. Even if it's for all the wrong reasons, I have found these two and am glad the other two revolutionists "chickened out."

It's only seven, but the sun is already setting and the long day of traveling does leave me pretty exhausted. We go back to the cheap hotel and Denise and I hardly chat before she's out cold. She's a snorer, but it's endearing . . . not unlike a cute pet who's drifted off and provides a soothing ambiance for the room. My eyes struggle to stay open, but I find myself wanting to do something completely out of character. So much so that I should be winding down, but I am too curious to leave it be. I get out of bed and quietly open and close the door behind me.

I gently knock on the outside of Kai's room, and my heart nearly stops at just that. What the hell am I doing?! What if he opens? Maybe he didn't hear me. That's okay. Cool. He's probably already asleep too—

The door opens.

I instantly regret all of this and want to crawl under the nearest rock I can find.

"Everything okay?" he asks.

I don't say anything and lean forward and kiss him.

Who is controlling me?! I wouldn't do this in a million years. The last guy I was intimate with was Omar, which was over fifteen years ago. I stop myself from letting it linger for too long and pull back. He looks completely stunned. Great. Just fucking great. Is this going to be another rejection like Santiago?

He leans forward and kisses me back, but deeper as he gently, yet firmly, grabs my hair. I melt. It feels like both kneecaps have locked and I'm about to fall over, but instead I lean into him. He closes the door behind us.

After we're done, I am physically exhausted. World War III couldn't wake me up after that.

*   *   *

Even with the adults around, I am way outside my comfort zone. The nurse seems nice enough, but the anxiety I feel about being around all these strangers is too much. Mrs. Thompson has to help

131

another kid who puked on the playground, which works for me because it's one less person that is around me. The assistant principal also seems kindhearted and even offers me some chocolates, but I'm not hungry and I have no interest in making friends. I just want to be home.

I get my wish as Mom walks through the door with her scrubs. She does not look happy. Her hair may be frazzled and those are definitely a patient's fluids stained on her work outfit, but she is still the guardian angel here to rescue me from this strange place. I know she senses my eyes on her, but she doesn't look at me and looks rather upset with the assistant principal.

"So, what was the problem?" Mom commands the room and a part of me feels bad for Principal Ed having to feel my mom's wrath.

"I am truly sorry, Mrs. Dunham—" Ed begins but is cut off.

"Nuciforo."

"Excuse me?"

"Miss Nuciforo. Dunham is her father's last name," she corrects him.

"Yes, of course. And soon to be Doctor Nuciforo, am I correct?" He attempts to butter her up, but she doesn't seem to be in the mood for compliments.

"Who knows if I'll even be able to finish my rounds when I have to drop everything to come pick up my daughter from school." She's irritated and I know that she'll be mad at me for a little bit, but she will definitely come back around.

"Ma'am, I understand your frustrations, but Isabelle went into the closet and locked herself in the room, refusing to come out for anyone. We had to get the janitor to unlock it—" he begins, but Mom's not the type to let anyone get a valid point in.

"Doesn't this school have state-renowned psychologists who work with varying types of children?"

"It does, but—"

"I'm taking out more student loans to enroll her in this school, and now I have to rearrange my schedule because you don't know how to handle one anxious kid?" My mom's stare is piercing, and she waits for the principal to speak up. "Well?"

"I've dealt with parents like you, Sydney. And I know there is nothing I can say to make you happy. Believe me, I would've rather talked with her father, but we couldn't get through to him."

"Asshole is fishing with his army buddies in Utah," she mutters. Sydney looks at her watch and swears under her breath. "Whatever, I might as well just take her back to work with me at this point."

My heart flutters. I get to go to Mom's work? This day turned out not so bad after all. She marches out with me in tow, and the door slams on her way out. We get into the car and I try not to grin. Mom's scorn has turned to me, though, and she knows exactly how to wipe that smile off of my face.

"Isabelle, what is wrong with you?! Do you know how hard your father and I work to give you a good education? A way better education than my parents could've offered me!" I have never heard *her yell this loud, and now I'm conflicted whether the stunt I pulled was worth it.*

"You have anxiety? Really? You know what that is? You're eight! And, my goodness, your dyslexia is not the worst disorder to have." She is seething as she is hyper focused on the road.

"I have to fight with the people over at the financial aid office to help fund this semester and pick up some shifts as a caretaker to that pervy old man, but do you ever see me curling up in a ball and giving up?" I know she's just talking to herself at this point, but I let her vent.

She lets out a primal, anguished scream and I can't help it . . . I begin to sob. I hate this side of her. The last three years she's started to go back to school have been horrible. I see her less and she's not as happy as she used to be. What's worse is that she used to pull me in her arms and apologize after little outbursts, but now those are becoming more and more infrequent.

When I stop crying and am only now sniffling, I wipe my face and look at her, expecting to see sympathy. There's none behind those hollow eyes.

"I need to finish my rounds for the day." My mom leaves the car running and speed walks back to the hospital.

*　　　　　　　*　　　　　　　*

The curtains open to the motel room and I groan as Kai and Denise are both there. I don't even have my clothes on! I pull the sheets over me, but Denise doesn't look amused.

"Get dressed. We're already thirty minutes behind. Kai wanted to let you sleep in longer." Denise woke up and chose violence, but to be fair, I assured her that Kai and I wouldn't be a distraction.

Kai avoids eye contact as I get out of bed and grab my clothes. I look down and notice that Denise has already packed my stuff. They are literally just waiting on me. I'm pretty sure my bra is inside out as I awkwardly rush through getting dressed. Denise seems satisfied enough as she grunts and informs us that she's already checked us out. We start piling out of the room.

"About last night—" I begin to Kai.

"Isabelle. You're amazing and I want to get to know you better. But first we need to get our heads back in the game." If I didn't know better, I would say that Denise has been talking to him.

Fuck the plan! Let the world burn for all I care. Last night was incredible, but classic Isabelle says, "You're right. Let's find this guy and burn his book to the ground."

His smile is more than enough to hold me over. Although if he had bent down and kissed me, I wouldn't have fought that.

CHAPTER SIXTEEN

We get to the beginning of a hiking trail that we think is not far from the commune. I feel like the amount of research the three of us have done over the past few days is just pinpointing general areas of where he could be. What if he lives here and isn't home? What if the information in the photos misleads us and we're in some random countryside where some hillbilly is waiting with a shotgun? Like Cain purposely did this to send enemies on a wild goose chase? What if he's not even real?

I've thought about the last one a lot. There are some people who believe that Shakespeare's work was not from one man but instead a collection from different authors. What if this book was engineered by a religion or the government? It seems to be doing a great job of convincing the masses to buy in, but I don't want to think too much about that. At work I would sometimes listen to Trey and Steve go down the rabbit hole of conspiracy theories, and it always struck me as idiotic. It seems like a lot of people who are uneducated crave to be in on "insider information" because the alternative is to actually be informed on the facts.

We get out of the rental and Kai has me carry a tripod and some lighting equipment. They're not heavy but definitely annoying to haul around. I try not to complain, though, because he has a rather big backpack and has to carry a camera that looks like it was built in the 1990s. Denise has assumed the role as our "on-air talent," and despite just rolling out of bed, she still looks stunning. She even has an earpiece that looks pretty convincing. I'll admit that if I saw the three of us, I wouldn't think twice about who we were.

The woods are damp from light showers the night before. I already hate not having heavy-duty hiking boots, but then again I was kind of thrown into the whole situation and didn't pack anything to begin with. Denise and Kai had obviously talked about this expedition for months, and I was the last-minute addition who has been playing catch up.

The three of us start on a trail and head north. I sincerely hope we are going in the right direction because our cell phones lost service on our way to the trailhead. I take out my phone in between shifting the gear in my arms and look down to see the lack of bars. Denise observes this and places her arm on my shoulder.

"This will be good for all of us. Even those who are not as vain could stand to spend a little less time on their phones." She walks past me. I'm already a hermit who doesn't live on social media apps, and I have no one contacting me. Even Dad has been quiet for the past couple of days outside of an occasional apology text. I'm more worried about our safety if we run into problems. Then I remember: we are the problem.

We're alone for miles and the three of us barely exchange words. I wonder if Denise regrets bringing me into the fold because of whatever this is between me and Kai. And has Kai thought about last night, or was I just another notch on the belt? I remember when I first tried to get myself out there, I would go on the dating apps to legitimately meet friends and found out the hard way that a lot of men take that as a code for hooking up.

After a few seemingly innocent men were successful in having one-night stands with me, I swore off the apps. Even ones that were advertised as strictly platonic—and the few times that I did go out with women—they usually got bored with me within days. You could always tell when someone doesn't want to continue a friendship when you've texted them three times and gotten no response. Naive me used to think that people must've been too busy to text back, but after enough times and some research on the internet, I found out what ghosting was.

We hear voices and Kai motions for us to stop. We spot a younger couple in their twenties about thirty yards away from us. They're not hiding their presence and

laugh with one another about something. Kai turns back
to us.

"Denise, we've been over this before—talk loud
enough for them to hear, but do not make it suspicious.
Only mention the commune when we're within earshot,"
Kai orders Denise in a whisper, and her eyes are on the
prize. I wasn't given instructions so I just nod like I know
what they're talking about.

We continue to walk toward the couple and
Denise and Kai start conversing out loud. I just sit back
and listen.

"Mating season should've just ended, so we're
going to be catching them after the females are left
burrowing in their dens." Denise starts the conversation
and it seems well rehearsed.

"That's the idea. Although I hope that the mates
take advantage of the rainy season and hunt out in the
daylight. We're still months away from the winter season
where they usually thrive."

"I told you we should've waited until November to
start filming," Denise continues as we begin to approach
the couple. They've seen us and stop talking to each other.

"This was the only time we could get the grant and
it worked with our schedule. I still have a full-time job,
you know," Kai explains as he balances the camera to his
other arm. "They don't hibernate, so we should be able to
catch them—" we've crossed their paths and they look up

139

and smile, but they have excellent poker faces. I cannot read them. Kai breaks the ice with them. "Good morning."

"Good morning," the woman echoes. She has olive skin and green eyes. The man is tall and slender with dirty-blond hair and is the first to take the bait.

"I hope you three weren't hoping to see any grizzlies right now." It seems like a lighthearted tone, but I can still hear some hesitancy.

"Nope," Denise says with a chuckle, "we aren't that cool to be studying bears . . . just looking for your typical little weasel."

"Weasel?" the woman scrunches up her face in confusion.

"They're actually called Haida ermine, but most people don't know what they are," Kai pipes up and seems to give off a disarming-enough demeanor.

"Oh sure! Those little white-haired rascals? We see them all the time!" The man seems genuinely happy to talk about them.

Kai turns to Denise and widens his eyes, and she smiles at him without revealing teeth. A not-so-hidden gesture of triumph.

"I told you Margaret knew what she was talking about," Denise tells Kai.

The woman's eyes widen as she says, "You two know Margaret?"

140

"Not well. Only online. We were emailing her about potentially filming in the area. A lot of cities and towns are too crowded and scare them off. We were hoping to go somewhere where they thrive without much human activity." Denise sounds like a pro.

Bingo. The two of them have let their guard down completely and look genuinely pleased to see us now. The man is the first to speak. "That's a lot of equipment for you guys to haul around. Would the three of you like for us to give you a ride? We're heading to the commune's center right now."

"Commune? I thought we were near the town of Maple," Kai says innocently.

The woman and man laugh and now exchange their own looks as if saying, "We're off the grid and no one even knows about us."

"Margaret, ourselves, and about sixty of us live our own way, further away from the cities and general population," the woman explains.

"Sounds great for the ermine!" Kai has transformed completely into a wildlife nerd who cares about these little weasels. Even his mannerisms are different. I don't recognize him at all. Why should I? I need to keep reminding myself that he is Kyle now.

"Follow us. I'm Henry, and this is my wife, Azul." The three of us introduce ourselves accordingly: Kyle,

Danielle, and Sydney. When we shake hands, Azul lingers on my handshake longer than the others.

"Beautiful name." Her eyes stare deep into mine, and for a moment it seems like she knows I'm lying. How could she, though?

"Thank you." I pull back on her grip, which loosens. She tilts her head, smiling, and turns around for us to follow them.

Denise and Kai give the breakdown of the documentary while I add meaningless agreements and occasionally repeat the same words they say like a parrot. I am not as good at lying as they are, and I don't want to get caught in a lie that has them questioning everything we're doing. The only silver lining is that they only talk about the documentary for a short period before shifting to our personal lives, and I listen as they explain what they do back at home.

To my surprise, Denise actually still talks about the salon and her work as a hairstylist. With her going first, I figure there's no harm in telling them what I actually do as well. I'm about to tell them my company's name, but Denise swoops in and cuts me off and gives some bogus name. Maybe I am getting too comfortable with them, but I don't see the big deal. There's not an ounce of evil in our new friends.

In fact, it's probably better that these two live off the grid so they cannot be influenced with the teachings of *Your True Colors*. But then I remember that Cain grew up here. They have to know him, right? And, if so, wouldn't they have read a copy? Isn't that what supportive friends do whenever they make something of themselves?

I so badly want to ask about him but keep my mouth shut. If we're this close and are on the cusp of valuable information about Cain, then I cannot ruin it, and I find myself getting excited. I can only imagine how Kai and Denise are feeling. And, of course, tactfully they switch over the conversation to further talk about Henry and Azul.

They are about to go in depth when Henry says to Kai, "Jump in the front? We'll let the women ride in the back?"

We've approached a classic pickup truck that looks like it was built in the 1970s. I didn't even know these kinds of trucks were still in circulation. Azul picks up on my nervousness after jumping in the bed and leans down to extend a hand. "Come on. It's completely safe—I promise you."

I allow her to lift me up and the three of us settle in the bed. While the guys get up front I can hear Henry brag to Kai how he was both the homecoming king and valedictorian of his senior class. In response Azul rolls her eyes.

143

"He was one of ten people in his senior class, but he loves telling outsiders that." The joke has clearly been told hundreds of times but still brings a smile to her face. I admire that. The two have probably known one another their entire lives but haven't gotten sick of one another.

"Is that what we are? Outsiders?" Denise asks, and I instantly feel uncomfortable. It wasn't phrased like an offensive question, but I still feel like it could create tension.

"Well, sure. We don't really know you that well yet. Of course we'll give you the benefit of the doubt, but we don't meet too many people who are not from around here. In our community's history, we've been taken advantage of before and always need to remember that." I feel secondhand embarrassment and I don't know where to look.

It doesn't seem to be an issue with Denise as she looks deep into Azul's eyes. I feel an eternity pass and like I need to change the subject, but I am relieved when the homes begin to reveal themselves through the shrubs of the woods. I forget all about the conversation and am speechless as I see some of the most beautiful houses ever created.

There are only about two dozen of them in total, and they are spread out just enough to give each property their space, but not too far to alienate the nearest neighbor. The homes are unique. It's almost as if they were built like miniature castles yet have a dash of modernism to them. Even Denise marvels at the sight of the community.

I look back at Azul and there is a sense of pride in her eyes. For a moment I have forgotten all about our documentary charade, the mission, and even all the problems I have in my life. This looks like a haven. She reads my facial features and gently asks me why I am so surprised.

"I feel a lot of people think we live in little huts in the middle of nowhere, scrounging for food and barely civilized." Is it sad that that's exactly what I was thinking and am now blown away?

"It's beautiful." It doesn't take long before we pass a barn that I know was in the background of one of Cain's photos. I don't care, though. The community feels like a warm blanket on a winter's night. "How many families do you have here?"

"Sydney!" Denise insinuates in her tone that I'm overstepping and being rude. Isn't that the pot calling the kettle black? Wasn't she just antagonizing Azul moments ago?

"No, she's okay." Azul seems to sincerely mean it. "A lot of these homes are custom-built, and our families settled back here in the early 1960s. There were only eight to begin with, and now there's a total of fifteen clans. Homes were torn down and rebuilt in the late nineties, though. The grandson of one of the original families is an architect and thought about the winter life more acutely than his predecessors. He was also able to get the electrical grid to come from more than just generators."

We drive through the commune. Some sit outside on their porches and wave to us. Or maybe it's just to Henry and Azul. Regardless, the warmth of the blanket continues to be nurturing. I see crops off in the distance as well as hides of animals hanging in another person's yard. There's a brief glimpse of free-range animals in someone's backyard that look like goats, ducks, and maybe even a fawn. That can't be right, though . . . aren't they usually skittish around humans? Then again, what would I know? I guess I am a city girl.

"Your little friends are going to be further away from our commune, though," Azul continues, and I am briefly so confused, but thankfully Denise saves me.

"Don't tell me you hunted them off."

"Not necessarily, but they were unwanted visitors that often attacked some of our livestock. Despite their size, you'd be surprised the size of prey they are willing to take on. Never underestimate your opponent." Azul winks.

"Maybe this wasn't such a good idea, then." Denise sounds genuinely upset. "We thought this would be a perfect location to find them. We don't want to be too much of a burden. Do you think Henry could drive us back to our rental?"

And the Oscar goes to . . .

I would be so easily fooled. Denise is really selling this Danielle persona. I've seen so many versions of her in the short amount of time that I have known her that I wonder if she's actually friends with me or if all of that is a farce. The most passion I've seen from her is to locate this guy, and right now she's asking these strangers to take us away when we're obviously in his stomping grounds. My thoughts are interrupted by Azul's laugh.

"Don't stress it. There are still some around. We have definitely seen them on our walks further away from the commune, and I know Henry would be better than me at telling you the exact locations. We just don't let them get too close to our livestock. Trust me—you'll find your little rodents."

The truck comes to a stop. Kai and Henry help the two of us out of the vehicle, while Azul jumps out quite nimbly.

"I'm going to go check in with Walter. Meet up with you later, babe?" Azul kisses Henry, and she shakes our hands again and welcomes us to their community. She assures us we're in good hands with her husband and then off she goes.

"It's early, but around here we typically meet up in the dining hall to eat lunch around ten thirty. Would you guys care to join us?" Henry offers.

"I don't think it'll interfere with the schedule too bad, right Danielle?" Kai is not as good of an actor as his partner in crime, because he no longer seems nonchalant and even seems quite eager.

"Kyle, wouldn't it be better if we got at least some footage before calling it a day?" I don't understand. Isn't this all what they wanted? We're practically in the den right now.

"I don't want to intrude on your crew's plans." Henry opens his arms innocently. "I could always point you in the direction where they're at, and when you're done with whatever, we'll have someone drive you back."

"No, no, no . . . that won't be necessary. What do they say? Breakfast is the most important meal of the day, and that's what it'll be for us. We're in." Kai puts a stamp on it.

Henry's behavior transforms to that of a little boy. He seems giddy at the idea of having guests and tells us that we can walk the neighborhood. He just needs to let the cook know that they'll be adding three plates to today's meal. He asks us to meet up back at his truck in fifteen minutes.

This day has been the best in my life. I have never been on this much of an adventure. Nothing can ruin this mood. When he's gone I turn to them and am surprised to see that Denise and Kai look like they are about to fight with one another.

"We fucked up. We're all in danger," Denise whispers.

CHAPTER SEVENTEEN

The three of us walk the perimeters close to one another, and they talk in such low volumes that I am almost unable to hear them, and it seems even harder to keep on pace with them. Why walk so quickly? It's not like we can outrun anyone on foot even if we wanted to.

"There are eyes everywhere. This was a mistake. I thought we'd be able to scope out the area before stepping foot on their turf." Denise is in a sense of panic, but Kai heavily disagrees.

"Are you kidding? We're here! This is the spot. Did you see the barn?"

"Of course I saw it along with the other backgrounds in the photos, but now I'm realizing this wasn't a careless error on their part." I don't follow and wait for Denise to continue. "They lured us here. You think it was a coincidence we ran into those two in the woods?"

"Take the tin foil hat off, Danielle." Okay, I'll give it to Kai . . . he can stay in character. "They were harmless photos. Is it really hard to imagine a married couple getting some fresh air in the morning?"

"Yeah, it's hard to imagine because everyone here does a job and pulls his or her weight. The back of the truck bed was empty. If it were full of wood, supplies, or anything else I wouldn't be concerned, but the only cargo they shipped was us."

"Jesus Christ, Danielle, you're being ridiculous," Kai hisses, and even though I think she is being a bit overly paranoid to the point of crazy, I find myself now feeling slightly worried. What if she's right? We have no cell signal, and thanks to our careless car theft, no one can pinpoint where and when our last whereabouts have been.

And I was still mad at Dad so I didn't tell him where we were. The last sighting of both of us could've very well been when Denise barged into my work. I don't have anyone I share my phone's location with, but Denise has to. She's a popular person. People have to know when she would be missing, right?

"Sydney, what do you think about all of this?" Denise asks.

Fuck. My heart sinks. I never thought I would be a tiebreaker in any situation, and now the weight of what they're asking could very well be a life-or-death decision. Goddammit, I'm not that person. On one hand, if we stay and they're harmless, then we get further to our goal and could get answers as early as today with maybe even meeting Cain. On the other hand, the whole wholesome

151

country life could be a ruse, and they will be showcasing our hides on their front lawns come dawn.

Both sets of eyes are on me. I sigh.

"We've come this far, and they have visuals of who we are, so even if we were to be taken back to our car, wouldn't we just be coming back to them anyway? I think we should regroup after the meal." Kai is clearly happy with my decision, and rather than sulk, Denise locks eyes with me.

"This isn't a game, Sydney." Even though I think she is trying to intimidate me, I see fear in her eyes. I feel the need to channel my inner mother. If I'm going to assume her identity, I might as well act the part.

"If the lunch seems in any way sketchy, I'll let Henry know that I have a medical condition. Something like diabetes and that my HypoPen was left in the vehicle." Not bad for on the fly. Kai applauds my quick thinking as well.

"Oooo, that's good. Great job, Sydney. I can get on board with that exit strategy." He pats me on the back and looks down at his watch. He informs us that we have six minutes to meet back at Henry's truck.

If we're not careful, Kai is going to blow our cover. I don't think that Henry was literal when he said fifteen minutes, and ever since we drove into the commune, Kai's been letting his mask slip further and further. He's anxious and I can sense his energy. Omar used to try to act cool around me when we were kids, but I knew he'd had a crush on me since middle school. I know most women like the chase, but I found it endearing. Make no mistake—people are usually pretty keen on picking up true intentions.

Regardless, the three of us walk back toward the truck. Henry's not there yet, and I know that the real Denise is not comfortable. Her usual confident, carefree attitude has been replaced with this shroud of uncertainty. I hate that it reminds me of myself. I typically feel out of place and want nothing more than to leave and be in the comfort of my own room.

I reach out and gently scratch her back. She jumps a little at first but eases up and attempts to loosen up a bit.

"I want to be mad at you and tell you that you only took his side because you guys hooked up last night, but I know what you said makes sense." If that's an apology, it was a clunky one, but I don't say anything and let her finish. "Do you think he's here?"

"I honestly don't know." She knows that I don't know all the answers and nods her head in disappointment. "But with a haven like this, I think he'd be crazy to spend time away from here and not return. I'm not a betting person like my father, but if I had to guess, I'd wager he's around."

I feel like Denise has had tunnel vision since we've arrived and only now looks around at the community that they've built. She seems to appreciate it because I can see her shoulders loosen and the tension eases a bit.

I don't tell her about the hidden camera that lurks on the side of the truck. Everyone keeps their property guarded. It's probably nothing and I don't want to make a big deal out of nothing. Why stress Denise out further?

Henry joins us along with a man who looks like an older version of Azul. It's no surprise when he introduces Javi as her older brother. This is not at all how I imagine people from the country to look like. They both were obviously blessed with good genetics. It has to be a prerequisite to live here, because the two of them could easily be models in the real world.

"Would you guys like me to take your equipment to the barn before the meal?" Javi asks. I feel like hitting my forehead with the palm of my hand. I almost forgot about it. I look inside the bed of the truck and it's all still safely there.

"We can't keep it in the truck?" Denise questions.

"I mean, you can, but I don't know if it's going to rain soon, and I think Henry has to go run errands later, so it'd be a tight fit in the front seat with him." It makes sense, but I can see why Denise is apprehensive. I'm not sure how much she spent on these supplies, but they definitely look like they're worth a lot of money. Even if this is all an act, I wouldn't want to lose out on thousands of dollars' worth of equipment either.

Both of them are falling apart. If I hardly knew them, I would have at first thought that both of them could've had a career in acting, maybe even Broadway, but now Kai is eager, borderline desperate, while Denise is cracking . . . attempting to act cool, but she is a bundle of nerves. If the wheels are already falling apart for them, then what type of energy am I giving?

"Where will you be taking it?" Denise asks as Javi assures them it'll be safe in his living room and nods over to a beige house that's at the end of the street. He offers for her to accompany him, and I can tell that she really wants to but lets it go and assures him that she trusts him. He hauls all of our belongings with ease. I know that I would need to take two or three trips.

"I hope you guys brought your appetite. Elk is on the menu today." Henry's smile is warm and friendly, and if I look really hard at his true emotions behind this mask, I cannot find any. His surface seems one hundred percent genuine.

It's less than a fifteen-minute walk to the town center where the commune is going to be gathering. In the center of the commune there is a building that looks similar to that of a recreation center back in the city. The doors are open, and although we get some confused looks here and there, most people go about their own business and smile politely when we walk by.

Tables are all aligned within the dining hall, and people have already helped themselves to plates, while there is a small group of people who serve those who approach them. It actually reminds me of my junior high years when there was a lunch line and the cafeteria employees would serve us. But now instead of an access card, it appears to be free. Although I definitely don't ever want to assume anything.

"Would we be able to pitch in for today's meal?" I ask Henry. His laugh booms throughout the hall, and he politely pats me on the back.

"Most definitely not! It's not a bother for any of us here. If you want to go the extra mile, maybe collect some of the kids' dishes since Betsy's got her hands full babysitting today. Even then I think she'd want the older kids to get in the habit of pulling their weight," Henry informs us.

"How does that work?" Kai inquires. "Pulling your weight around here?"

We all get our food and join Azul and some people who are closer to our age at the table. They've made sure there's enough room for all of us. "It's not that foreign of a concept. We all do our part to make sure that we look out for one another. There is, of course, the basic necessities we need like clean water, food, and shelter . . .

156

but we have all those departments covered and even train ourselves on a lot of DIY projects when it comes to fixing things around the houses."

"What about legal and medical assistance?" Denise asks. I'm a little embarrassed because she hasn't touched her food and I wonder if they can see how guarded she is.

Me, on the other hand . . . I'm already eyeing my seconds. I don't know what they used to season the elk with, but it's some of the best food I have ever had. Not that I travel much outside my own backyard.

"Our community does travel outside of here. No one is a prisoner. The ones who choose to study law and medicine have been offered lucrative amounts of money, which some of them have taken," Azul explains, "but you'd be surprised how many of them give up their wealth to come back home. We currently have four doctors and three lawyers in our compound."

"Five doctors," Henry corrects.

"Oh, right! Victoria joined us not long ago." Azul hits her forehead with her palm, "She's been such a welcome addition to the community."

"Has anyone ever left and become famous?" Kai asks. Under the table I can feel Denise kick him in the shins. None of this has been subtle, but these people don't seem like murderers, so I don't feel the need to ridicule either of them. I'm honestly halfway tempted to just to point-blank ask them: "Hey! Doesn't Cain Skaggs live here? And, if so, which one is his house? I don't know if you guys know, but you have a psychopath mastermind living among you all."

"Like we've mentioned before," Azul is onto them and now her facade is slipping, "we've had success outside these walls. A lot of our community has gone on to accomplish a lot of glorious things."

"Kyle . . . would I be able to have a moment with you, outside, about the documentary?" Denise hisses. He hesitates, and I know he wants to press further into whatever cryptic message Azul was saying, but reluctantly he gets up and joins her.

I think I'm off the hook until Denise marches back and quite forcefully yanks me out of my chair too. I instantly regret not eating more as the plate gets further away from me.

"What the fuck was all of that?" Denise has pulled us over to the side of the building where there are no visible windows for eavesdropping.

"What's your problem, Denise?" Kai snarls.

"Danielle. My name is Danielle," she hisses through her teeth. I'm extremely uncomfortable. I've spent my whole life actively avoiding confrontations and now find myself in the middle of these two vigilantes. Please, God, don't let them ask me to choose a side again.

"In case you haven't realized, we're on his turf. We're practically here! It shouldn't be too hard to find the guy, and the community seems like pacifists." Kai's voice starts rising.

"Except they're not," I quietly say.

They both turn to me, and I instantly want to cover my mouth and act like I didn't say that, so I try to tell them that I misspoke, but then Denise presses me further until I further elaborate what I said.

"They're hunters. All of them. Even in the short conversation we had with them, it's clear that they are equipped with all the trades—including hunting and gathering their meals. Henry had guns in the back of his truck, stashed in the cab, but even driving into town I noticed younger kids target practicing with adults in the backyard with BB guns." I know it seems like I'm choosing a side right now, but I'm honestly just stating facts. Denise is practically gloating.

"See! We're in over our heads. I say we regroup in the forest with our equipment. Get further away and then only go back when we have a better plan." I wasn't agreeing with Denise and am actually slightly disappointed upon hearing about leaving. I've grown quite attached to this little pocket of the world.

"You two do whatever you want, but I'm getting answers." Kai turns his back to us, and I can tell that Denise wants to stop him but is afraid to attract attention, so she settles with hissing his name. He turns the corner and then suddenly we don't hear him anymore. No footsteps. No breathing. It's oddly still.

"Kyle?" I ask. The two of us inch around the corner and are met with the butt of a shotgun to the back of the head. Everything goes black.

CHAPTER EIGHTEEN

I groggily open my eyes, but the world is still blurry and swaying back and forth. The back of my head hurts. I groan, but my throat is on fire. I don't know if I was drooling a lot while I was out or what, but I am definitely dehydrated. Kai is tied up to my left, and Denise's screams are distinct and feet away from me.

"You're going to be sorry! You think we'd come out here without a contingency plan?" Except we did. Jesus Christ, this whole trip seems so stupid when you think about it. Who did we even tell that we're out here? My boss just thinks I'm gone for the week, while my dad still thinks I'm mad at him. It's amazing how quick you forgive when your life is suddenly in danger.

We seem to be in a barn of some sort. There are haystacks and some barn animals corralled inside. The three of us are tied up in heavy-duty ropes. Denise and Kai are on their knees with hands tied in front of them. Meanwhile I am swaying back and forth with my hands tied over my head.

"Did you all write the book together and use Cain as the face of it?" she screams. "The world is burning out there and this Manson rip-off family is all to blame!"

161

Azul laughs and turns to her husband. "Manson family? That's a new one." She motions her head toward me and Kai. If I could back up, I would.

My eyes go wide as Henry approaches, and I pee my pants. Henry looks down at me and shakes his head. "Relax. I'm just cutting you two loose." He nods his head over to Denise. "Her, on the other hand . . . it's in our best interest she stays tied up for the time being,"

"We won't say anything." My voice is hoarse like I've been the one screaming this whole time, and Henry notices this. He whistles. Javi tosses a bottle of water that lands near my feet. Even if it were to be poisoned, I don't care. When I'm cut loose and my feet touch the ground, I unscrew the top and instantly gulp down half a bottle.

Kai is the next to be let loose, and he seems perfectly motionless. Javi tries to untie the knots but struggles. He hollers over his shoulder for a hunting knife. Henry jokes that he purposely tied Kai too tight because he had a bet with Azul whether or not he'd be able to loosen it. Javi flips him off but accepts the hunting knife and begins to loosen Kai's ropes.

"He's a genius," Kai says so softly at first that the room almost cannot hear what he has to say. His head lifts up and he looks at Javi square in the eyes. "Cain is brilliant, and I've never met someone so well-versed in the art of manipulation. I applaud him."

162

Javi and Kai look into each other's eyes for what seems like eternity. Then in a quick instant Kai grabs the hunting knife and Javi instantly backs up. In a very swift movement, Azul reaches for a shotgun and levels it at Kai, but he doesn't lunge at the captors . . . he steps behind Denise and puts the knife to her throat.

"Kaiiiiii," Denise's voice cracks as it raises three octaves, "what are you doing?"

"I saw through it the first time I read it but knew it had a deeper meaning." Kai ignores Denise and her pleas. "The intentionally split-up sentences and clunky dialogue—it triggers parts of the brain, and it's working."

"Kai, please just take the knife away from my throat." Denise's fight has been expelled out of her completely.

"I want in. I already traveled to Wyoming and Arkansas to take care of the users on the forum board who were planning on killing him," Kai confesses.

A small sob escapes Denise's throat, and she would cover her mouth if she could. "The other crew members that were going to meet up with us."

"Make no mistake, Henry, even though one of them was a fourteen-year-old . . . he was figuring out what your community was up to. You have to weed out the nonbelievers and those who won't let chaos unfold."

"He was a child, Kai. Oh my God, you've gone insane." Denise is more horrified at the thought of a child

163

being killed than the knife to her throat. I would agree but cannot find my voice. This all seems like a very horrible dream that I walked into.

"At first I thought I was insane as well! Why wasn't it making sense the first time around? Colleagues and family were all reading it for what it was, and I was over here analyzing it like it was a manifesto that needed to be debriefed." Kai acts as if his confession is somehow justified and that the people around him will accept him. Will they?

There's a moment's pause before Azul finally breaks the silence. "You should step away from the woman, Kai." Her voice sounds calm and rational, but the shotgun is still trained on him.

"This is a test, isn't it?" Kai speaks as if suddenly enlightened.

"It is not," Azul assures him.

"Of course! Anyone could say they killed the nonconformed, but seeing is believing." In a quick motion Kai's knife opens Denise's throat and crimson red spills to the floor.

"Jesus Christ! Grab her!!!" Azul barks.

I pass out. Before I am completely out I could swear that I hear Kai ranting like a madman that he has Isabelle Dunham. He brought Isabelle Dunham to their camp. What would someone want with a nobody like me?

CHAPTER NINETEEN

It's evening out. I squint and notice that I am now sprawled across a hospital bed in what seems like a nightgown. That can't be . . . the nearest hospital has to be miles away. Where am I? Denise! Where is she?!

I sit up and have an instant headache as I force myself to lie back down. The lights turn on and I can see Henry in the doorway. He talks into what appears to be a walkie-talkie but far more sophisticated. Is it a military phone? "She's up."

He walks into the room but keeps his hands open in a nonthreatening way. Naturally I curl up and start to panic as I hit the wall in an attempt to keep as much distance from him as possible.

"Relax," he assures. He stops walking into the room and beelines toward a chair in the corner. He nods his head to the chair. "Is it cool if I take a seat?"

I don't say anything as I look out the window. His eyes follow mine and he sighs. "I suppose you could try to jump from three stories, but I wouldn't suggest it."

"Is she alive?" I meant to ask where Denise was, but I'm happy with my question. It seems like the more appropriate one.

165

"Yeah. He ruptured a vocal cord and she lost a lot of blood, but I'm optimistic." Henry leans back in his chair. Was this an effort to have the least threatening body language? I hate to say it, but if it was the goal, then it's definitely working. I climb back into the bed, never taking my eyes off of him.

"Kai on the other hand . . ." he smirks.

"Dead," I suggest.

"Most likely. Obviously there will be a town meeting on it," Henry states so matter-of-factly like this is a simple occurrence.

"Why not just take him to the authorities?" I ask. I'm proud of myself. I am still in shock and am using the innocent, injured, distressed woman to my advantage. Even though the mission is most likely well over, I'm still trying to get intel and a feel for the place.

"That's not how we do things," he responds. Great. Not that helpful, but what did I expect? Before I can ask another question, he interrupts my thoughts: "Do you want to see her?"

He motions at my clothes sitting in the corner of the room. Pretty neatly folded, I might add. I don't know if he plans on killing me, but at least he's somewhat of a gentleman. He turns around while he lets me dress, and I feel there's a lot of trust in his having his back to me. If I were stealthy, quick, and had a backbone, I could grab the handgun in his holster.

166

Before he changes his mind, I go ahead and put on the shirt. Those aren't my pants or underwear though. I am momentarily confused until I remember that I did, in fact, pee myself in front of everyone. Not that I'm ashamed. I feel most people would do the same when death is staring them in the face. I am reluctant to put a stranger's clothing on even though it feels and smells new, but what other choice do I have?

When I'm finished I notify him, and he looks over his shoulder and then motions toward the door, indicating he wants me to follow him. I leave the room and notice that it's not a hospital at all. Of course it's not; why would it be? I haven't left the commune, but I suppose a small part of me was hoping there would be nurses, doctors, even a janitor I could cling to and let him know that I have been taken hostage.

I don't even care that we were trespassing or that I helped steal a car and was potentially part of an assassination attempt. At least in civilization I could plea my case and maybe go back to my boring life where the biggest dilemma I would face is what to cook at night or what movie I should watch on Netflix.

We pass the halls of the rather large home. He wasn't kidding—it is three floors, and if I studied architecture, I would appreciate the non-tour I was getting right now. But instead my eyes are searching the halls for an escape route. Am I supposed to run on foot? I'm horrible with directions and couldn't tell you north from south. Steal keys and drive off? Again, assuming I made it past the commune, would I be going further into the woods or toward the next town? The roads were rocky when we got here and were barely made for off-roading.

I don't have my cell phone. I don't know my dad's number. If I did manage to make it into town, how would I explain the stolen car, or in this case cars plural? What would I say—a guy I hooked up with last night slit the throat of my friend and these people patched her up? Oh, by the way, we were only trespassing because we planned on killing this author.

We reach near the end of the hall where Henry gently opens the door to a room. It's rather lavish, and I don't know if it was designed to have a surgical table, but sure enough, there are medical tools and blood stained on the table. But I see Denise intact and strapped to a hospital bed. She breathes heavily and is wide-eyed like a caged animal. I know that I should be cautious, but I cannot stop myself as I run into the room and hug her.

"Oh my God, Denise!" I choke up. Instantly my eyes fall to her straps and I begin to try to undo them, but Henry advises me against that.

"I wouldn't do that," Henry warns. "We had to give her strong meds to knock her out while patching up her throat. I told our doctor that we should sedate her more because she's going to rip her stitches and potentially lose more blood, but she was insistent that we don't medicate her too heavily without knowing her medical history."

"That makes sense." I stop untying her, but Denise gives me an expression that I can read all too well.

If she could talk I could easily see her saying, "Fuck this guy. What kind of sorry excuse is that?"

I can't help it. I laugh a little even though I know she's not joking, and she exhales through her nose. "You're right, I'm sorry. That's not funny."

Henry speaks something unintelligible into his walkie-talkie and then confirms a command. He taps me on the shoulder. Of course I jump, and he backs away, arms and hands again. "I have to go check in with the others. Can I trust you alone for five minutes?"

I didn't realize how much I needed privacy with Denise, so I enthusiastically nod my head and promise him that I won't do anything stupid. His hospitality has been pretty good for being a captor, but I know he probably has his limits. Henry sizes me up and further emphasizes how much trouble I'll be in if I break anything on the property or cause any trouble.

When he leaves, I turn back to Denise, who attempts to speak. Obviously her voice makes no sound, and she winces painfully after each attempt. I am no doctor, but I can tell that's probably not the best idea, so I soothe her and caress her head. She grunts angrily and

169

knocks my hand away with her head . . . pretty hard too. That kind of hurt.

She abandons talking and tries to mouth words. I know what she's trying to do, but I cannot read lips. I apologize and let her know that I can't understand her. Denise is obviously frustrated and tears well up in the corners of her eyes. She sighs and rests her head on the pillow but then jolts up. Denise grunts and my eyes follow hers. On the table there's a medical notepad and a pen.

I hurry over and grab them. I look down at the straps that restrain her.

"I'll untie you, but please don't do anything stupid, Denise. We're on thin ice as it is." Her eyes tell me that she cannot promise anything, but what choice do I have?

I undo one of the straps and didn't even think to ask if that's her writing hand . . . it is. Thank God. All of a sudden I hear a pair of footsteps approaching. I panic and tell Denise to hurry. Denise starts writing two words and underlines the second one. She shows it to me and I am instantly flustered. It reads: OTN ICNA.

The second word is underlined numerous times and I look at it blankly. I try to decipher it quickly but feel like a gun is to the side of my head. "Ton cina? Action? Contain?"

Denise grunts and shakes her head, pointing to the second word and circling it over and over. It's too late.

They're here. I turn behind me where the siblings Azul and Javi await.

CHAPTER TWENTY

"Okay. You've seen her. Now let's get you back to your room." Azul wears a great mask, too, because this doesn't seem like the same person that I met back in the woods.

"I would like to stay with her." Even my voice sounds tiny compared to hers. Who wears the pants in her relationship, because even I flinch before she speaks.

"That won't be good for anyone. Your friend over here did herself no favors with how irrational she's been acting. Maybe if she were more like you, that wouldn't be too much of an issue." I hate to admit it, but Azul actually makes sense.

I turn back to Denise and give her an apologetic look while I watch as Javi straps her back in again. To give her credit, she doesn't put up much of a fight. Maybe she is listening to our conversation and starting to realize you can catch more bees with honey versus vinegar. It's my turn to communicate without words as I try to assure her with my eyes that I'll think of something to get us out of here.

It dawns on me that this in itself is a very scary thought. This isn't me. None of this is! If anything, I'm

172

supposed to be the voiceless one chained to a bed while the badass Denise goes full Rambo and breaks me out of here. And even though Kai turned out to be the biggest two-face, I'm sure if he were who we thought he was, then he'd use his brain to charm the community members to let us out.

What am I supposed to do? Apologize my way out of here? I follow the two as they escort me back to my room. Across Denise's room there's another patient hooked to life support. I definitely recognize the sound of the machines and not from movies. When I was a little girl, I would occasionally visit my mom at her job, and the sounds are rhythmic . . . borderline hypnotic.

I don't see the patient, but I can hear his or her steady breathing. They seem in stable condition, but I sense that whoever is connected is a fighter. I guess it makes sense that this house/building is their hospital. It would probably take at least a half an hour to fly to the nearest major hospital, and something tells me that these are not the type of people who want to get involved in public affairs.

They stop at the bathroom and tell me that I have to go now because I will be locked in my room for the rest of the night. Great. I'll be locked in there? It seemed comfortable enough, but what the hell am I supposed to do, think of some shitty plan to get us out of here?

I didn't think I could go to the bathroom on command but hadn't realized how much I was holding it in. It comes easy, and I splash water into my face as I look into the mirror at myself. This is it. I'm staring at the face of the person who's going to rescue Denise and get us out of here. I break down. First it's light sobbing. Then a full-on cry.

The door creaks open and Azul's face softens. She ushers me out of the bathroom and allows me to cry into her arms as she walks us over to the room and gently sets me on the bed.

"Do you think we're going to hurt you?" Azul asks.

I shrug my shoulders and try to compose myself. It's irrational, but suddenly I find myself embarrassed about crying in front of Javi and Azul. I guess it's better here than in Denise's room. Had she seen this, she would've truly given up on me and probably finished Kai's job.

"Think about things from our perspective. You came into our home with false names, brought recording equipment, conspired against us, and not only did we save your friend's life, we also housed you in one of our hospital rooms instead of the lair." Her words were comforting until I heard the word "lair." Is that where Kai is? Do I want to know the conditions of that?

174

This is where the strong, independent woman comes to life. I see through her good cop ruse and basically spit in her face that I am not intimidated by them. I'm going to break out of here and she could send the whole village folk on us, but that won't deter me. Instead, of course, I mumble the words, "I want to go home."

Goddammit. I can be so pathetic. With this response, Azul doesn't say anything as she leaves the room. I visibly hear the lock. I know I should go check it to make sure that it's secure, but I don't. I'm left alone and looking at the four walls, thinking about all the horrible choices I have made in the last five days.

That stupid book.

Outside of some embezzled funds, a prostitute in my house, and being caught knowing about an office affair, what harm was it doing to me? I should've just kept out of it altogether and gone on with my head buried in the sand. I've done that my whole life and have been just fine.

My eyes get heavy and I realize that I haven't slept in a while since passing out. Or at least I don't think that I have. Then again, I was out the whole time they stitched up Denise, and I don't think this dusk is from the same day. Maybe all this stress and action have exhausted me. I can't say that I'm surprised. What else am I going to do? I lie down and further run away from my problems.

*   *   *

I wake up.

It's still evening. I didn't even dream. It'd be one thing to be in another reality where I'm living my mundane life from a week ago only to slowly remember where I am, but sure enough . . . yup. Still living in the same nightmare. But I look over the room and notice something off. The door. It's ajar. Did someone come in and leave something? I look to the side and, yes, there's a water bottle that wasn't there before.

Great. Either this is a test, and if I try to escape I'll just end up sharing a lair with Kai or, worse, they truly don't see me as a threat and are willing to bet I won't do anything even if I leave my room. Somehow I think it's the latter. But then again, I try to be optimistic and think that maybe this was a human error. How often do they have people locked in these rooms? Maybe they really did accidentally leave the door open.

Whatever the reason, I am wide awake and will not stare at it all night. I approach the door and look through the crack to see if someone is standing guard. There's no one there. I open it further and the door does not creak. So far, so good. I peek my head out into the hallway and look left and right. Coast is clear. The socks I am wearing are pretty layered, and I cannot hear my footsteps as I move.

I still err on the side of caution and slowly make my way down the hall. It's not that far of a walk, and I see Denise's room. My goodness, the dyslexia is going to kill me, but maybe if I give Denise the notepad again, I can read better when not in a tense situation. I'm sure she's had time to think about what we're going to do too.

I almost open her door but hear the machines from across the room and see that that door is also ajar. I am curious to see who's on life support. I don't watch many horror movies because they pump my blood too much, but I know enough to know that this is the beginning of every one of those types of movies. The stupid girl who goes into a creepy room in the middle of the night when help was on the other side. People want to laugh at them and talk about how they wouldn't be such an idiot, but what if it's someone who also needs rescuing?

I approach the door and push it open, and I notice that the man is decrepit and has a very aggressive form of cancer. Not just any man. Cain Skaggs. I cannot believe what I'm seeing as we lock eyes. He's awake and the look in his eyes is that of acknowledgment.

I'm so distracted that I don't realize that I've walked toward him. I don't notice when the door closes behind me. I'm broken out of my trance when a familiar voice speaks out to me.

"Hello, Isabelle."

I lose my breath when I turn around.

177

Your True Colors

"Mom?"

Your True Colors

Your True Colors

PART II
SYDNEY

CHAPTER ONE

Eugene, Oregon, 1999

It had been a week and it was only Tuesday. My car was in the shop, and it was an uphill battle convincing Tanner to let me take his Jeep. Heaven forbid he have his military buddy pick him up for three days. But, no, cool— let's let the parent going through med school take public transit all while I made sure Isabelle got to school.

This wasn't even mentioning that he could walk to the local bar anyway. But after downing four or five beers, he often drove with no regard for the law or his own well-being. I used to get worked up over his long nights but realized that I was sacrificing sleep which, in turn, affected my schoolwork. I began taking downers when I went to bed. Get shitfaced and die for all I care—just don't wreck the vehicle. Mine was barely on life support as it was.

I had to do some digging at the hospital and made friends with this incredibly awkward receptionist when my Corolla started acting sluggish. It was simple to turn the charm on, but Beatrice was clingy, and I could not handle another one of those in my life. But I toughed it through and listened to boring stories about her cat named Musket. When the subject of her husband came up and she mentioned he was a mechanic (I already knew that, though), I casually mentioned that my car was on the fritz.

She offered, quite eagerly, to help get it fixed, so I put on the performance of a lifetime to act simultaneously surprised and grateful for the hookup. Of course I had to include the "barely making it on my student loans" broke-college-kid excuse, but she waved her hands and insisted that it wouldn't be a problem. We could even laugh about it at happy hour sometime! Yeah, that would never happen. It was definitely nice having a kid as an ultimate get-you-out-of-anything excuse.

I would've had to dip into the secret "webcam" fund if the plan fell through, but that was the only nest I had at the time, and it was hard making the right kind of connections online that could get me money under the table and paid in cashier's checks. I knew the hacker I was working with was skimming me and taking more of a cut than he should, but this was probably as good as it was going to get. I'd already been burned, financially, with three other online "partners." Thankfully Tanner thought I was just doing more schoolwork when I locked the door, and he was too thickheaded to think otherwise.

I did love him, though. We met at the lake in my high school years while he was getting back from basic training in the military. He wasn't my type, but his confidence won me over. Plus, he liked teasing me about my liberal views and told me that I would be the type to vote for Gore in the next election. He wasn't wrong, but what did that say about him? He was supporting a candidate who was only there because his dad was president. One-term president, mind you. It didn't matter. He'd lose. Now if the Republicans had chosen McCain, they would've really had a shot.

I pulled up to the school and was instantly worried when I saw a vacant parking lot. At the front of the school I saw Mrs. Roberts with Isabelle clinging to her leg. My eyes shifted left and right while I tried to remember what time it was. I looked at the clock . . . I wasn't late, was I? Fuck! Early release because of half day. Dammit. I was on thin ice with this school as it was. How much charm did I have left today? It was going to take a lot because I could tell that she did not look happy.

I was tempted to leave the car in neutral, but I knew that'd piss her off even more if I seemed like I was trying to avoid the conversation. Nope. This was on me. I had to own up to that even if I did have a million other things to worry about.

"It's a half day!" I tried to sound ditzy, which worked sometimes. I opened my palm and hit my forehead.

"Mommy!" Isabelle ran rather quickly into my legs and nearly took me out.

"Hey, Izzy." I hugged her back and patted her head as I returned my gaze to Mrs. Roberts. Okay, be cool. Don't make any excuses, I told myself. People just wanted you to listen to them and hear their problems. Don't be combative.

"Sydney. This is the third time." I nodded and agreed with her as I waited for her to continue. "We've had five incidents this whole school year, and your family has been involved in three of them."

"I know. You're right." I wanted to pile on more excuses, but I was still feeling out her emotions. I studied her face and found an opening. "You have a million other things to worry about, and my daughter shouldn't be an additional problem."

Her face softened. "Isabelle is not a problem child, and I love her, I really do—" There was the opening. I took it before she piled on more blame.

"—but she's not your responsibility twenty-four seven. She's mine. You're completely right, Mrs. Roberts." I sympathized with her and let my body loosen. When approaching a bear, you needed to puff your body out and act bigger, but it was better in these situations to seem as nonthreatening as possible.

She opened her mouth to speak but then closed it. She looked me up and down and nodded like she understood what I was trying to convey. "Tough day at the hospital?"

186

Like there were ever easy ones? Sydney, stop, I commanded myself. She was extending an olive branch. Take it.

"You know, some days I wonder if it was the right decision to even tackle this while being a parent." Mrs. Roberts was caught off guard and rubbed my shoulder. My goodness, I hated to be touched.

"Hang in there, Sydney." She was comforting me! "I know it's probably tough right now, but it's going to pay off so much when you get past this." This was the part where I had to act completely idiotic.

"You really think so?" What a dumb question, but it worked.

"Oh, you're going to look back on these days and laugh. You know a lot of our students' parents are also in the medical field." She beamed.

"You don't say?" I acted surprised, but no shit, lady. This was the nicest school in a thirty-mile radius.

"If you'd like, I can get you in contact with some of the doctors here. I'm sure they're always in need of more nurses." She seemed genuine, and it was so hard to keep up the fake smile, but she had no idea. My face muscles were screaming at me to stop smiling, but I didn't waver.

I was going through med school to be a doctor. Not a nurse. I had no desire to live in Oregon when I was finished with school. Half the dads here had creeped on

187

me at least once whenever Tanner hadn't been present. But I said none of this.

"You know, I would like that!" I apologized again for forgetting Isabelle's pickup time, and she insisted that it wasn't that big of a deal but to be more mindful next time. When I saw her drive away, my face dropped and could finally relax.

It took thirteen muscles to smile versus fifty to frown, but lately it felt like they got those numbers mixed up. I sighed while Isabelle did her happy dance to the Jeep. It was cute, but my social battery had been pushed to its furthest limit and I had hardly any energy for her.

"Come on, kiddo, let's go home." I ushered her into the passenger seat.

"Mommy, I'm starving!" I was halfway tempted to turn up the knob on our car's radio. I think Britney Spears was in the CD player, but I tried to compose myself mentally and turned to our daughter.

"Well, T, do you want to help me make some salads when we get home?" I asked.

"No way! Dad got us McDonald's last week." What a confession. He must've had her brush her teeth after they ate the evidence, and I didn't see any of that in the garbage bin.

"Honey, that's not real food. Your father knows better than to eat that," I explained to her, but she wasn't listening.

188

"And then there was another time we went to Taco Bell. I love their soft tacos, but not their hard ones. Dad usually gets a Meximelt," Isabelle went on.

"You don't say? Okay. Well, we're not having that tonight. We went grocery shopping over the weekend and are going to put the lettuce to use, and I've already diced up the veggies."

"But I don't want a salad!" Isabelle groaned. She was just a little girl and my only child, but sometimes her complaining was like nails on a chalkboard.

"That's too bad, Izzy. We're having salad." I gave my stern voice and knew I could skip all the way to the shouting, but that'd only upset her and make her cry. And even with her upset with me, she'd still look to me to comfort her after I scolded her. It was a never-ending cycle.

We really needed to work on getting Tanner to be a better good cop.

"Listen, Isabelle. How about if you eat your salad like a good girl, then I'll read you more of your bedtime story tonight," I bargained.

"You said I was too old to be getting bedtime stories," Isabelle responded. She was too old, and although it was a good practice when she was a little kid and opened her mind more, it was a hindrance and she needed to start being more like the kids her age. But I was far too tired to be fighting with an eight-year-old.

189

"Only if you're a good girl and eat your salad, use your indoor voice at home, and do your chores." I saw she was thinking about this. Good. I thought for sure that would've been a good deal, but I was relieved when she accepted.

"Two stories," she demanded. You had to be kidding me.

"Honey, one story." I was getting irritated.

"Two—" she began

I wanted to snap and yell at her, but of course I didn't do that. I had to be far more tactical in life, even with my young daughter.

"Okay, two. But they're going to be short ones. Mom has to study tonight." And do cam work, and check on the bills, and get to bed at a decent hour.

"Deal!" Isabelle shrieked, accompanied by an obnoxious scream. I had to remind her to use her indoor voice, which she then did.

Before she could ask more questions, I turned on the CD player and let Britney sing about being hit one more time. Completely relatable.

I, of course, had to bite my tongue when Tanner got home from work. I had to listen to him complain about his overwhelmingly simple problems as a maintenance assistant. When he told me how irritated his bosses got with him, I could easily see it from their side. I would be mad at him too for not picking up the most basic ideas about the tools they needed. It wasn't like he was even doing the actual work. He was basically a glorified errand boy, and I hoped he'd able to keep this job because despite its decent size, this city didn't offer much, and I alone couldn't support us even with all the jobs I had.

He was eager to get his vehicle back. Trust me, that made two of us, because I didn't like relying on anyone for anything. And Tanner didn't seem too keen on me going through medical school, so I had to assure him almost on the weekly that it'd pay dividends if we just rode it out. Isabelle was looking at us through the kitchen door, and even though I should have been happy she wasn't loud or getting into trouble, I really just needed to be alone. The two of them were suffocating me.

"Izzy, don't you have homework that needs to be done?" I gently asked her.

"It's already done." Her eyes fixated on me. I was her world, and I should have been be honored that such a well-behaved little girl thought so highly of me.

I couldn't fight; I bottled my feelings up, a prisoner of my own emotions. I waved her into the kitchen to help me finish preparing dinner. Tanner may have been dumber than a box of rocks, but he could sense when I was at my limits and didn't protest about the greens I was about to serve them for dinner. It was a small win, but I took it.

CHAPTER TWO

Austin, Texas, 2004

We pulled into the neighborhood and I was completely smug with my own thoughts. They were speechless—as they should be. I worked my tail off during my first couple of years on my own in Oregon and waited for the right moment to purchase. The housing crisis was about to leave the whole country in shambles, but I was able to capitalize off the opportunity because of my signing bonus and found a great location in the Southwest. Arizona was my first option, and the state did offer mansions on the outskirts of the Phoenix metro area, but I did my research and couldn't tolerate moving to a red state. I'd already had to bite my tongue with Tanner and his military buddies and couldn't bear to do that with future neighbors, coworkers, and colleagues. No. This move was strategic. Texas was as red as they got, but Austin was a pocket of blue where a lot of enlightened minds could express their opinions.

The new car was pretty comfy too. Why not splurge? I was in high demand out here. It wasn't hard to pass the exams, and they were desperate to have me added

193

to their team. So much so that I had to put my foot down and allow myself a two-week break before they corralled me onto their schedule. If it were up to them, I would've left the hospital in Eugene Friday and started first thing Monday morning.

No, I needed this.

"There's a Whataburger. Hmm, I wonder if it'll live up to the hype." Tanner pointed at the fast food location in the distance. I just nodded and refused to let it get to me anymore. They'd been sneaking fast food here and there, though Isabelle was older and knew how much I disapproved of it, and she stayed away from it for the most part. They still had their moments, though, and I knew that within the first week of my work schedule they'd be sneaking out to clog their arteries.

I did have to remind myself that it was father-daughter bonding, which they didn't do enough of. Tanner had tried to get his daughter involved and vice versa, but they seemed to be from two separate worlds. She just couldn't get into basketball. It didn't help that the SuperSonics hadn't been relevant for the past ten years. And Isabelle may have been quiet, but she was actually quite talented on that cello. It was a shame that Tanner had no interest in classical music.

Then again, did I even like either of those hobbies? I'd paid a lot of lip service for the two of them over the course of the past ten plus years just to appease them. I knew Isabelle was getting older and it probably wouldn't have been the worst thing to finally get the divorce, but then I remembered that she wasn't like ordinary girls.

Just the week before I'd had a set of twin sisters come in who had hurt themselves roller-skating in a derby. They slammed into one another and coincidentally both broke their left arm. How on earth did that even happen? What were the odds? When taking their X-rays and assessing their damage, they both chatted animatedly about the boys in their class and then would shift their conversation to their friend group. They were both even polite and treated me younger than I was. When I told them that I had a daughter their age, they became interested, even though I knew they shouldn't. During that doctor visit I think they said more in those two hours than Isabelle said all year.

Of course I didn't bore them with the details of her shy demeanor or how she was super anxious on top of being dyslexic. When she was younger, I used to think she was borderline autistic, but I had to dig into some new technology that would help her with her dyslexia, and once we became accustomed to how it worked, we found out that she was actually pretty bright. From there I never really had to worry about her grades. She was a straight-A student and more responsible than most of the kids her age. I just sometimes longed for her to be more like them.

I used to create fake business trips and not even go anywhere special. Sometimes I would drive a few towns away and rent a cheap motel just to have some peace and quiet. Isabelle was great, but my goodness, she needed me in her life more than anything or anyone else. If Tanner and I were ever to divorce, they would both insist on me getting full custody, and then I'd really have her attached at my hip. Although the child support that Tanner could potentially get from me might be tempting enough for him to try to be a halfway decent dad.

When we approached our house in the suburbs, it was better than the pictures that the real estate agent sent me—light-years better than the shack we had been living in back in Oregon. Hopefully this was incentive enough for Tanner to stop sulking. He soon found he had no opinion on the matter because I was the one who held all the cards. It was better to let me make the decisions.

I looked in the rearview mirror and saw Isabelle's mouth fall open. When I turned to my right, Tanner looked impressed. The car was not even in park before the two of them jumped out and rushed to the front door. I tried to act annoyed, but I smiled—genuinely smiled. I had worked so hard for the past three years and I was the biggest hero today. My vision was simple and attainable but so much more than the doubters expected.

We were home.

It wasn't long before I made friends with some of the neighbors. It wasn't hard when I saw the Kerry-Edwards signs in their front yard. Stacey was nice and lived with her partner, Ari, and daughter three streets down. I started off by waving at them when I was on my jog and then found myself helping them with a newly bought couch they were struggling with. They invited me in for some brews after placing it in the living room, and we got to talking.

They weren't really gossipers, but they did tell me about who to steer away from in the neighborhood. A couple of sex offenders lived at the far end of the block, but a nice Middle Eastern couple just moved from Pakistan. We all decided it'd be a good idea to bring them housewarming gifts and let them know that they were welcome in this country.

When we did, I was pleasantly surprised to see that they had a son who was Isabelle's age. He was even in a few of her classes. He was almost as shy as my daughter, but his parents seemed very traditional and almost had to force him to hold a conversation with me and Tanner when we visited with the homemade muffins.

The adults decided to set up a playdate. God. They both sounded way too old for that term, but I was surprised when it turned out to be a success. The two apparently liked the same cartoons and listened to the same trendy emo music. I felt like most of my life I'd been so angry at the world and like I was fighting a current, but I finally felt at ease. My daughter had a friend. My job at Heartwood had been fulfilling and life-changing so far. Even Tanner had been nicer to me lately. A lot nicer. What could go wrong?

One Year Later

How could I be such an idiot? Like seriously. Was I that gullible to miss all the warning signs? Tanner wasn't cheating on me, but I would almost prefer that to be the case than what was really going on. He owed money. And I mean *a lot* of money. When I heard it was over fifty thousand dollars, I nearly had a heart attack at the hospital.

A sketchy-looking goon came into my work and said he had a family emergency to talk with me about. He laid it out to me straight. Tanner had been going deeper and deeper in the hole with these loan sharks, taking bets that were absurd. I guess Tanner didn't break his arm helping Eddie on that construction gig. I think most women would be intimidated by this wannabe gangster, but I had the money to make this go away . . . even if it was at the expense of Isabelle's college fund.

I was livid and didn't think this week could get any worse. It was bad enough that Isabelle and Omar went through a breakup. Most parents wanted their teenage daughter to be single, but I had a solid year where she was

198

spending time with someone else, and I was able to do some of things I always wanted to do, like take up pottery and Pilates. I even considered having an affair with my yoga instructor, but I didn't want to ruin the good life I was just getting. So much for karma.

After all was said and done, I headed into a side room that was completely dark and got to the sink, exhaling loudly as I splashed water into my face. When I looked up, I didn't recognize the person in the mirror. I wasn't even that old. Why did I look like I was approaching my fifties? Was this the effect of supporting a family of three and cleaning up all of their messes?

My phone started vibrating and I took it out to see that Dr. Campa was texting me. He wanted me to meet him. Now. The director could wait. I needed a moment to compose myself. But the texts started bombarding me and didn't stop. I was about to turn off the phone when I noticed I accidentally answered an incoming call from him. Great.

"Dr. Nuciforo? Are you still in the building?" Dr. Campa asked without even a formality. What could be so goddamn important that he was calling me like this? I decided to meet up with him because I didn't think it'd take longer than fifteen minutes.

I didn't get flustered often, but this took the cake.

"You were having sex with dead bodies?! For fuck's sake, Jose!" I exclaimed as I sat down across from

Dr. Campa and a woman I didn't even know. Apparently she was an attorney.

She'd been speaking for him while his eyes were glued to the floor. I was at a loss for words as she continued explaining the dilemma.

"A colleague of ours has an inside person at the local news station, and this is going to be big when the police come and arrest him. We're having him step down as soon as possible and for the well-being of the hospital. We'll need a new chair." The attorney looked at me and waited for me to respond.

"A board member? One of the board members?! That means you'll be taking me off of patient outreach." It was funny how most people would do backflips to get to where I was, but it wasn't about power or money with me; it had always been about the job.

"Obviously the compensation will be much more substantial than what you're getting now, and you'll have complete oversight of the entire hospital," she continued, obviously not caring about my concerns.

"There are far more qualified doctors in this hospital who can do the job. I don't think I can—" I began to protest. The words were stumbling out.

"You're the best we have, Sydney. We've followed your career, and I have seen you work. You're good. You can't teach that level of charisma, and we're going to need a good new face for the hospital with Campa out." She complimented me, but my head was spinning. I was going to puke.

There was a knock at the door. We looked up to see another doctor in scrubs who had peeked his head in, and he informed us that the detectives were coming up with the handcuffs. The two looked at me in desperation. I begrudgingly signed the papers and accepted the role as the new director of Heartwood Hospital.

I drove toward home and saw red. How could all of this happen at once? I didn't remember leaving the hospital parking lot, and I ignored all the buzzing from my phone as I received alerts of messages from coworkers, unread emails, and even a ton of voicemails. I just needed to get home and process what had been thrown at me.

That was odd. Why was Tanner's vehicle in the driveway? Shouldn't he be at work? I knew I should be, but I had a damn good excuse not to be.

I walked into something I never thought I would see in my lifetime: Tanner with his head deep in his hands as he sobbed. He was actually crying. Could this day get any worse? I was guessing there was a death in the family. Not Isabelle, obviously—I would be the first notified. He looked up through bleary eyes, and at the sight of me he instantly toughened up and wiped the tears away.

I then realized the mobsters must've said something to scare him stupid, and normally I wouldn't want to kick a man while he was already down, but today had brought out a whole new side out of me. I kicked him in his rib cage . . . hard. He tumbled over and struggled to catch his breath. Tanner was livid. When he regained his composure, he balled up his fist, grabbed the collar of my scrubs, and threatened me.

"The hell is your problem, Syd?" He was about to swing that punch, which would have been the biggest mistake of his life. I didn't flinch.

"Put your jeans on. Wipe off those tears. I'm going to our bank and we're withdrawing the money right now," I snapped. He let go instantly and looked relieved but confused.

"Did you have to get a second mortgage on the house?" he asked.

"What?" My face scrunched up. "God, no. Tanner, I have my own life and bank account separate from you." He dropped his jaw, literally . . . not unlike a cartoon.

"How much do you have?" He did not have the nerve to just ask that question out loud. I shoulder checked him as I reached for my coat.

"Not much after your little stunt." I'd used this exact same tone with Isabelle, and Tanner knew he just scored a get-out-of-jail-free card. He retreated back to the room to get his jeans.

We withdraw the funds and got a cashier's check for the amount. This much cash would be hard to get at one time, and I wanted this as far behind me as possible. The silence was rigid and I knew that Tanner wanted to ask tons of questions like, "How much money is in that account?" and "Were you ever going to tell me about it?" and "What were you going to do with it?"

The dive bar came into focus and Tanner reached for the cashier's check, but I snatched it from the dashboard before he could touch it.

"Babe, you can't come in. It's kind of an all-guy's club—" I didn't let him explain further as I parked the car and walked toward the entrance.

I could hear Tanner swear as he clumsily unbuckled and followed me in. When I got inside, there were a couple of bikers and a busty woman with a hardened face behind the bar. She was probably in her forties but looked like she was in her sixties. I was blunt with her.

"Where's Isaiah?" I demanded. She arched an eyebrow and Tanner finally burst through the door and curtly nodded to the bartender.

"This your woman?" Her voice was raspy and matched her face.

"I'm here to pay off my tab." Tanner was such a moron.

"He's not paying shit. I am." I was not trying to be a comedian, but the bikers laughed and even the bartender got a chuckle out of it.

The bartender was probably breaking a lot of protocols with their little operation, but she motioned for me to go in the back, and Tanner was as white as a ghost when he saw me march in there. He even hissed at me to not go in there and to just let him take care of it.

I walked through a piss-smelling grunge hall to find a table of four men playing poker in the back. Most of the men were checking me out, but a bald Hispanic man, who I assumed is Isaiah, shot me the coldest look.

"Who the fuck are you? Get lost on your way to the ladies' room?" Tanner was afraid to go in but meekly peeked his head around the door. "You get your five thousand you owe me for the day, or do I have to call back the hounds?"

I reached into my pocket and handed over the check. He looked down at it and looked back up at me. He smirked but smiled afterward. "This ain't real. Shit's going to bounce."

"I'm still wearing my scrubs. Does it look like I'm the type of person who is hurting for money?" The men were all watching the two of us lock eyes.

"Sugar mama ain't playin'." He snorted some laughter and his men echoed him. I reached into my wallet and whipped out more hundreds. Tanner's eyes widened. "What's all this?"

"Here's an additional five thousand to ban my dumbass husband from this place." Now the men were roaring with laughter, and my husband's shoulders sagged. He was contemplating whether or not he would've rather been jumped.

"Why would Isaiah take that deal? We just suckered your man almost half a hundred. He's one of our best customers," a man with tattoos on his face chimed in.

Isaiah shook his head at his man and gave him a look that instantly shut him up. He turned back to me and nodded. "Homegirl here ain't a cash cow and would leave this bag of bones for dead if he pulled this kind of shit again. And she's no narc. No cops, debt paid, and an upfront payment shows good faith. You've got yourself a deal, *chica*." He looked over my shoulder at my husband, who instantly darted his eyes away from Isaiah. "Hey, white boy, if I ever see you in our bar again, I'm breaking your fingers myself. Especially now that I know you have a woman who can patch you up."

"Thank you," I said in a quiet voice meant for just the two of us, but I was pretty sure our entire crowd caught it.

"Don't worry, sugar mama, I'll also reach out to the other sharks in town. Your family's money ain't no good there either." For a hardened criminal, this man was actually pretty reasonable. I genuinely smiled at him, and the two of us moved to exit before he hollered again to Tanner, "You're one big *puta*, white boy. You have a woman like this in your life and you choose to piss it all away?"

That's what I've been saying! Finally, someone who said it how it was.

CHAPTER THREE

Austin, Texas, 2008

Bureaucrats . . . they had to be the worst people on the planet, and now I was one of them. Growing up in a poor family, I always thought that the scum of the earth were the people who did the petty crimes, but I was quickly seeing that they were too narrow-minded to pull the shit that kept the world turning. On a daily basis it was about putting on a front to investors and politicians to keep the boat afloat.

I'd even stooped further than I thought I would go. On my own I had hired at least seven different private investigators and hackers. I had been quite successful in pulling up dirt on many of the politicians in the area. And you would think I'd be a merchant of death with the deals I made, but nope, it was just to keep the air conditioning on in the building. We were privately funded but got a lot of the tax breaks that public health organizations got due to the strings that I pulled.

It didn't hurt that I was ruthless when going toe to toe with them. They threatened my husband, my life, and even Isabelle's, but what were they going to do? Spill our "darkest secret" about Tanner's old gambling habits? That'd barely make a two-day news cycle. Would they be ballsy enough to physically go after Isabelle? A girl who suffered from anxiety and dyslexia—yeah, good luck with that one. They knew that'd only paint me in a better light.

No, they'd leave me alone because they knew I didn't have time for their bullshit as it was. When I met up at discreet locations to get them to vote a certain way, I could hardly stay long as it was because I had to babysit the staff I had underneath me. It was exhausting always trying to get grown-ass adults to do their jobs correctly.

I found myself working eleven-hour days and, if I was lucky, I caught one of Isabelle's orchestra concerts. I tended to just let the two get dinner without me and hired a chef who prepared my nutritious meals for the week which, more often than not, I ended up eating on the drive home.

Isabelle loved *Grey's Anatomy*, and though I absolutely despised the show because it was nothing like reality, I bit my tongue because this was an activity that required very little from me when I was already mentally and emotionally drained for the day. I would rather be watching *True Blood* or *Dexter*, but Isabelle got too squeamish with it and Tanner thought both shows were "too gay" for his liking. If he would've roughed it out to season two, then he would've at least had some eye candy with Lila West—a pale, voluptuous woman who Dexter ended up having an affair with.

Tanner had befriended a couple of the army buddies at the local American Legion. He never even saw any wartime action, but the bar had like-minded customers and aired all the Spurs games. He wasn't gambling, but he had fallen in love with the local team. How could he not when they were winners? I was grateful that they both had their own lives, because I couldn't handle another ten years of working double time at my job and then doing the same thing in my home life.

When I pulled into the driveway, no one was there. That was new. I was sure a note was in the house, but I took out my phone anyway and texted Isabelle. She responded right away saying how there was a group project she had to be at but she could be home right away! If I texted back rapidly, she'd get upset that I was trying to get rid of her, so I had to hold off my excitement and then collectedly text her that I would prefer for her to focus on the group activity and to take her time.

A house to myself?? That never happened!

I went into the spare bathroom, turned on the television, and hooked up the DVD player to put in an old episode of *Dexter*. The bubble bath felt like a bed made from the clouds of heaven. I even lit candles around and sunk inside with a deep sigh. This was the happiest I'd been in months. So of course the doorbell rang.

I nearly cried. Go away! But the ringing continued, and I submerged into the water to let out the most visceral scream that could probably be heard from downstairs. I put a robe on and was prepared to kill whichever Mormon was on my front doorstep, but I was pleasantly surprised to see it was Stacey. I exhaled, and she noticed.

"Well shit, boss woman, I didn't know you were having alone time. I can come back." Stacey was really good at reading people, and honestly if it were anyone else, even my own mother, I would have turned them away, but I welcomed her like we hadn't seen each other in ages.

She waited in the living room while I put on a change of clothes, and together we shared a bottle of wine and caught up. She and her wife were doing well, and the accounting firm she was working for needed a new part-time assistant. She was the only person who knew how ruthless of a businesswoman I was and loved hearing the stories. Stacey was such a cheerleader that she wanted me to get into politics myself. I laughed. I didn't disagree that I would kill it, but I couldn't imagine the added stress that it would bring. Finally we got to why she had come over: she found something for me.

"Doctors Without Borders?" I asked. I had never thought about the organization.

"You always said you wanted to go to Colombia!" Stacey exclaimed. Apparently her cousin said a doctor backed out and to ask around.

"I don't know . . ." I thought about all the people who needed me right now. Tanner could hardly tie his shoes without my assisting him. Isabelle couldn't imagine two weeks without me, let alone two months, and the hospital . . . that damn hospital.

"You know what? Don't think about the big trip first. Do the smaller stints!" She further explained how there were trips to poorer parts of America and quick flights to closer foreign countries like El Salvador and Guatemala. I admitted that a week did sound nice. I took the brochure she gave me and knew that I'd already made up my mind before getting past the first flap.

*　　　　　*　　　　　*

Alabama was really eye-opening. I wasn't in charge, which was a breath of fresh air. I was assigned to do rounds at an underfunded hospital that was obviously committing numerous health code and construction violations. I never thought twice about Heartwood and its conditions, but then again, I was ruthless back at home and made sure we got more funding than any medical office within that part of the state.

Given ten months with this place I could turn it around in no time, but I had to stop myself. This was just a short stint. Free medical services I was providing, nothing else. No one asked for my business input and I didn't need to provide that to them. Even though this was just charity work, my advisor, Dr. Sheldon Banks, had taken a liking to me.

As someone who oversaw other people, I understood. I did what was asked of me. I didn't complain about the conditions or the lack of medical supplies that were provided. There were a lot of doctors I worked with over there, and the amount of smugness and entitlement was astounding. Dr. Jacob Juarez was the worst. He was from a town not far from Scottsdale and reeked of privilege. He was under the impression that we'd be getting our own medical bag and not have to use the communal supplies. I almost laughed out loud and snorted on my Diet Coke when he started protesting that we were also in charge of sterilizing the tools we were using. This wasn't a five-star vacation, sweetheart.

What the hell was he even doing here? No one forced a gun to his head and made him fly out to BFE Alabama. We were all volunteers here. It wasn't until I caught him sneaking off to a room with a girl clearly half his age, one of the interns our program hired on. Then I realized that he oversaw all of the collegiate girls and a lot of them wouldn't even complete the full three weeks here.

It made sense. These naive girls would get the experience on their résumé and not have to serve the whole time. In exchange they would have to bite the bullet and sleep with a man old enough to be their father's age. I was tempted to stick my nose in all of this but realized that it'd create more of a shit show, and I didn't need any of that in my life. Instead I watched him and one of his victims sneak into a room, then I followed a few minutes after.

His pants were down to his ankles, naked ass midthrust, when I entered the room. He swore obscenely as he scrambled to hide himself, but I played it cool.

"Dr. Juarez? Alexis? What's going on here?" She scurried off while Jacob blabbed about how it was a one-time, heat-of-the-moment kind of thing and that it was a complete lapse in judgment. I was fascinated by the lies he was spinning because this was obviously not the first time he'd done this, and he was acting like I was one of his wife's best friends. Was he worried I was going to tell?

"Jacob, shut up." He stopped his explanation and waited for me to speak again. "I'm flying back home tomorrow and could give two shits about what you do in your personal and/or work life."

"Why'd you follow us in then? This room is off-limits and abandoned. I don't believe you randomly stumbled in here." He had me there. Why did I come if I didn't plan on doing anything?

213

"I wanted to meet the real you," I told him, and I surprised even myself when I continued talking. "The fake voice you use—your holier-than-though shtick you use with Dr. Banks and pretty much everyone here . . . You hate this work, but this is the only time and place you can do your dirty little habits. Let me see who you really are."

He didn't seem to believe that was all I wanted, convinced I was looking to blackmail him. But when he studied my face long enough, I saw a subtle shift in his demeanor. The good-guy act was gone and I was looking at his real face—the one that had been hiding for God knew how long. There he was. Satisfied, I tossed his pants to his chest and let him know that there were still patients in wing three that needed attention.

I finished my work there and even connected with a lot of the local kids who invited me out to their little league baseball game afterward. I was the only white girl in the bunch and didn't know another person there, so why not? I hated my colleagues anyway and I'd rather spend time with the underprivileged locals than these fake, rich phonies.

The week was an overall success, and I couldn't believe how fulfilled I felt doing this work. It was a rare instance where I didn't feel suffocated both in my work and personal life. After the eleven-hour days were over, I would either meet with Banks or one of the patients would suggest a local dive bar where I would watch the Saints.

Football was not my sport, but I was able to watch two games while I was there on a Monday night and Sunday afternoon. Maybe it was the crowd or being around locals, but I definitely got caught up in the atmosphere.

It also felt great to help others again. Like really help them. I did the people back at home a solid by creating one of the best hospitals in the state, but being a pencil pusher was not in my nature, and I wasn't in the trenches helping those who needed me. I knew my shit and doing this charity work was something I would consider doing full time.

I thought about all of this on the plane ride back and couldn't even settle in to watch a movie. My mind was working overtime and I was already committed to another gig with Doctors Without Borders. Dr. Banks was ecstatic that I was able to check out Honduras next. He did warn that the supplies and hospitals there would make Birmingham, Alabama, look like a paradise.

I was not deterred and in fact welcomed the challenge. He did tell me that I'd likely have to expedite my passport and wanted to be sure I gave my actual job enough heads-up to be able to commit to this stint. Please—that place could not afford to tell me no without the threat of me leaving. The family on the other hand . . . Jesus, that was when the anxiety started kicking in.

Would Tanner and Isabelle still be in one piece? What was I going to do if I made this a regular thing?

215

Should I get them a dog so they felt obligated to care for another living thing, and that'd keep them distracted? I was doing this no matter what. I had more than earned this. Some people liked traveling the globe while others liked going to the beaches of Hawaii. This was definitely my calling, and I wasn't abandoning it just because my husband and daughter would miss me for weeks at a time.

I didn't tell them my flight number and had googled the pet stores between the airport and our neighborhood. There was even a cute dachshund that I thought Izzy would take a liking to. I realized almost too late that my phone tracking had been on since leaving Alabama. Ugh. Sure enough, she was on her way to "surprise me" and pick me up. There went the dog idea.

I was a bit of a paranoid parent before I found out how well-behaved Isabelle was. I thought about how I was as a kid and knew I had to jump on the location tracking so I could always know where my family was. I didn't think of it as a two-way street, and she was bright enough to realize that she never really had to ask where I was because she could always check.

What felt like the shortest flight landed, and the serenity I gained from my trip was quickly fading. I could feel a mental countdown for Honduras starting in my mind already. I gathered my things, the irritation rising, but I did what I do best—bottled those emotions up and put on a big plastic smile as I grabbed my luggage and acted surprised when I saw Isabelle waiting for me at the gates.

CHAPTER FOUR

Austin, Texas, 2010

I had a routine down to a T: Book my trip, plan it around sweeps, and then watch as work would try to guilt me into staying but eventually give in because they understood that they were dealing with a lion and could only push me so far. My family life had even improved a bit. Tanner successfully enrolled into Gamblers Anonymous and had even kept the drinking down. For a while I was worried that he'd even be a little bit preachy.

Isabelle was still a shy girl and didn't like when I went on my trips, but I tried to instill into her the confidence she needed to be the woman of the house while I was gone. Despite my husband's massive leaps forward, I'd never trust him with our finances and even considered a dark account that would be opened only in the event of an emergency. Who knew? I could push a politician too far or piss off the wrong person. I needed the two to be okay, because even though my insurance policy was quite generous, a backup plan should be in place.

218

Isabelle and I went to the bank together and opened the account, and I even encouraged her to regularly put money into it. It was a Roth IRA, and if she put the same amount into it every month, she'd be able to retire in her fifties. Kids didn't want to hear about that far ahead into the future, but she saw how much it meant to me, so she went along with it.

Of course it should go without saying that she couldn't tell her father, but I brought it up anyway. She was going into her senior year of high school and the grades were stellar, but she lacked direction in life. I encouraged her to get back into music, but she worried that the kids were going to be in a clique and not accept her. Silly, because it was just the band geeks! I was pretty certain they hadn't changed since my high school years.

Regardless, I made sure to spend extra time with her two weeks before heading out on each trip and even took her to her favorite ice cream location. I purposely did it when Tanner was at work because I knew she liked the time spent with just the two of us. While out, I also got her to be my little study partner. She typically opened the Spanish book and would ask me to repeat back certain phrases and words, and I typically aced them. Damn straight I did.

Normally I'd only spend a night or two each week with her after my babysitting duties at Heartwood, but this week I made sure to spend a whole five days in a row with her. I was heading to Colombia, and no one knew that I was going to be there for three months. The straw that broke the camel's back was when I found out that three of my best employees were attempting to mess with the books. Thank God for Izzy.

She'd gotten good at accounting and noticed an odd tax that was higher than before after looking at one of my pay stubs. At first I didn't really care about a measly hundred less dollars each check, but something nagged at me, and when I looked into it further, it was nearly all employees who were getting deducted. And, of course, those three smiling backstabbers were not.

I lost it and nearly got fired right there and then. When I cornered them into my office, I made sure the door was locked and pulled up each of their files. Of course they denied the embezzling, but they got deathly white when I laid out the photos of them running a massive grand theft auto scheme here in Austin. The press has been on it for years, and I should've guessed that it was educated people behind it. My private investigator was good. He definitely got compensated well for this discovery.

I had a lot of dirt on them and they went rabid. It went from stress to panic to violence really quick. I allowed Kara to grab the surgical knife and hold it to my neck. Julian was yelling for her to do it, but man was I waiting for that coolness of the blade to be placed next to my throat.

I elbowed her hard and twisted her arm, sending her nose straight into my desk. It shattered it instantly. I kneed her hard in the stomach and she gasped for air as I took the knife and cornered Gilbert next. He backed off quickly and went for the door, but I wanted this too bad. I lunged at him, and that was when Julian hit me across the face with a bedpan.

That was probably the best thing to happen that day, because he was going to go further as I got up, but Gilbert told him to stop and asked me if there were other copies of the three of them.

"You're too late. I already sent the images to all the local agencies. I just wanted to see the look on your faces. The look of the people I trusted for the past five years." I spoke through bloodstained teeth. "Kara, your husband knows about Julian too. I sent him those pictures as well."

"You didn't . . ." Her voice cracked, and she was about to cry tears of sadness versus pain.

In the distance I heard the police sirens and cracked my neck as I got up and readjusted my office. The three were stunned, and Julian revealed his true self to me for the first time . . . the mask slipped.

"You could've just gotten the money back if you knew about the car ring too. This felt personal." Julian's eyes narrowed on me.

"You're damn straight it's personal. Do you know what I have to do on a daily basis to keep this place running and my inner circle compensated well too?" I knew I needed a therapist and also should've just talked to these backstabbers first, but I was too hurt. "And for what? You undermine me and take more of the pie."

There was a banging at my door and I looked at the three of them. We exchanged no more words. It was almost unspoken that they'd not bring up the assault on me, and they wouldn't tell the officers I was seeing red when I lunged at Gilbert.

I spat a wad of blood into the sink and calmly readjusted my hair before opening the door, allowing the cops to come in and take the three of them away. I looked through my window from the top floor as I saw the three of them handcuffed and being escorted into the back of the cop cars. Cameras and reporters flooded the parking lot, and I'd been so mad that I hadn't had time to feel the true emotion that was at the root of all of this: betrayal.

I thought about how much trust I had put into these three and how we'd go out for karaoke on drunken Friday nights. I supported Gilbert when he came out of the closet and even went to some of Kara's daughter's dance recitals. If these three were capable of this after all the work I'd poured into the place, who was going to be the next to burn me?

My time at Heartwood had run its course. I ended up taking no more calls that day and had our intern deal with a lot of the press that wanted a statement from me. I contacted Dr. Banks and asked him about an extended stay in Colombia. Of course he was enthusiastic, but we'd gotten to know one another well enough too, and I hate to say it, but he was more of a father than my dad ever was. He listened to the conversation and picked up on my sadness.

"Maybe it's not the best idea, kiddo." Banks had always been too good at reading the room. "What's this really about, Syd?"

I knew that I should lie and do whatever was possible to get on that flight to Medellin, but I was about to break and I didn't know what to do. I cried. Over the phone I told Dr. Banks about the hospital. I told him about the family and how much responsibility I had carried my entire adult life. He didn't say a word and listened to me completely. I half expected him to tell me that he wasn't going to accept my application and that I should probably spend more time at Heartwood while seeing a licensed therapist, but that wasn't what happened.

"Three months will be a great time for you. I should've suggested it a long time ago. When you're away and we book these missions, I don't recognize the person you are in your personal life. You put on this show for the public, and I admire your commitment to your obligations, but when you step foot on that airplane you look out for the person that matters the most—yourself. I'll book the flight and I'll see you next Thursday, Sydney." The line went dead.

*   *   *

I looked at all of our assets as soon as I got home and made sure that it was all reasonable. Thankfully the three of us had been pretty frugal despite the great income I made. I even started a college fund for Isabelle when she was in grade school that had more than enough. Even despite Tanner's stupid mistake. She was a smart cookie and I didn't think it'd be bad if we had to dip into that, but honestly, I'd always have a job. Four agencies had tried to headhunt me while I'd been at Heartwood, so working full time would always be an option for me.

The way I saw it, I could actually go eight years with no income based on the projections of my family's spending. Sure, we couldn't go to Hawaii or anything, but that was a long time they'd be okay. For these three months, they'd be just fine. To be certain that things were even more secure, I went ahead and transferred the majority of the money from my joint account with Tanner into Isabelle's. I also checked on the life insurance policy that was separate from Heartwood. Heaven forbid some anaconda ate me or something.

The next day I went to the board meeting and, of course, they were all in shambles over our three stooges. But what I found the most amusing was that a lot of the board members were not worried at all because they knew that mommy dearest would fix it for them. Those arrogant motherfuckers. How had I not seen this before? One of them even had the audacity to be on their phone, probably checking Instagram or something.

Oh, they were in for a treat.

"Dr. Nuciforo, what route do you think we take? PR hasn't been this bad since Campa's necrophilia here on the hospital grounds," Betsy Cunningham asked me. She had always been the biggest brownnoser, but at least she shut up when I needed her to. I ignored the question.

"Dr. Greene," I addressed Chad, who had been the one so engrossed in his phone. "What do you think we should do in this situation? How do we approach it?"

This was indeed out of character for me, so the board was silent and all eyes fell to Chad, who put his phone away like a teenager who'd been caught in class. He straightened up and shrugged his shoulders. "I mean, we certainly can't ignore it because they'll only pester us more. I'm sure your statement is going to be sufficient enough. It always is. You're great in front of the camera."

225

I smiled. I wanted to punch him so hard in the face. The blood boiled, but I kept my cool as I laughed. The rest of the board didn't know what to do and some of them laughed along with me.

"I'm not going to make a statement."

"That's an odd strategy, Dr. Nuciforo," Betsy began, but before she could go further, I continued.

"I'm not going to do anything, because as of today I resign as the Director of Heartwood." The room was dead silent and then a few of the board members began to laugh again.

"That's funny. You're funny, Dr. Nuciforo. It's great to lighten the mood around here. I think that's the breath of fresh air we need."

"I'm not joking, Betsy." Even though the rest of them hadn't bought it, Betsy could see the seriousness in my eyes. "The board can vote for a new director, but I assume it's going to have to be Dr. Greene, who has the most seniority here."

Chad shifted uncomfortably in his chair. After studying my face he realized that I was not joking either. His face turned whiter than a ghost, and as I got up out of my chair, the room erupted into a panic. I smiled. A genuine smile. I actually felt like I'd just received ten years of my life back. I sauntered back to my office and took out a cardboard box.

There were some reporters camped outside in the parking lot, and I didn't even mind telling them what just happened. What was funny was that there was a time not long ago where Heartwood's reputation meant everything to me. The empire I had built since arriving in Austin six years before was now about to be the fall of Rome. The trio served the role of Casca well because it was time for Caesar's reign to be over. Let it be someone else's problem.

CHAPTER FIVE

If Isabelle were ten years younger, she would've had her arms wrapped around my legs like she did when she was in elementary school. I was hoping I would be able to fly out before she got back from school, but I anticipated her skipping out early. What was really unfortunate was that she picked up on my extra suitcases and put two and two together long before I was in the air.

I was excited for the trip, and a large part of me thought that I could still get there with little to no guilt, but I did find myself needing to comfort Izzy before I headed out. She was still just a kid. I assured her that everything was going to be okay and that her new job would be just fine. I knew that it was a bit of a dick move on my part getting her a job without her permission, but dammit, she needed to start socializing, and with how good she was with numbers, Stacey was getting a solid employee.

Stacey was still one of my closest friends, but sometimes we did not see eye to eye with one another. She was constantly complaining about the young people in her office who didn't take work seriously, lied, and were immature. So she was excited to get Isabelle, who checked none of those boxes. I told her how I hoped that some of the troublemakers stuck around, because it'd be good for Isabelle to get out of her shell.

I'd asked Stacey to keep an eye on Isabelle while I was gone; she was one of the few people who knew that this was going to be an extended trip. She gave me her word, and I was grateful. Stacey told me Isabelle's pay and, for fuck's sake, Isabelle, what I wouldn't have given to have that high of a starting salary as a first job! When I first started as a file clerk back when I turned fifteen, I was only able to get a little more than five dollars an hour.

Maybe it was too good to be true to really expect to be gone before Tanner broke the news to her. He obviously didn't mind. They were both horrible with confrontation, and I honestly would've paid to see how that conversation unfolded without me being there to take charge, but while she was off in the bathroom at Applebee's, I was stern with Tanner on making sure she made it to and from her job.

He waved his hands and agreed that she'd be there alright, but I pressed him further anyway. I knew he was irritated because I quit my job and he would have to find work soon; he'd gotten comfortable with his fishing and drinking schedule. But he bit his tongue, knowing that I still held all the cards.

The bribing and blackmail of politicians, the self-defense classes, the real dark side of me I'd hardly shown to him, but he had been married to me long enough to know that it existed, and he knew when to not push his luck. Sometimes I wondered if he was afraid of me. It was crazy to think that someone who went to Iraq would cower from his woman, but then again, I knew *he* knew I was a force to be reckoned with.

When Isabelle came back from the bathroom, she continued to sulk, and I was halfway tempted to cut the dinner early and just tell her that I could get a taxi to the airport from there, but now it was my turn to bite my tongue. She was just a kid. I had to keep reminding myself of that—I was her world and needed to be motherly with her.

So I ignored the sour attitude and ordered us the most unhealthy appetizers along with the dessert I knew she liked the most: the apple cobbler. She ate it, and I made myself the life of the party for the dinner, massaging her ego the best I could. I talked about how I thought it'd be a great idea to adopt a puppy or a dog when I got back and wanted to hear their input.

"What kind were you thinking?" Tanner didn't seem opposed to it, but unfortunately Isabelle hadn't come around completely to the idea and just shrugged her shoulders.

"C'mon, Izzy, have you seen how cute dachshunds are?" I pulled out my phone and showed her pictures of some of the ones that I had been eyeing.

She only got excited because of how excited I was about it, which was the best I could hope for, I guess. I had been so focused on the aftermath of me leaving my job and getting all my ducks in a line with this trip that I completely spaced the whole dog adoption. I honestly thought it would've helped these three months without me go by so quickly. Then she could have had a taste of what it was like to have a living being who needed you desperately for their survival.

We laughed at one of the TVs that was broadcasting a bunch of sports bloopers, and I got Isabelle to sulk less and come around enough for me to put my arm around her and let her rest her head on my shoulder. Sometimes it was like pulling teeth, but at the end of the day, she could never stay mad at me for too long.

I got to the airport and Isabelle helped me unload my bags. She begged to join me at the airline counter and check the bags in, but I had to draw the line somewhere. I told her that I needed to be in a good mental space to go from there and get situated on the plane. I also explained that a colleague I hadn't met would be joining me on this flight, and I needed to talk with him before we got there to establish a solid game plan before reaching the village.

Isabelle was heartbroken but honestly handled it better than I would've hoped. She even sensed not to push her luck with me. We hugged one another, and I gave

Tanner one of the most passionate kisses I had given him in a long time. I felt him get a little hard, and he probably regretted not trying to make a move back at the Applebee's bathroom.

I didn't mean to tease him, but I was genuinely excited for my trip, and that must have brought out the best side of me. I did him a solid, though, and gently rubbed his bulge before leaving. I whispered to him that when I returned, I'd make sure it was taken care of.

Like a turtle on its back, I completely disarmed him. He said he loved me, assured me that he'd get Isabelle to her job, and that she'd be taken care of. I left them and was genuinely proud of them. They were about to go three months without me and hold the fort down. But then again, what choice did they have?

*   *   *

Isaac Winters, a registered nurse, was tall and lanky with an obnoxiously big nose. He was also quite socially awkward. I could see my daughter so much in him that at first I didn't have any desire to get to know him despite the fact that he'd be joining us. But, of course, we got seated next to one another on the flight.

Then, to my surprise, despite how nice I was to him, he didn't pester me during the flight. He obviously didn't feel the need to cling to me or delve more into the details of our trip. Instead he read to himself, so I decided to take off my headphones and strike up a conversation with him.

"Book any good?" God, what a stupid question. No one liked being asked that while reading, but he was polite and put it down, and smiling at me.

"I've read it before. I'm a huge fan of Crichton." I looked at the flap and felt like a complete idiot because I only now realized that I didn't know much about pop culture.

"Oh yeah . . . he's big, right?" I genuinely had never heard his name, but did I really know any current authors?

"He's the author of *Jurassic Park*." When he told me this, there was no trace of arrogance or judgment. It was actually quite sincere, but I still felt like a complete idiot. He watched as my face turned red and laughed. "Don't worry, that was his biggest hit. He's big in the sci-fi world, but I don't expect the general mass audience to know him."

"Mass audience. What do they read?" I was genuinely curious, because I didn't know what genre I would be into.

He thought about the question and mulled it over.

"That's hard, because the top authors kind of corner different markets. J.K. Rowling does the whole young adult fantasy. Stephen King is the biggest horror writer, and James Patterson does well with his political thrillers, but I think a lot of people also like *The Secret*." I knew the first three but was a little bit lost with the third one.

"*The Secret*?" I asked.

"It's a self-help book. It took the public by storm and basically encourages people to go out and get what they want. It has a lot of Christian fundamentals in there as well, so I guess it doesn't hurt that its teachings are not too far off from the biggest bestseller of all time," Isaac explained.

"What's the biggest bestseller of all time?" I was so far removed from pop culture that I felt like a complete moron even asking.

"The Bible." He smiled, and I hit the palm of my hand to my forehead.

Duh. For as smart as I could be, there were some basic things that I was surprised I didn't pick up on.

"Are you religious?" I regretted the question as soon as I asked. That was too personal and I had just met this guy. To my surprise he shook his head.

"I am agnostic and even read *The Secret* because people wouldn't stop raving about it, but it did nothing for me. I think books can be successful in convincing you to go for things, but you have to be buying into whatever it is they're selling."

I pointed to the book he was reading. "But *that* you'll buy into?" I also regretted saying that too. Why chastise the guy for having a hobby? What was wrong with me?

"Of course I bought into it," he said with a laugh. "The author is basically writing science and poetry. The words run smoothly together and take you into a whole other universe while exploring the scientific subjects that should be addressed. He was truly an author ahead of his time."

I found myself envious of his passion. Why didn't I feel that way about art? I made a mental note to buy a book when we landed at the airport in Medellin.

CHAPTER SIX

Tayrona, Colombia (three weeks later)

The chicken bus stopped for Isaac and me as we ventured outside of the village, leaving our medical supplies at the main base. We both carried light backpacks that had just enough clothes for the weekend, and a few toiletries.

Isaac was hesitant to join because he was a boy scout who only signed up for the mission to further add to his résumé and give him an edge in a competitive upper class Boston market. Plus, despite being three years in the field, he was still up to his head in debt with student loans, but I assured him that the whole thing would be covered by yours truly.

The hostel we were planning to stay at had limited internet access, so I made sure to find an ATM to withdraw a bunch of cash before heading out. But the mystery surrounding our itinerary for the next four days was what made it so much fun!

The local minister had to leave town to tend to a family member in Bogota, and our work was pretty caught up. Dr. Banks told us that we'd essentially have a four-day weekend. Isaac instantly retreated back to his hut to put his nose in the same Michael Crichton book, but I invited myself in and threw his book to the ground.

"Fuck that. We're going to stay at a hostel!" It sounded so filthy when I said it. I didn't say we were going to be in a five-star hotel or a really nice rental house, but what Isaac didn't know was that I did my research. The photos of this hostel looked like it was located in heaven. There were private rooms that I booked for each of us, gorgeous views that overlooked much of the forest, an infinity pool, and I went ahead and paid extra for the open bar. We'd be getting our money's worth.

"Dr. Nuciforo—" he began.

"Sydney," I corrected him.

"Sydney." He smiled. "I cannot afford that. Even if it is a hostel."

"Too bad. I already put it on my card and you can pay me back after you land your gig in Boston."

Excuses kept pouring out of his mouth, and I knew he was just nervous because he was shy, but I even looked up some of the other guests on the hostel website who were checking in, and there were a ton of cute girls his age who would go crazy for a tall, skinny registered nurse. I made sure he didn't have a choice in the matter and even pulled the guilt card about how I didn't want to be a single girl traveling in a third world country by myself.

And like that we were off to Tayrona. My Spanish had gotten serviceable enough to go without a guide. I made sure we got off at the right stop, and we tilted our heads up at the hostel. It was breathtaking but also intimidating. The hostel sat atop a steep hill and was a hike just to get to the top. It was a good thing we packed light, because I already felt exhausted just looking at it.

We made our way up the stairs, and Isaac was holding up better than I was, but then again, I was starting to get a little soft before I left for trip. The stress back at home paired with a semi–fast food diet clogged up my arteries a little too much. This was a great wake-up call, and I vowed that when this trip was over, I would go back to eating healthy and not let a job, family, or stress get me this out of shape again.

The receptionist was a cute French girl named Claire, and I instantly looked at Isaac and her side by side to see if she was his type and would treat him right. Stop. I had to stop while I was ahead, but I couldn't help it! I was wrong about him from the get-go and now felt that he deserved the world. I didn't tell him this, but I intended on being the best wingwoman on the trip and to at least land him a kiss from some foreign hottie. Why not? He deserved it.

Claire led us to our rooms, and I was grateful that they were close to one another. Isaac got acclimated with his space and obviously preferred to be alone, while I was

ready to be a social butterfly. But something told me I'd
want to be attached at the hip with him for this short
vacation. I unloaded my belongings and went to use the
private shower I had but realized that I'd forgotten
shampoo. I swore, put a towel on, and walked to the
dormitories to see if one of the other guests had some.

"*Buenas dias! Tiene . . . lo siento, pero no sé cómo decir esto
en español, pero es para lavarme el cabello.*" Shit, I thought as I
looked at three girls half my age . . . I didn't know
shampoo in Spanish.

"Shampoo?" one of the pretty girls suggested and
then laughed. "That's better Spanish than we could ever
do." I heard a tinge of an Australian accent or maybe New
Zealand.

"Oh, thank God. I felt like an idiot for not
knowing that one."

The girls ended up being from all around.
Christine was the Australian who spoke up, while Andrea,
a British girl, retrieved some of her shampoo. Hera was
from the Netherlands and informed me that Isaac and I
were the only Americans outside of a young man who had
checked in the day before.

We hit it off really well, and I made sure to bring
out a deck of cards so we could get to know one another
before hitting the bar the next night. I already knew of
some drinking games from my high school years, and by
midnight we were wasted. I whispered into Andrea's ear

about how shy Isaac was and that he would never make the first move.

That was all that was needed. By the end of the night the two were practically glued at the lips and off in the corner. One of the girls giggled and told them to get a room. And even though Isaac did have one, I knew he was too much of a gentleman to take it further because they were both intoxicated. The night wound down and eventually everyone went back to their own rooms, but I just admired the sky.

In the night the stars really popped out at you, and I didn't think the air was this clear back in Austin, but to be fair, usually at night I was so focused on getting home from work that I may have developed tunnel vision. I thought I was alone until I noticed a young man sitting by the infinity pool, reading under one of the few remaining lights.

"I really need to get in the habit of doing that." I interrupted his read, but I was too intoxicated to care about manners.

"Everyone could benefit from a book," the young man said with an obvious American accent. So this was the fellow Yank that the girls were telling me about.

He was about ten years younger than me with curly hair and an innocent face. Something in his eyes was kind but also full of wisdom. He was obviously younger but at the same time looked like more of an adult than most of the adults I'd met throughout my time on the planet. I pulled up a seat next to him and dipped my feet into the infinity pool.

"You mind?" There were still a few manners left in me.

"Not at all." He put the book down completely and followed me to the pool, where he sat next to me and also put his feet in. "My goodness, that still feels just as nice as it was this morning."

"It's paradise," I agreed. I didn't realize it, but I guess something inside me cracked because the young man studied my face.

"What's wrong?" he asked. I denied that anything was wrong, but he didn't let it go. His eyes pierced into me, and I felt him catch my mask slipping. "You don't have to tell me anything, but I hear that it's good to get things off your chest and speak your mind."

There was a good period where I still denied that there was anything wrong, but then tears started welling up in my eyes and I began to sob. I told this complete stranger about how this had been the happiest I had been my entire life, which was unfair to the people that I had in my life. My husband, my daughter, coworkers and friends who relied on me back home had always been grateful. but it was too much and I didn't think I could handle it anymore. I almost didn't want to go back home. I'd rather help people who really needed my help and was tired of putting on this mask for everyone.

I wiped tears away from my face; he didn't say anything for a long time. I regretted essentially dumping all of my problems on this poor man, but he didn't seem bothered by it at all.

"You're entitled to your emotions," he finally said, which at first I thought was such an odd statement. "We're all allowed to be the truest versions of ourselves, and you're not crazy for thinking that that face you put on is a facade that most people have learned to also wear on a daily basis. It takes real courage to look inward and be your true self."

What did I say about those eyes? Who was this young man? The next Dalai Lama? He gently scratched my back and told me that he had to get some rest but he'd be here tomorrow. I sat with his words and heard him walk off before I realized that I had completely forgotten to introduce myself.

"I'm Dr. Nuciforo by the way." Oh my goodness, what was that? "I mean, Sydney. Please don't call me doctor. Just Sydney." My face reddened, but he genuinely smiled at me.

"My name is Cain Skaggs. And I guess you can call me doctor if you want."

I laughed as he retreated. Cain Skaggs . . . who are you?

Your True Colors

CHAPTER SEVEN

We had decided to all meet in the common room for breakfast. The girls couldn't hold their liquor well and were sluggish in joining us, and I found myself running on fumes—I hadn't been able to go to sleep. I acknowledged Isaac and each girl who exited the dorm, but despite the coed dorm being emptied, I still saw no sign of him. I tried to hide my disappointment but was not all that successful. Christine asked who I was looking for.

"The other American. Cain. Have you seen him?" If I were as young as these girls, I may have tried to play it off cool, but I was past the point in my life where I cared what others thought.

"Cain?" Christine's eyebrow arched, and I could tell she was teasing with the question.

"Please. I'm practically old enough to be his mom." I rolled my eyes at the girls.

"Don't be ashamed, queen," Andrea chimed in, "my mom ended up marrying fifteen years younger with her second marriage."

"Yeah, well, *I'm* still in my first marriage, so there will be none of that." I could keep defending myself, but I

244

honestly didn't care if they thought I was interested or not. I was just wondering where he was.

"He left early," Christine explained, "but his backpack is still here."

"Who're you guys asking about?" The French receptionist joined us. The hostel staff was able to enjoy the breakfast after being sure all the guests were fed.

"Sydney is looking for Cain," Christine sang mockingly.

"Oh yeah, he signed up for our sunrise hike. They'll be back around noon. It's an early one. He showed interest in seeing the spider monkeys that are in the area."

"That was an option? Damn, that actually sounds fun." I was happy he didn't leave but also a little disappointed I didn't join him.

"We could probably catch up to them," a voice said from behind me. I turned around to see a muscular Latin man. He had droopy eyes and was taller with dark features. "I was going to go into town to pick up some supplies and could swing you by. I've done the hike with the travelers many times and have a good idea of where they are right now."

He didn't need to say more. I downed my orange juice and retreated back to my room quickly. Before I could get too far, Isaac reached out and grabbed me by the wrist.

"Hold up." Isaac smiled politely to the local but pulled me aside. "I'm not letting you get in someone's truck by yourself."

"Isaac, I appreciate the little brother role, but I'll be fine," I assured him.

The man didn't seem concerned or offended. He chimed in as well. "My truck can fit the whole bunch of you if you want to join."

I look back at Isaac like to say, "See." He reluctantly let me go and told me that he'd go get dressed. Andrea joined us too as we retreated back to our rooms to hop in the shower and be out the door as soon as possible. I considered taking my portable makeup kit with me, but what was the point? We were just going to work up a sweat and it'd smear anyway.

We were on the road within the next half hour, and while Isaac and Andrea sat in the bed of the trunk, I accompanied our new friend in the front. He explained how Cain was actually not American at all but a Canadian from a really remote village. He was actually a staff member who had worked in the hostel for the past month. Really great guy, he assured me.

"That guy taught me things I didn't know about myself," the man said. "Oh, and I apologize for my English."

I was caught off guard. Sorry for his English? The man spoke better English than my husband, and this was this man's second language! I assured him in Spanish that his English was far superior to my Spanish, and this time he lifted an eyebrow and told me how impressed he was.

"You're just saying that. Liar," I teased him.

"No, ma'am, I don't lie anymore, not after meeting Cain. Those days are behind me, and outside of not lying to others, I mainly want to make sure that I'm not lying to myself."

I studied him hard and could tell that he'd being truthful. "I am so rude. We've spent this whole time talking and I haven't even introduced myself. I'm Sydney."

"Javier, but you can call me Javi if it's easier." His smile was sincere, and I looked at him and realized he'd be a great match for my daughter. He was built, had a kind heart, and didn't lie. Shit, that was better than more than half the men in America.

He later explained how his younger sister met Cain a while back and how they were both kind of doing a foreign exchange program but with adults. Her name was Azul and she was really thriving over there. He didn't go too much in depth about what Cain's home was like, but the way that Javi talked about it made me curious.

We got to a clearing where Javi followed a path off the main road. He drove steadily, but I still looked back at Isaac and Andrea to make sure that they were okay. They gave me thumbs-up and we soon approached a group of six people hiking through the forest. When they turned around, Javi honked and the tour guide gave him the middle finger but was smiling the whole time.

While the four of us unloaded, Javi talked with the guide rapidly in Spanish. I got lost in the translation but then saw my new friend, who waved at me. I didn't play it as cool as I would've liked as I eagerly brought Isaac and Andrea over to him and introduced everyone to one another. There were four other travelers who had joined the hike as well.

"See any monkeys yet?" I asked.

His face transformed to that of a little boy as he explained the different breeds they'd seen and how there was a little village that they weren't too far away from. It contained hot springs and they were excited to relax in them for a bit.

"Javi, you didn't tell me that." I was genuinely upset because I didn't pack for that.

"You didn't ask," Javi said with a shrug, "but you'll be able to go in your underwear. Tourists do it all the time."

I mean, he had got a point. How would it be so different than wearing a bikini? Javi finished chatting with Emilio, the tour guide, and he was about to leave when he saw another truck approaching.

"*Mierda*," he swore under his breath and shot a look at Emilio.

The two locals looked petrified, and that genuinely worried me. Emilio moved to stand between the approaching truck and all of us in the group. When the vehicle got closer, I could see some men standing in the back with what looked like warpaint covering their hardened faces. Tats filled their arms, and they held automatic rifles, machetes hanging around their belts.

"Let us do the talking," Javi hissed quickly in English.

The main guy hopped out of the driver's seat and approached us. Though my Spanish wasn't very good, I was able to pick up most of the conversation.

"What a good group you guys have today. They pay well?" the man asked, and I automatically saw what he did: privileged, rich travelers.

"We work off tips, Pedro, you know that."

"That's funny, Emilio, because I also work off tips. I love them. Either hand over what you've got, or I take that skinny one over there." Pedro nodded his head in Andrea's direction, and despite Isaac holding her hand, she gasped and squeaked out a cry.

"Hey man . . . there will be none of that. I can give you what I have." Emilio emptied his pockets and handed over the equivalent of thirty American dollars.

Pedro laughed as he let it fall to the ground, then explained that that was definitely not enough. He began to walk toward Andrea while Emilio, Javi, and Isaac

249

surrounded her. Some of the men jumped out of the truck, and as they got closer, I interrupted the scene.

"Stop," I said in my best Spanish accent, "I'll pay."

"Oh I see . . . rich *mamacita* was holding out on us over here." He looked over at me. I was just grateful I brought my purse with me because something told me that these guys didn't take loans.

"How's two hundred American sound?" I prayed to God that was enough because I left the rest back at the hostel.

"Take the money, Pedro," Javi insisted. "There doesn't have to be a scene, and you can be on your way. You know messing with the tourists can get messy for you guys."

Pedro thought this over while I showed him the money. He sighed and nodded for one of his goons to approach me and take it. Pedro began to walk away when I grabbed him by the wrist.

"Give me your number," I commanded.

"You crazy bitch, why would I do that?" Pedro's eyes blazed into mine.

"As insurance you don't mess with us for the rest of the trip. Especially the girl." My eyes darted to Andrea. "How do I know you won't just change your mind and come after us again anyway?"

He looked amused but gave me his phone number. I dialed the number right away to see him answer it in front of me. He called me crazy but definitely memorable. I handed over the money and told him that my phone was being tracked and his contact was in it. I said this even though I doubted this threat would really bother him.

The bluff seemed to work as the men retreated into the truck and drove past us on their merry way. Pedro and I stared at one another as long as possible until he was out of sight. We collectively exhaled when he was over the horizon.

Javi turned to me. "You're an idiot, Sydney. They have your number now? You don't give Pedro Juarez any sort of information at all. He may change his mind later and hit you up for more money."

Oh I planned on it. The darkness in me rose so much that I was seeing red. I wanted nothing more than to be in contact with Pedro and take down his entire operation brick by brick until I had him alone in a room where he was begging me to put an end to his misery.

I knew this was out of my league, and I'd never messed with criminals ranking this high. Blackmailing politicians and taking some martial arts in the safety of America was nothing like dancing with the cartel members. These guys even made the bikers in the sketchy bar back at home look like Disney characters. I was way in over my head, but oddly I found myself welcoming the challenge.

"Sydney." My trance was broken when Isaac came over and put a hand on my shoulder.

"What?" I realized that he had been talking that entire time and I didn't hear one word he said.

"Andrea is really shaken up, and I think it's probably better that we go with Javi back to the hostel," Isaac said. I looked over his shoulder, and she did indeed look as pale as a ghost. I didn't blame the girl. She was two hundred dollars away from being a worst-case scenario as a woman traveling the globe.

"Yeah, you guys do that." I nodded my head in agreement.

"You're not coming with?" Isaac really didn't like the idea of my being alone in the forest, but I didn't want to give him an ultimatum.

"I'm here for the vacation and I'm not going to let some thugs stop me from checking out some hot springs and monkeys." I played it off light, and it took a lot of acting and convincing on my end, but eventually I was able to get him to let it go. He even approached Emilio and sternly told him to keep an eye on me. My heart melted. He was like the brother I never had.

"Shit, man, she's fine," Emilio responded in Spanish. "If anything, she needs to protect me."

I laughed. Isaac's Spanish wasn't as good as mine, but he liked how high-spirited I was. We hugged one another and I whispered into his ear that I promised I'd be fine and would even pull some of the self-defense moves I had taught him in our tents back at base if I needed to.

The three of them took off.

I was grateful that the truck was traveling in the opposite direction of Pedro's people but was almost secretly hoping for the cartel members to come back; because even if I died in this forest, I'd make sure Pedro Juarez would be dickless by the end of it all.

CHAPTER EIGHT

The remaining group members were still on edge when we made it to the small village. The group consisted of Cain, Emilio, me, and a guy from the Dominican Republic—Carlos. I must have been insane because all the women who were with us hightailed it after that encounter. If I weren't so stubborn about secretly wanting those men to come back just so I could teach them a lesson, I would've gotten in the back of Javi's truck and left too.

Carlos had taken a liking to a local spider monkey that he fed an orange to. Emilio was decompressing and talking with the villagers about his close encounter. His spirits had been dampened since the confrontation, and I could tell he was doing his best to put on a brave face.

That poor tour guide stood in front of Andrea and probably thought that he was going to take his last breath. Despite his joking banter, I he was scared, grateful, and happy to be alive all at the same time. I studied him from a distance while Cain and I were alone in one of the hot springs.

"He'll recover." Cain followed my attention, and I realized that I didn't need to hide anything from him.

"They were willing to die to protect her," I stated. I was so used to seeing the shittiest sides of people that I forgot that humanity still existed.

"They were on the other end of a losing battle, that's for sure," Cain agreed.

"You didn't step in front of them." I turned back and redirected my rage at him. "I know you probably don't think much of yourself physically, but they could've used all the help they could get."

"I thought about joining them," he agreed, then continued, "but I was watching his eyes the whole time, and the added men were just a bonus to him. It almost made him want her more."

"Coward." I didn't buy whatever Zen bullshit he was peddling.

"You can think that if you'd like, but I think if you look back on the situation and saw it for what it was, you'd know I wouldn't be wrong."

We didn't say anything for a moment, and I thought about the money. Two hundred dollars wasn't that much in the grand scheme of things, and they could've taken it by force.

"Why did he take the money?" I asked, more to myself than him, but Cain's face genuinely lit up like he was waiting for me to ask that question.

"He took the money in front of his men for the optics, but that's not why he stopped the potential kidnapping," Cain explained. "It was because of you."

I eyed him and waited for a further explanation.

"All 5'6" and 115 pounds of me. So scary," I mocked him.

"You're not the only one with eyes." Goddammit, he was talking in riddles again. I hated and loved it at the same time. When I finally pieced it together in my slow, nonphilosophical head, I asked another question.

"What did Pedro see in my eyes?"

"Fire. And, sure, he could've had his men go for you, but he saw that you were the only one who wasn't scared and, well, that fight-or-flight response is the reason he's been able to operate that gang for so long." Cain could be pulling all of this from his ass, but I didn't think he was.

"So you don't think he'll contact me?" I asked. I didn't know which response I wanted to hear more, but he shook his head.

"I can't tell the future, but I do know that he didn't buy your 'tracking phone' story one bit. If it's any consolation, I think you'll be safe once you're back at home in the States."

I needed to learn to let this scumbag go. I found myself agreeing with Cain and eventually decided to let the conversation drift off. Besides, the whole reason I came out here was not for the monkeys or discussing the cartel's next move, it was to get to know this young man better. He was an open book and left no room for riddles or mystery when I began to chat with him.

He was from a very remote area of Canada like Javi had told me earlier. It was so remote that they lost their village status years back and were basically a commune—Black Wolf Creek. It surprised me that he lived so far off the grid with a group of other people that I couldn't help but think of some backward-minded survivalists with tin foil hats, but he assured me that it was nothing like that.

It was a community where everyone had known everyone for a long time. Everyone pulled their weight and wore many different hats, ranging from carpenter work, gardening, hunting, and even educational instruction. They weren't completely cut off from the outside world, but they preferred not to interact with it too much.

When he talked about it, it didn't sound so foreign anymore and actually sounded better than the busy life that Austin provided. I guess I'd always been a city girl and wondered if I would thrive or not as a country person. He talked about how the community always encouraged foreign traveling and to see the world . . . even though it could be a negative place.

There were stories he told me about friends and family who had been too trusting and taken advantage of.

257

Some of the members of the community had lost all of their money, been thrown in jail, or worse. But when they returned back home, it only served as a reminder that it was better to just stay with the community.

I asked him about how they added new members and what it cost to join. When those words left my mouth, I instantly realized that this could be some kind of scam. He already knew that I made comfortable money as a doctor, but to my surprise he didn't seem to care about that.

"We don't charge people to live with us, but we don't just accept anybody," Cain explained to me. "Our policies used to include more people, but over time there have been too many who freeload or have caused trouble in our society, like my parents, so we've learned to be limited."

That was interesting. His parents didn't even live there anymore? That just brought more questions than answers, but I found myself longing for acceptance instead of pressing him further on this topic.

Did I want to be a part of this group? What if they weren't all like Cain, and he was the enlightened one of the bunch? Was I seriously entertaining the idea of moving my family to the middle of nowhere where I would make Isabelle even more of a recluse? And what about Tanner? Oh God. Talk about the least educated and most freeloading person on the planet.

Cain laughed as he read all of these thoughts that were racing in my head.

"We're not taking applications. No offense," Cain told me. I laughed but then realized that he was talking about me.

"Wait? Are you saying that I wouldn't be allowed in your little club?" I probed.

He dodged the question and attempted to shift the conversation to the diverse wildlife that was available in this part of the country, but I didn't let it go.

"Cain, what the fuck?!" I was offended, but on a deeper level I was just more hurt than anything.

"Sydney. You're an interesting person," he began, "but you're holding on to too much and are too afraid."

Afraid? I had never been afraid of anything in my life. I went after what I wanted and would burn down anything in my way to get what I wanted. I'd been doing this my entire life and had never taken no for an answer. I'd never backed away from a fight or a confrontation.

"You're afraid of being your true self. Our community only wants people who fully embrace their true selves."

I hold on to this as he downplayed his home and acted like it wasn't a paradise. He further went on to how great of a person I was (apparently behind this fake version of myself) and how we should continue to enjoy the beautiful earth and the wonders that Colombia had to offer. I'd zoned out and was reevaluated everything in my life yet again.

Who did he think he was? I had more than embraced my true self. I got gritty and nasty with politicians. I quit my job. I traveled halfway across the world away from my daughter for Christsake! He was still rambling about some sort of local fish that was only found in that part of the world when I cut him off and leaned in to kiss him passionately.

He reciprocated, and this was the first time I'd see him flustered. He clearly liked it but then thought about what had just happened and turned sad.

"Sydney, I'm not trying to play hardball. You being affectionate with me won't change the fact that I cannot bring you back home." He sincerely meant this and honestly thought that was the only reason I went for it.

"I know, but I wanted to kiss you and stopped caring about what was right and wrong," I confessed.

CHAPTER NINE

The next two days went by too quickly. There was a little bit of everything—clubbing, exploring, hiking, swimming, and no more close glimpses of death with guerrilla soldiers. Isaac and Andrea were almost as inseparable as Cain and I had been. I didn't press him about moving to his commune, and besides, I didn't know how that would work. Would I leave Tanner? Isabelle would still have to be a part of his life, and I just didn't see her adjusting to their ways. Plus, what would his adoptive aunt and uncle think about his dating someone eighteen years his senior?

Cain's parents were kicked out of the community when he was twelve, and when he observed the outside life, he decided that his parents' way was not the answer. The world was an ugly place, and everyone was trying to take advantage of you one way or another. The problem was that people in the world packaged it as something really nice and smiled to your face about it. It took a lot of courage for Cain to basically turn his back on his parents and go back to his real family: Black Wolf Creek.

I understood I was not allowed to live there and needed to learn to accept it for what it was: admiration.

They lived a life in way that a lot of people would call too simple, but it was much more than that. There was zero tolerance for lying or being two-faced. To be a part of their home you had to be your true self, and I really wished people back at home would do the same.

It was time to report back to the campsite, and although Andrea and Isaac had exchanged numbers and their socials, I decided I didn't want to be tempted with having Cain's information. I had to rip the band-aid off so we could go our separate ways. He hugged me and I found myself clutching him harder than I had with any other person I had met in my life.

"You'll be okay," he assured me.

"Liar," I said back, even though I knew he was right. I had navigated this life this far on my own and had come out unscathed. Surely I could go another forty-five years. "I'll be your first reader when your book comes out."

He'd only written ten chapters, but it sounded like a unique tale about a boy going out into the world only to return home. I bit my tongue and didn't tell him that the main character was clearly himself and he wasn't writing for, as Isaac would put it, the mass audience. Still, there was some good content sprinkled in there, and he was a true poet in the way he wrote. It was such a catch-22: on one hand I should tell him the issues with his novel because truth was valued more than anything in his world, but I just didn't want him to get discouraged and abandon the project altogether. Maybe I'd been living in the real world for too long to where I was no different than the people I lived among.

There was one last deep kiss. He didn't think it would be a good idea for us to have sex the night before because of lingering feelings between us, but I assured him that it wouldn't be an issue. Afterward I realized that he may have been right; the moments of intimacy were fresh in my mind, and I was already beginning to feel hollow inside. Even though it was essentially a one-night stand, it felt so much more real than that.

We made our rounds to everyone else and said our goodbyes, and before I knew it, we were on the chicken bus back into town. Isaac had always been observant and aware of his surroundings. He pulled me into his shoulder and I was able to be sad in the arms of someone who could sense my pain. It didn't fix my heart, but at least there was some comfort.

The next couple of months were fine. The local village had a lot of problems, but we were able to leave most of them better than they were before we came. My Spanish had gotten so great that I began dreaming in Spanish. Isaac and Andrea became more serious than I initially thought they would, and I teased him constantly about the perks of having a British girlfriend. His family was traditional and he worried that his parents wouldn't approve, but I assured him that that shouldn't be a problem. She treated him well and that was really all a person could ask for.

"Dr. Banks, I lost my file on Robert Diaz—" I began as I walked into a patient's room where Sheldon was adjusting his pants. He was just telling a young boy in Spanish that the exam was over.

"Sydney! I didn't hear you coming," Sheldon said too brightly. The boy's eyes were glued to the floor as he walked past me, and I felt instantly dizzy. The whole world shifted.

Not Dr. Banks. Really? He was supposed to be one of the good ones. I became intensely nauseous as the world continued to spin. I tried to rationalize that maybe it wasn't how it looked, and I smiled my best fake face to him. He didn't let on that I knew, and we continued to talk about the patients and the rest of the work we needed to be prioritizing for the next week before going home.

We finished our conversation, and I told him that I was going to call it an early night. I waited patiently for the camp to fall asleep, but I was wide awake as I camped out fifteen feet away from Dr. Banks's tent. The mosquitoes were relentless, but I paid no attention to them as they bit. I waited. Sure enough, sometime around midnight Sheldon snuck out, and it wasn't long until he was returning, his arm around the same boy, as the two of them walked back to his tent.

I clutched the dirt and vomited. Afterward I paced back and forth outside my tent. There were many animals in Colombia, but none sicker than this invasive species that had plagued this village, no matter how much good work we'd done. I contemplated sneaking into the tent myself with a surgical knife and going straight for his crotch. He'd never touch a child again, and he might go after me, my family and even my license, but it'd be one less predator in our society, and I could at least stop some of the kids' suffering. But I thought about how it would all play out.

If I went in there and even killed him, then there would be witnesses, and I was not prepared to go to a Colombian prison. If I confronted him, then he could, in turn, come back at me and jeopardize my career and even go after my family. He was well-known in the medical world. I needed to be smarter than this.

It dawned on me what I had to do. I went inside my tent and dialed someone's number, embracing my dark side as I set a plan in motion.

The day we were set to leave, the villagers insisted on cooking us a feast. I was sure to grab Isaac's plate and take it off to the side before bringing it back to him. He left some food on his plate, and I lectured him like a mother would and insisted that he finish his food. He rolled his eyes but did as he was told. I hugged the locals and said a special goodbye to Mia, having taken a liking to my little assistant. She was fifteen and wanted to go into medicine, which softened my heart. I ended up leaving all my medical supplies with her and even hid a few thousand dollars within one of the pockets. There was a note that instructed her to only use it for schooling. Maybe that was too trusting, but I could tell deep in my heart that she'd obey.

The whole community came out and waved goodbye to us, and the three of us were en route back home. Isaac wore a pained smile as we approached the airport, and I did my motherly duties of checking his forehead.

"Everything okay, Isaac?" I asked with a concerned expression.

"I'm fine." He grimaced as he ignored the problem and grabbed his luggage. I watched him wince occasionally as we approached our terminal.

"This is getting ridiculous," I said when the three of us sat down near our gate. I checked his vitals and then he excused himself and bolted to the nearest toilet. He was in there for a long time before shakily coming out.

"I'm sure the long flight home will be okay. I'll just sleep." he assured us.

"You're not coming with us," I sternly told him.

"Sydney, Isaac is probably right. He could've caught something, and all his body needs to do is relax." Sheldon chimed in.

"Exactly. An airport isn't the best setting. You see how tall he is? He needs a bed. I saw a hotel that's close by. He can check in there for a night," I rationalized.

"Syd, that won't be necessary." He was woozy and nearly collapsed. Both Sheldon and I jumped up to hold him up before he fell to the floor again.

"Okay, Dr. Nuciforo, your word overrules ours. Let's get him checked in," Sheldon assented. The three of us backtracked through the airport, and I was able to go to a nicer hotel and book him three nights to be safe. I didn't like how much I put in his system, and though I knew he'd recover, I didn't want him to rush getting better overnight because of financial obligations.

Part one was done. Now it was time to get Banks on that plane. I was glad I insisted on our leaving early so we could get Isaac a room and be back in the nick of time to board. Banks and I were accounted for and sat next to one another.

"Just know that you brought this on yourself and everyone's lives were lost because of your perverted ways," I said, then turned to him and stared deep into his eyes.

"What?" Sheldon was taken aback and not sure if he had heard me correctly. "Sydney, I don't understand."

"I need to use the restroom," I said as I unbuckled my seat belt.

"We're about to take off." He looked around me, but I paid no attention.

"Have a safe flight." Those were the last words I would ever say to Dr. Sheldon Banks.

I got up and walked toward the end of the cabin. I gave a bribe to the flight attendant, who opened the door to the back of the plane and allowed me to get out with maybe only one or two passengers noticing. After stepping onto the tarmac, I approached some of the airline employees and told them I had an emergency. They allowed me to get on one of their carriers, and we cleared the space as I watched the plane take off in the air.

When it was barely a speck in the air, I pulled out my cell phone and called Pedro. He assured me that the explosives were planted and would go off in about two hours' time. A part of me wanted to watch Dr. Banks explode in person—even if my last seconds were the most agonizing pain I had ever felt—but I knew where my true calling was. It was time to go back to Tayrona.

CHAPTER TEN

Two hours my ass. The plane exploded maybe fifteen minutes after I got off the phone with him, and it was evident in the airport as the whole place was in a state of panic. Employees were running in opposite directions, and I could see that the civilians knew as well as they began to exit the airport and had to reassess their travel plans.

The local law enforcement was present, and I did my best to blend in with the crowd, but I was discovering new obstacles in my plan . . . like how little money I had actually withdrawn before I thought this through. Sure, I had about five grand on me, but what was I supposed to do after that was out? Before the panic set in, I reminded myself that I was bilingual and could easily work at a hostel here in South America. There was room and board and a lot of food accommodations. When I realized this, I laughed out loud and was left wondering if I was really doing this or if it was all a dream.

Did I really just kill Dr. Sydney Nuciforo? Tanner and Isabelle would be more than okay financially. I always figured there would be a risk when I traveled internationally so I took out a very expensive and

269

generous life insurance policy. Izzy was a smart cookie and could be okay the rest of her life if she truly lived frugally.

I no longer had the responsibility of the household or the career or even friends and family; I was free. I could be my true self and not worry about the whole thing falling apart. It just fell apart fifteen hundred feet in the sky, and now here on earth I had a second chance at life. Fifty was around the corner from me, but it was not too late to start living life how I wanted to live it.

Without thinking much about it, I absentmindedly got to the chicken bus and took the route to the small town outside Tayrona. I didn't even know if they'd need my services or if they kept up with the news and would think that they were seeing a ghost. I guess I was just winging it from there on out and I was completely okay with that.

Isabelle Claire Dunham, how I had failed you. I thought about the motions that were about to be put into effect. The plane wreckage. The realization for her that Mom was gone. I could see how her emotions would play out, and a small part of me panicked: what if she ended her life? No! She wouldn't do something that drastic . . . would she? With enough luck, she'd realize that I wouldn't want her to abandon her father like that.

And Tanner? Oh my goodness, wouldn't that be rich? He'd going to have to go from relying on his wife to relying on his daughter (assuming she kept it altogether). I had watched him attempt to flirt with servers when he didn't think I noticed or was around and, holy shit, was it cringeworthy. I sometimes had to clear my throat or make my presence known to get him to stop. Not out of jealousy but out of genuine pity for whatever girl he picked on.

The news would spread quickly to Heartwood and that'd squash whatever hopes they had of convincing me to return. I sometimes wondered at the beginning of the trip whether I was going to return or not, but after meeting Cain I knew I couldn't do myself that type of disservice. I'd outgrown that place and wouldn't return even if they doubled my salary.

The thought of that place in shambles brought a new smile to my face.

I thought about how to approach this new life. I could always work at the hostel and only accept management if they'd offer it. And I didn't even think I'd be deterred by the staff. They all seemed genuine enough, and if they were ever out of line, I could find replacements that fit my new "no bullshit" model. If low seasons were truly hard financially, I could always contact Pedro about side hustle . . . NO.

I had to stop myself even in my hypothetical reality. Just because I was going to embrace the person I truly was, that didn't mean that that true person had to fully embrace the underworld. I could make it work legitimately the right way and, at the same time, not be a stranger to myself. With this new life in mind, I went back to thinking about my daughter. I never even gave her a chance to meet this new version of myself. Would that have changed our relationship?

Had I told her that I needed healthy boundaries and for her to leave my shadow, would she have listened and become the independent woman I always wanted her to be? I had my doubts, though. I had listened to serial killer podcasts and learned that sometimes victims would get Stockholm Syndrome and look to their captor about how they should feel or what they should be thinking.

I wasn't saying that Izzy was as helpless as a serial killer victim, but I knew that she struggled with independent thoughts, and a lot of this was my fault. I had failed her. I shouldn't have coddled her so much at a young age, and I should've really laid down the law. I could have shown her my real self ages ago and forced her out of her comfort zone. I guess there was nothing like throwing someone in the deep end.

As much as I worried about her and all the other people that were in my life in Austin, I knew that I was not going back—only forward.

After I stepped off the bus, I began hiking the road, no luggage, making my way to the hostel. Nothing but my small purse and the shirt on my back. I was slightly hungry and wondered when the hostel was going to serve dinner. When I arrived I was famished. I was practically skipping to the top of the hill when I stopped in my tracks. Waiting at the front of the hostel, all packed up, were Javi and Cain.

Cain's mouth dropped along with the phone he was holding. He ran to me and lifted me in his arms. Despite his size, he picked me up all the way off the ground and was crying.

"You're alive!" he repeated over and over. Javi joined in on the group hug and I began to realize how selfish and reckless I may have been. What if Pedro had miscalculated the explosives and I were still on the plane? What if I had chosen not to get off because that was how much I truly wanted to watch Dr. Banks suffer? It was one thing to embrace your true self, but it was another to be completely blind to the people in your life who cared about you and your well-being.

"I'm fine, really." Now I felt guilty and couldn't look Cain in the eyes.

When he got a grip on reality, he noticed the change in my demeanor. I could lie to a lot of people, but he was not one of them. He studied my face and asked for a moment alone with me. We went back to one of the empty rooms in the hostel where I confessed everything. My voice was calm and collected. If this were any other person, I would expect nothing but disgust and maybe even a slap to the face. Another person, maybe a saner

one, would even go to the authorities, but I saw something
else in his eyes: acceptance.

He leaned forward and hugged me without saying
a word. We embraced one another and then he took my
hand. We walked out of the hostel and approached Javi.

"Change of plans. We're taking one more back
home with us," he said, and I instantly stopped breathing.
Was I dreaming? Javi must have had some idea that
something shady had happened with the plane, but he
didn't question it and only nodded his head.

"Wait until we get to the commune to get her a
new wardrobe?" he suggested. Cain nodded, and I realized
that it wouldn't be easy for me to travel, especially with the
news spreading of what had just happened to me.

"Would Pedro be able to get me access to a new
identity down here in Colombia?" I asked Javi. He seemed
upset that I had been in contact with him, but he shrugged
his shoulders.

"He'd probably charge a lot, and you may not even
pass customs," he suggested.

"Over five thousand?" I asked sheepishly.

"That's how much you have on you?" Javi asked,
even though it was more of a statement.

"We'll make it work. I'll get money from the
community if need be." Cain assured us.

And with that we changed my name to a missing
hiker from Northwestern Canada. A woman with parents

who had passed and who had no children. Victoria Cross. Sure, I could get on board with it. She was a bit of a recluse and it was hard to find any of her social media accounts, which further added strength to my assuming her identity.

I knew there would be no records of Cross leaving the country or even being found, which I worried was going to be big news, but Pedro told me that his forger was used to having a lot of heat on American passports, which was why they could not guarantee their safety. When I pressed him about Canadian documents, he shrugged his shoulders and said it wasn't often they came across them.

I guess I'd just have to cross my fingers and hope that I could make it to Canada in one piece. Cain bought me a plane ticket after canceling his and Javi's original ones. This really was fate. Had I showed up at the hostel just minutes later, then I would've missed the train and life would've put me on a different trajectory, but here I was being admitted to Eden.

CHAPTER ELEVEN

Black Wolf Creek, Nova Scotia, 2015

It was even better than he described, and I discovered that I had no problem doing laborious work. Some might have thought I was kissing ass, but I genuinely didn't mind volunteering to tend to the farm animals or helping with plumbing. I remembered that at Heartwood our janitorial staff would skimp on some of the duties, and I would end up working even later hours cleaning up after them. This was no different. And with these gestures the community had welcomed me with open arms.

Of course they diverted me away from a lot of the smaller duties when Cain told them over dinner one night that I used to be an ace in scrubs. Welp. There went my new life. I had already been secretly observing the other medics in the camp and had no complaints with what they did, but then again there were no complaints with anyone because they all lived by the same rule: no lying. They were the most honest people you'd ever meet in your life, and Cain's aunt and uncle accepted me no matter how much older I was because they knew we were honest with our hearts.

Even though they took me off of a lot of the grunt work, I still insisted that I wanted to know how to do everything there. I could be persuasive, and they couldn't argue with my logic of wanting to be a Swiss Army knife of skills and knowledge. During the next five years I became skilled in hunting, gardening, fishing, and even carpentry.

Cain had his own place already—the home his parents used to occupy. I read through his first book and hated it. He sure loved his science fiction, but it was a story that I felt couldn't keep up with the likes of Andy Weir or Michael Crichton. I smiled every time I thought about how proud Isaac would be of me if he knew that I was a frequent reader of all types of books now. It had become my favorite pastime.

Speaking of Isaac, I stalked him online and was happy he and Andrea became more serious than they anticipated. They were expecting their second kid and it truly blew my mind how magical Colombia was. Maybe that was where Cupid had been hiding all these years. I did feel a huge pang of guilt when I saw the anniversary of when I passed and how much Isaac had gone out of his way to set up an organization in my name.

Of course information came out later about Dr. Banks's secret life, and Isaac was not a dumb person. He must have put two and two together and known that I poisoned him. I did feel bad that he had survivor's guilt but also knew that his life was better because our paths had crossed. Cain agreed with me and told me to let go of my guilt, and I knew he was right.

He was always right about everything in life, and I realized that he'd been focusing on writing the wrong things. Cain should have been focusing on his strengths as a philosopher. More people needed to live like this community, and I told him this one night when we were up late after an amazing session in bed.

"Your story needs to be told," I pressed him. "Imagine how much better society would be if they were truly honest with themselves."

He looked at me with a saddened expression, and I could tell he wanted to say something, but he held back. "But Syd . . . never mind . . ."

"That's not fair! You would never let me not speak my mind." I knew how ironic that sounded but I continued, "What are you so worried about?"

"You killed a lot of people on that flight," he reminded me.

I lay back down in the bed, and a lot of mixed emotions rose inside me. "Don't you think I know that?" I muttered. Why was he bringing that up? It had almost been an unspoken rule since we arrived in Canada and got past security in New Brunswick.

"I know that you'd do it again in a heartbeat if you could," he stated matter-of-factly.

I opened my mouth to object but knew that that wouldn't be true in my heart.

"And I love you for doing what you felt was right, but those souls weigh in on my conscience as well. The pilots, staff, and other passengers," he continued.

"You didn't kill those people, though," I reminded him. My heart began to ache.

"No, but I played a pivotal role in your life and showed you how you should be," he explained, like this was some kind of intervention I had no intention of being a part of. "Now imagine if even a handful of people read my book and decide that they were going to be their real selves."

He had a way with words, and I guess I never thought about the gravity of the situation, but the idea didn't scare me as much as it did him. In fact, I thought the world would be a lot better without the fakeness.

We went back and forth on the issue before he grew exhausted and told me that it was time for bed. I didn't sleep well that night because I felt like there was something he was hiding from me, but it wouldn't be until much later that I found out he wasn't hiding anything from me. He still was not aware of how much more restless he'd become or how easily he tired. Had he not been my partner, I would've seen it for what it was: terminal cancer, but I guess love was truly blind.

*   *   *

Black Wolf Creek, Nova Scotia, 2020

The outside world had been cruel to say the least. Even as a ghost I was able to pull a lot of strings and get Cain the best medical help any person could ask for, but after five of some of the best doctors money could buy, they all told me, Victoria Cross, to come to terms with the situation. Even with the best technology he'd be lucky if he lived many years more, but they explained how wasteful it would be to pour those kinds of resources into him.

I was also winning no votes with the council. I'd brought it up at our community hall on numerous accounts, and even though the citizens loved Cain like a son, they were not going to spend all of their resources on keeping him alive. I was tempted to do a lot of things that I knew I wouldn't be proud of, but that life was behind me and I needed to do things the right way.

How did people inherit large sums of money? I considered snooping on my daughter and former husband to see how much they had squirreled away, but I knew that confrontation would only lead to further problems and,

280

worst-case scenario, lead to my arrest—spending time fighting the courts while Cain's life drained away.

It was a sick joke that the world would lose such a creative mind. That was when it came to me. While I was in our backyard gardening, I realized that it was so simple. I didn't realize why I hadn't seen it before. I ran back into the house where Cain was playing chess with Henry.

"Write the damn book." I didn't waste any time or explanations.

"This again?" He halfway smiled and let out a gruesome cough.

"Listen. You have been taken off all duties and all you do in the house all day is read anyway. Wouldn't you like to make one lasting impact on the rest of the world?" I reasoned with him.

"You want me to write it because you think it'll sell and keep me alive for maybe a few years longer." He said it how it was.

"Yeah, so what?" I don't bother arguing. "But your pages will keep you alive, and you know I'll keep that book close to my heart."

He didn't have the energy to argue with me and closed his eyes as he allowed Henry to win the game of chess. Then he promised me that he'd give it a go. I squealed in anticipation and hugged him. He embraced me while coughing, and some blood stained the shoulder of my shirt. I caressed him and did not want to let him go.

The first draft was good, way better than his fiction, but there was a lot that was missing. He was not getting through on the page like he did with me. I took his pages and analyzed them. I had to grab Azul's cousin, Randi, who studied linguistics at an Ivy League university. She told me how I could structure words to have a stronger impact, and with enough patience, a lot of subliminal messaging could be inserted with the right kind of clunky sentence structure.

"Some people are going to read it as conversational but it'll feel off—kind of like when you're speaking with someone who's learning English as a second language." I wrote down notes as I listened to Randi speak. "Without realizing it, they're going to be subconsciously thinking about things from different perspectives. This will be because the writing is going to force their guards down. It's almost like a confession with priests . . . a lot of people will feel freer to be themselves."

"Can you help us with his pages? You're a part of this community too and know the kind of values that we share." I asked her because I knew that I could study this all I wanted but wouldn't have the intellectual ability to pull this off.

"I don't know . . ." Randi hesitated as she jumped to the same conclusions that Cain had earlier.

"How about this: we write this draft and then show it only to our community before we go to distribute it." My heart sank because our word was everything here, and I realized that if it didn't make it past the votes, then his words would forever be lost here, and I wouldn't stain his memory by going behind his back.

This won her over and the three of us were hard at work every day. Cain wrote, I revised, and Randi basically rewrote. The three of us went over draft after draft, rewriting until we felt confident enough that it was complete. I knew how different my life would've been had I never met Cain and instead read this at any point in my life. I would've been liberated and done things differently because these words were true.

The final product was good, and it killed me to know that I basically volunteered it for a game of Russian roulette. I had a good consensus from our peers but I didn't know if they would want this unleashed into the world. Best-case scenario, it landed in a handful of people's possessions and some took it seriously enough to chase their dreams and better themselves, but even I wasn't not that naive enough. The worst-case scenario was that world leaders were curious about the buzz and we all ended up nuking one another.

It may have sounded vain, but I believed in the work enough to know that it could really reach the depths of people's souls. Plus I cheated . . . a lot. When rewriting

283

the pages, I made sure that I read all of the best-selling books within the last twenty years and would mimic some of their writing styles where I could. We still needed the subliminal messages, but I had to see which authors were making enough buzz and noise. I had to mimic their habits and make sure it stood a fighting chance on the bookshelves.

The moment of truth came when I passed out copies at the town hall meeting. They all liked Cain, and some of them liked me more, so there weren't many in the commune who weren't willing to read it. They agreed that the next town hall would be when they would vote for the blessings of the distribution of the "self-help book."

Cain had come to peace with his work and his life as a whole. He was on the fence about whether he wanted it to be unleashed on the world, but it had become so much more to me. What started out as funding for his health took an entirely new path of its own, and it scared me how much I wanted it to be out there and to watch the world reveal itself for what it was. Cain sensed all of this.

"You need to learn to let the outside world go," he gently told me as I checked his vitals and used the makeshift hospital bed that I spent all my earnings on.

"Easy for you to say. You only spent four years on the outside with your parents. Imagine over four decades." I knew that I sounded bitter, but I didn't care.

"I sent a copy to my parents." I stopped looking at his paperwork and my jaw dropped. "They liked it." He laughed and continued, "They're even coming back to the commune next week to make amends with me while probably cursing the whole town out."

"Were you writing it for them?" I had been so caught up with my own world that I forgot about the most important person who was sitting right in front of me.

"I can't lie to myself any longer, Syd." He had tears in his eyes, and I realized that I was not the only one who was benefiting from this book.

While all my frustrations and anguish had been put into those pages, Cain was writing to his estranged parents who hadn't seen him since before his diagnosis. I'd had no problem leaving my family behind, but it must've been a lot harder of a choice for him. He basically emancipated himself as a teenager and chose to leave his parents, who were lost in the real world. I never pressed him on this subject because I knew how much he didn't want to talk about it.

"They've spent a lot of their life swimming through molasses, and I'm just grateful that they can let that part of themselves go, even if it means they won't be the best people afterward." He grimaced as he said this last part.

"Sydney, my parents were their true selves; but because of that, they were not allowed in the commune.

They're horrible people at their core, and the community saw that I was different. But just because they're monsters, it doesn't mean they shouldn't be given the same rights we have."

I was unsure what to say, so I stopped being his nurse for that night. Instead I crawled into bed with him and allowed his head to rest on my chest as I caressed the little hair he had left, gently humming lullabies until he was asleep.

CHAPTER TWELVE

The night before the morning of the vote I was hardly able to sleep. It was not a secret how much this book meant to me. Cain's parents came and went. Things were cordial for the most part. The two were insufferable, and I was curious how they were allowed to live in Black Wolf Creek in the first place, but now I could see why Cain had never brought them up.

They were friendly enough to me. His dad was perhaps a little too friendly. I kept forgetting that I'd aged backward since living there. Even though I was in my fifties, I could easily pass for midthirties if I went on dating apps or spent a night in town at the local bars. Of course I ignored his stares and his wife's jealousy. They didn't hide their true emotions; the book really did do its job. I thought Cain's dad was half tempted to make a move on me but decided against it when he saw his son fighting for his life. Had he been healthy, I may have had to put him in the hospital bed instead.

The two did renounce their religion though, which surprised both me and Cain. His father told his son that the false prophet had led them astray for too long and that he and his wife were finally going to undo the damages

287

they had done with their strict religion. I didn't know what that meant. I knew that during Cain's younger teenage years they had traveled the world as a family to spread the word of God, but I assumed that because they were kicked out of this haven, they must've had questionable methods to get what they wanted. I knew I had in the past.

When entering the town hall and as I made my way to my seat, I received numerous compliments from a lot of the members of the community. Henry's father, Stewart, started the meeting, and we went through the numerous items of business that had to be addressed. Toward the end of the meeting it was asked of the community if anyone had read the book. All of their hands reached in the air.

We got to voting, having beforehand agreed that it would be majority rule. The 435 people voted 220 to 215 in favor of the book going out. The votes were counted three times, but that was the end result. Many cheered, but this brought a new order of business: security.

It was widely assumed that this book would be successful and that all the proceeds would go to the community as a whole. At first I was livid because all of this was to go toward the equipment I needed to keep Cain alive, but I bit my tongue because I didn't want to make enemies. It was also agreed upon that our names could not be on it. Too much attention would get drawn to this place, which is why we voted to create the alter ego: Rex Sutter.

Then it was also decided that we needed to get more involved with technology and to set up a secure perimeter around the community. There could be fanatics who would try to infiltrate us, and we needed to be prepared for them to come around. Finally, I was in charge of the task force that dealt with the outsiders. I made Henry's wife, Azul, my second-in-command, and we made sure that a handful of us were trained in self-defense techniques and handy with firearms.

It was unspoken, but I knew a lot of these precautions were not just because we thought that there would be fanatics who would trace the work back to our haven. If people really did read our work at face value and enough people bought into it, we could be looking at complete anarchy happening in the real world, and things could get ugly quick. I was glad to see that my paranoia about the book wasn't isolated. This literature ran the risk of making people act out uglier versions of themselves, but at the core of it, it preached what a lot of us were practicing already—living honestly.

Cain was excited, and I asked for his permission to use some older photos of him in his youth as the images of "Rex Sutter." He didn't mind, and I got to the next hurdle: the marketing. It received fifteen rejections before a publisher picked it up and was obsessed with it.

Thankfully that printing press had just sold a *New York Times* bestseller the month prior and people were starting to notice it as a legitimate source for new books.

It wasn't necessarily a bestseller its first year, but it did well enough on its own. And because of our legal team, we made sure we were not screwed out of the deal. That first year our community celebrated with a fancy dinner, and some wanted to spend all of the hundred thousand dollars on things that were needed, but I put a halt to all of that.

I explained how it was a great start, but I felt that all of the current earnings needed to go back into the book. They were confused until I told them that if we hired the best campaigns and marketing, then it would skyrocket our sales even more. Of course, many saw this as a gamble, but I wouldn't let it go, and as one third of the authors, my weight held true.

We held off on spending, and I did my research alongside other great minds in our community. We realized that copies needed to be sent to important figures—celebrities, athletes, politicians, musicians—to get it into their hands and let the work speak for it itself.

Some even suggested audiobooks, but Randi assured me that the rhythm of reading would unveil the curtain and it would lose its glamour. She was the Ivy League grad, not me, so I took her word for it. We executed our plan and waited.

Nine months later we were rewarded tenfold. Sales skyrocketed, and suddenly my hundred-thousand-dollar investment brought us back millions. We even considered translating it into other languages, but to create the subliminal messaging in the English language was hard enough, and Javi and Azul could only write five chapters before saying that they needed helpers that they could genuinely trust to pull it off. We got to work on contacting our people back in Colombia, and soon they were translating it to the best of their ability.

The compound had to be reinforced with invisible security in all of our homes as well as with cameras throughout the woods. The council had been right—we had a few fanatics who found us, confessed their love to Rex, and even slit their own throats when they approached the community. It was concerning, but not as concerning as the crime statistics I read up on.

Homicide up by nearly forty-eight percent, rape was up nearly seventy percent, and petty crimes over two hundred percent. And these were just the cases where people were caught. We had truly opened Pandora's box and there was no going back. Police forces were worn thin.

I didn't trust our own people for hacking and digging on the people who were digging into us, which is why I convinced the council to hire professional hackers. I became a little obsessed with its success. Naturally, there were a lot of people who were against the message that we were putting out there, and it was the first book in a long time to get banned from some libraries throughout the States.

I stayed up late at night to watch coverage of the book and the psychotherapists and professionals who tried to urge people to take the book at face value and not literally. A dark side of me longed to have the critics killed, but I had to dial back my rage and remind myself that these people had good intentions, even if they were lying to themselves.

There was a lot of buzz online about Rex Sutter. People wanted to know who he was, and I assumed due to a publisher that paid them off, his real name was briefly slipped on a message board on the dark web, but I sought to take care of that leak. That information had been scrubbed from existence and only a handful of people could truly trace back to the real Cain Skaggs.

It was a bad idea to use his photo on the back of the book, and before we could truly dismantle all the images of him from his social media accounts, some of them made their way on the web. The trolls made sure that no matter how hard I tried to get rid of those images, they were still alive and well online. A constant reminder that any photo you took in this digital age would forever be in our society whether you liked it or not.

Black Wolf Creek was never outright mentioned on the messaging boards, but there had been people who had reverse image searched those photos and were able to trace them to nearby villages and towns. It definitely scared me to think of fanatics at the doorstep. Not because I didn't think we could handle them, but because I knew that we had made a lot of enemies, and Cain, for better or worse, was the face of the book and all of its ideas.

Sure enough, the dark web and corners of Reddit were catching people like Kai Saito, and I wanted him nowhere near our community. He had indeed murdered critics of our book, and he even recruited some girl from my hometown to help him find us. Denise's record was clean though, and, if anything, it seemed like she wasn't a fan of our book at all. She didn't follow the social media pages or gush about it online.

Kai and I embraced our darkness, but we were not the same person. Sure, I silenced the critics online and scrubbed their disagreements out of existence, but he took the book's ideas even further and actually killed those who were against us. I should have be flattered that he was true to himself, but he was the kind of person we were trying to eradicate, if I was being completely honest with myself.

The whole idea behind the book was to bring the truly vile people out of hiding and then let the outside world burn itself into the ground. There were people out there who could reveal their true colors and not harm a fly—though even then, I thought the book could help empower them to no longer take shit from those who had bullied them. Kai and I believed strongly in *Your True Colors* but for different reasons. But who knew . . . maybe I was still lying to myself.

Something felt off about the whole thing. Tracking him online, I saw that he stopped in Austin for longer than I thought he would. I wasn't really surprised when they told me that a third person had joined this little crusade, but I was watchful. The original plan had been to capture them and maybe scare them into never visiting our property again, but all of that changed when I looked at the footage through the woods and saw their car parking off in the distance.

They took out their camera equipment and my heart sank when I saw the third person who joined this little expedition. Was that . . . no. While I studied the security cameras in the footage room, Azul notified me that Kai had arrived with his guests. My second-in-command watched the life drain from my face, and I actually collapsed when I saw who had joined Denise and Kai.

Isabelle?

CHAPTER THIRTEEN

Azul caught me pretty gracefully for having no heads-up. She sat me down in her chair and quickly got me a fresh water bottle. I felt like I could not breathe, and the room had gotten smaller.

"Sydney, speak to me." Azul could tell that I was rattled, and we don't lie here.

"That's my daughter," I whispered as I felt the world spin and like I might vomit.

Azul's eyes widened, and she looked back at the footage and then back at me. The resemblance was faint, and I'd always argued that she looked more like her father than me. She even got his last name and his codependency to go along with it.

"Do you wish to not see her?" Azul had always been tactful. Even with this big of a bombshell, most people in the community would urge me to look inward and maybe even confront her about why I chose to abandon her, but Azul saw me better than most people.

"I-I-I don't know," I stammered, and those three words were basically forbidden here because we always asked for resolution, but the truth was that I still stalked

295

her every once in a while on LinkedIn and even hired someone from the dark web to hack her room's computer.

Her home life was more boring than a sixties sitcom. It was repetitive, and she hardly broke her cycle. She knitted and occasionally went out with Tanner to dinner or the movies. It was hard to pick up their conversations because their computer had a cheap microphone attached to it, but I knew that she'd wasted the life that had been given to her.

Well look who decided to start living? This was such a mindfuck because this was the last thing I imagined she'd do. I was honestly somewhat proud of her. Was it the book? She couldn't read! I once got irritated enough by her condition that I forced her to read *Lord of the Flies*. Hey, look, I never said I was going to win Mother of the Year.

It had taken her five times longer than the other students in the class, and the assignment was due before she could finish it, but because she was completing it from front to back, I did her a solid and just wrote the paper to get the A. I thought she would hate me for making her do something that obviously took a lot out of her, but I found that she actually liked it.

I had read the same book in high school so we ended up having an in-depth conversation about the characters and how the kids acted once they were abandoned on the island—the true nature of the children and the demise of Piggy. It was one of the most riveting conversations I had ever had with my daughter. I wanted to encourage her to read more, but I saw how difficult it was, and I knew she wasn't faking her condition.

Maybe she sat down and actually read *Your True Colors*, though? If this was a new version of Isabelle, then I knew she'd not be like the rest of the monsters in the world and might even have a role in Black Wolf Creek. But what were her thoughts on her father? I was never seeing that man again, that was for sure.

"Go get them. I want you to do it. Take Henry with you," I ordered Azul. After the world stopped spinning, I got a better grip on things.

Azul was not the type to be told twice and she instantly packed her firearm, but unspoken words were passed between our eyes: don't kill my daughter.

"One more thing." I grabbed her arm before she was out the door. "You and Henry will have to put a mask on for this situation."

"You want us to lie." She understood what I mean. "No problem."

We spent so much time in the camp being our true selves that we didn't get much opportunity to be other people. It also helped that Azul was a part of theater in high school and organized plays for us every six months. She was a heck of an actress, and I would definitely give her a Tony. Her husband was okay, and I hoped his performance wouldn't blow it.

I didn't want this all going sideways before I got a chance to confront my daughter.

Luckily some of the cameras had audio, and I followed their every movement. Ron, in tech, showed me how to change the audio levels for each device, and I heard them talk. I stayed focused, but I nearly lost my breath when I realized they were not here to give their regards . . . they wanted to kill him. Cain, the love of my life, murdered at the hands of my daughter. The thought was so absurd that I could not help but to laugh.

"Yeah, I don't feel threatened by them either," Ron mused, but he was unaware of how harmless Izzy had been her whole life. I thought she would cry if she accidentally squashed a butterfly.

"I've got a hang on the cameras. Can you do me a solid, Ron, and get the background information on this Denise Harrington?" Ron could have pressed me on why I wanted this information, but he just nodded and started to go through the database of the Austin metro area.

"Never underestimate your enemies?" he probed while looking through her information.

"Yeah, something like that." I thought about it and then added, "I also want you to look up the people in her life: family, friends, coworkers . . . someone had to have a tragedy recently to get her to fly across the country and make this trek."

He nodded and continued to dig while I further listened to their conversations. When I heard that Isabelle was now calling herself Sydney, I snorted in amusement.

"You wish," I muttered.

"What's that?" Ron perked up.

"Not you." I waved him off and continued to follow their path to the dining room hall. I felt like Kai was not being so covert anymore. If he was not careful, the stealth mode would be completely deactivated and it could get ugly quick.

The three of them retreated to the dining room hall, seemingly unnoticed by most people, but I saw Azul note their departure. If I had zero faith in her methods, I would have asked her to just stun them, but I knew that wasn't necessary. She was a pro through and through.

Behind the barn they were subdued. Javi and Azul had made sure of that. It was almost underwhelming to watch on camera. A lot of people watched too many James Bond movies and thought they could successfully pull off a heist or infiltrate an operation, but the sad reality was that a lot of them would be killed off by goons within the first ten minutes.

A quick blow to the back of the head did the trick while Javi got creative and held Kai in a sleeper hold. Show-off. Although I did smile because I was pretty sure that I had taught him that one. To be fair, Javi had eight inches and nearly a hundred pounds on Kai. It was a pretty easy target. Azul had to chase down Denise a little bit, and the tackle was clumsy, but soon she was subdued too.

Some of the residents came out to watch the commotion but didn't question anything as they watched Henry and Javi lift Kai and Isabelle off the ground while Azul has her hands full with Denise. A strong part of me wanted to go out there and assist her, but if Isabelle woke up too early, then it'd just ruin everything. Besides, we didn't get much live entertainment, and even Ron had stopped his research to watch the scene unfold.

"We've got a fighter." Ron laughed.

"She's scared shitless," I observed. "I really hope Azul takes it easy on her."

"Yeah, I wouldn't go that far." I turned around to look at Ron as he had her information pulled up on the screen.

Jesus Christ. Her youngest brother almost became a school shooter. *Almost* being the key word. He was stopped on his way to school that day and almost withdrew a handgun. Apparently his frequent bully was stunned at finding the gun, and the other two who terrorized him on a daily basis opened his backpack to find explosives, guns, and, sure enough, a copy of *Your True Colors.*

When the police showed up, they didn't account for the bullies to not frisk him. In his back pocket he had another gun and tried to get a good aim at the main bully only to be shot by the police. Head shot. Closed casket funeral. Within his bag was also a manifesto that said some pretty damning things. I had to do some digging on social media, but I found that his family pleaded he wasn't like this and that he had been influenced by the wrong group of people.

Well, at least that's what the parents said. His older sister, on the other hand, remained silent, and I knew she knew. Photos of the family that were released on lowbrow news outlets showed a sulking Denise, and in those eyes I saw the fire that burned within. If she were to be let loose, something told me that she would burn this whole compound to the ground.

Had we underestimated her?

The barn was darkly lit, and I was again tempted to just go observe in person, but it was too much of a risk to even try to hide in the background. I had to settle for the cameras again. Technology had come a long way, but we never really thought there would be much use to having better cameras installed on the inside of the barn.

We weren't monsters and it wasn't some place we went to torture people. It was just a barn. Farm animals, their food tucked away, and maybe some gardening

301

supplies. Although I could see Isabelle shaking, and my heart did flutter. I did have a natural instinct to go and hold her in my arms, but I had to push that down and let Azul do her job.

It didn't help that Javi and Henry could look pretty intimidating due to their size, and the gardening supplies on the wall probably looked more sinister than they were. And Denise probably wasn't calming Izzy down either. She was like a madwoman. My goodness . . . Ron was right about her. She still had fight in her and was not intimidated by anything.

What was Kai's move, though?

We didn't have to wait long as both Ron and I watched like we were glued to a movie during a climax. Both of us visibly gasped when Kai took the knife in his hand and used Denise as a hostage. Holy shit.

"Holy shit," Ron echoed my thoughts, but I was too stunned to reply.

Azul, of course, tried to deescalate the situation. She was actually pretty calm when she wanted to be. I probably wouldn't be able to hold it together were I there.

Then the whole world turned upside down when I saw Denise's throat slice open and Henry lunged to cover her wound while Javi tackled Kai and pinned him to the ground. She needed a medic. Stat. I ran out of the computer room and was sprinting toward the barn.

302

Fuck. Fuck. Fuck. Fuck. Fuck. Please be okay. I looked behind me to see that Ron was not far. I told him to go back, but then I noticed he had my medical bag with him. Oh my God, yes, thank you, Ron!

"Thank you." I was already out of breath and took it and then continued toward the barn.

"Everything okay?" Gina hollered at me, and I screamed at her to get Joseph, Sally, or really any of our other medically trained community members to assist me.

I burst through the barn and was grateful that Henry still has pressure applied to the neck. She was still conscious, which was remarkable because most people would've passed out after that. I wasted no time wrapping her wound while continuing to apply pressure. My daughter was less than five feet away from me, but I had no time to focus on her.

She fainted anyway. I couldn't blame her for that. Most people would do the same. Javi had subdued Kai a second time and this time tied him up with no intention of the knots getting loose.

It wasn't not long before Joseph came through the barn door accompanied with other people who had, thankfully, gotten the gurney. She'd lost a lot of blood, but it looked like it was patched enough. We'd have to get her to the makeshift surgery room we had in the medical ward.

I looked down at Denise, and she looked about ready to pass out.

"Stay with me, okay, Denise?" The mentioning of her name snapped her back to reality, and she looked into my eyes. I couldn't tell you how she knew, but she did. She must have seen a resemblance between me and Isabelle, because now she was fully distracted.

I did my best to ignore the double take and stayed focused on her as a patient. "You've lost a lot of blood but you're going to recover."

I had to stop myself from saying "full recovery" because the truth was that Kai could've very well sliced through her vocal cords, and even Jesus himself wouldn't be able to get her to talk again. But after today and now knowing the person she was, would that necessarily be a bad thing?

CHAPTER FOURTEEN

Word spread quickly in the community and now I felt like I was on trial. My daughter was on the premises and had brought a lot of trouble with her. No one ever lied, so it was obvious that Isabelle was way in over her head and may have been influenced by Denise. I did not omit Denise's history and included everything that Ron and I had uncovered together.

Kai's future was unclear, though, due to the fact that he attempted murder on our premises, and we did not like police presence on our property. Even with the video evidence, they would want to analyze the scene and intrude on our community. It was obvious that we had to deal with this on our own, but I wasn't not sure what that would entail.

For the most part, Black Wolf Creek had not had a history of bad apples. There was a holding cell we'd created for the teenagers who got a bit rowdy, but overall it wasn't like we could keep him there permanently. During the town hall I listened and gave my input when it was asked. The two culprits who drew the most interest were not my daughter.

"Eye for an eye?" Henry suggested. I could tell his tolerance of Kai had run thin, and it didn't help that he was there when a murder almost took place.

"It seems like the most obvious answer," agreed Kendra, who managed the building maintenance.

"This could be someone who is mentally unstable, though, and it seems a bit inhumane to punish someone who doesn't have a full set of tools up there," Josie suggested.

"He was bright enough to track us down and seemed coherent enough to really study the work of Cain's book. His toolbox seemed pretty full to me," Ron chimed in, and it was hard to disagree with him.

The meeting had been hijacked by Kai and his actions. Denise and Isabelle were an afterthought. But if we went through with executing Kai, then I wondered what Denise's future held. Kai had proven he was willing to follow through with murder, but Denise could prove to be the same or back out. She'd probably reconsider if she ever saw the real condition that Cain was in.

Then it hit me. She would reconsider when seeing him in his current state. I'd been trying my hardest to extend his life, but I knew his days were limited. Would she rest easier if she knew that he was on his final days? Maybe she could get out of this scot-free and we could let all of this be water under the bridge.

The community had to vote on Kai's fate and would decide that in a few days' time to give everyone time to really weigh their options. When I returned to the hospital ward we'd created in one of the historical houses, I was informed that Isabelle was awake and locked in the room down the hall. It may have seemed like I was holding off this reunion, but I was genuinely trying to give her friend a fighting chance at a life outside of this. I walked past my daughter's locked room and went visit Denise, who was wide awake.

She flinched when I approached her, but I assured her that I was not going to harm her.

"Even though I don't necessarily have my license anymore, I still took an oath to protect my patients at all costs," I assured her, but she was still wide-eyed and looked cornered.

I sighed, unbuckled her straps, and asked if she could walk. She didn't respond as her eyes darted across the room, and I knew she was looking for something to attack me with.

"Please don't make me put you back in your place." I was exhausted at this point of the day after having had to take care of Cain, attend the meeting, and debrief with the council. I was confident I could take her, even though she was younger and more energized.

She got up and followed me out of her bedroom door, and I knocked on Cain's door. His eyes were heavy and he looked as sedated as I had left him. I knew I shouldn't get him so hooked on painkillers, but at this point, what was the harm of doping him up? He didn't have much time left.

"Hey, Syd." He gave me a weak smile and I looked back to Denise, who was momentarily stunned. She wouldn't be able to talk even if she could.

"Honey, this is Denise. She came here to kill you," I stated matter-of-factly, and Denise's face instantly reddened.

"Please do." He half smiled as he looked Denise in the eyes. "I'm sorry . . . though you probably don't want to hear that."

Denise's emotions were conflicted as she thought about everything. She pointed to one of my medical notepads. I picked it up and gave it to her. She quickly scribbled down a note. I read it out loud to him and also to myself.

"Why'd you unleash all of this into the world? You ruined my family's life." I hadn't realized that I was holding my breath and exhaled as I genuinely looked at her and apologized with my eyes.

"I'm sorry I hurt you and your family." Cain had a way of delivering his words straight to the heart, and I knew they were true because he didn't lie. "It's funny how you go along with the worst ideas if the person you love is so passionate about it."

She let the words sit and looked over to me. I knew I should have shown remorse for her, comforted her, and told her how I was sorry our book destroyed her family's life, but I wasn't sorry. Her brother wasn't as loving as he appeared to be, and maybe it was for the best that he was put out of his misery before he did real harm on this planet. Had we never made the book, he would have eventually shown the world his true colors sooner or later.

"He wrote more compassionate words, but I helped manipulate them to reach a broader audience and get it to be the phenomena that it is," I explained to Denise. "We shouldn't live in lies, and your brother may have done horrible things, but at least he was the truest version of himself."

She snapped and grabbed a surgical tool. She was slow, though, and I easily sidestepped and disarmed her. I bent her arm backward and pushed her against the wall. She fought a little but then quickly surrendered, the pain of her throat diminishing her fire.

When the fight was all out of her, her body went limp and she started to crumble and heave.

"You didn't have to be so cruel," Cain said as I pulled her back up on her feet.

"You'd rather I lie to her?" I didn't feel like being shamed right now or fighting with him.

"No, you've always been yourself," Cain responded evenly. "I'm the problem for not wanting to see the darkest sides of you earlier."

For fuck's sake. I'd spent all of my money, time, and energy prolonging this man's life, and now he was lecturing me about my character? What more could I give him? I twisted Denise's arm harder than I should have while she squeaked in pain, and I escorted her back to her room. When we were alone in her hospital room, I strapped her back up in the bed.

"You do everything for people and sometimes it's never enough," I ranted to her. "I got his work recognized and made him a crucial part of history but then he turns around and calls me a monster."

Some of the straps were tightened too tight and she winced, but I didn't care.

"Have you ever blown up a plane for love?" I asked her. "Have you ever abandoned your daughter and husband to be with the person who makes you feel special?"

These were rhetorical questions, but she nodded to the medical note pad. I let her scribble awkwardly with one hand and I read the note: YOUR SICK.

"I assume you mean to put an apostrophe in there." I crumbled up her piece of paper and threw it in the trash as I left her alone in the room.

310

I just saved this woman's life and let her meet her intended assassination target, and now I was being judged by her as well. Well fuck it. I knew which way I was voting for both her and Kai's fate when it came down to it.

I take a much-needed nap and didn't even go back to my home for it. There was a perfectly furnished guest room on the first floor of the house that I utilized. I had a spare change of clothes that was in the bottom drawer because you never knew when patients could get messy. The scrubs we used were sufficient, but it was surprising how much seeped through and could ruin perfectly good outfits underneath.

I wanted to crawl in the bed for the rest of the night, but I woke up sometime in the middle of the night and decided to go upstairs to check in on our two guests. Isabelle's door was locked and no one guarded the door, so I unlocked it. I checked in on Denise who was either sleeping or heard me walking up, so she shut her eyes and was pretending to be passed out.

Cain could sense that I was still mad at him, but he wouldn't apologize for his remarks. It was one of the reasons I loved and hated him so much. I knew he'd be dead by the end of the week, and I didn't want him to leave this world with us on a bad note, so I apologized.

"You know that I love you because of who you are . . . all of it," he told me.

311

A tear formed in my eye, and I leaned forward to hug him. We embraced one another, and I almost crawled into his bed with him to hold him for one of our final moments, when I heard the door from down the hall open. Isabelle. She was up.

Cain knew this too, and I watched through his cracked door as she was about to enter Denise's room. Well, she wasn't going to say anything. I had nothing to worry about there. But then she stopped and turned around to face the door I was looking through. She was coming here instead.

I retreated to the corner of the room in the shadows. My daughter opened the door, walked in, and saw Cain. The two of them locked eyes, and she began walking closer to him as if hypnotized. No words were spoken between the two as I went to close the door so we could have some privacy.

"Hello, Isabelle."

When she turned around, I saw a beautiful young woman who I had abandoned nearly twenty years before. I hardly recognized her.

"Mom?"

Your True Colors

Your True Colors

PART III

ISABELLE

Your True Colors

CHAPTER ONE

This cannot be real. Am I dreaming? I lose my grip as the world begins to tilt. I lean on the door for support. My mom. She's aged gracefully. Grays, thinner, but still flawless skin, and her demeanor hasn't changed. She even has that sympathetic look she used to give me as a teenager that I was never completely sure whether to be insulted or comforted by.

"This is a lot to process," she tells me. "I think you should sit down."

"You're alive? How?" I'm surprised she hears my voice, because it comes out fainter than a whisper.

"Sydney." Cain coughs and looks worse for wear. Why is my mom here with him? I have so many questions. "I think you should take her somewhere alone, and I can notify Azul to give both of you some privacy."

For a dying man, he certainty has manners. Mom looks back at him, and I can see her protest with her eyes, but she quickly accepts what he says and kisses him on the cheek. A kiss that was very close to his lips. He's closer to my age than hers! What on earth is going on?

Mom gently corrals me by the wrist and I almost well up and cry at that touch alone. When was the last time I felt my mother's hand on my skin? It's definitely

318

not a dream because I'd recognize those hands from anywhere, and it's the same firmness that no one could mimic. We go through the house and downstairs to what looks like a lavishly furnished guest room. There are two chairs. She motions for me to sit down and I do. I cannot stop looking at her. It's really her.

"Black Wolf Creek is a community where lying is not tolerated. Ask me anything and I will be truthful. Besides, being completely honest with yourself and others is what *Your True Colors* is all about." Mom sits across from me with her hands in her lap.

We should be hugging and crying, but right now this feels like a therapy session. She watches me as if I were someone who got picked on at school and she is a counselor who's here to hear my problems. I study her in fascination and don't even know where to begin.

"Really? Nothing?" my mom asks all while sounding borderline rude; maybe because it is. Building in me is a new emotion I've never felt toward her—rage.

"You didn't board that plane!" I nearly yell at her.

"I did. But I got off before it took flight." She seems happy that I at least asked a question.

"There were rescue parties. You could've been found! Jesus, Mom, you could've come home." My voice rises octaves.

"Those aren't questions, Izzy," she points out.

319

Of course that's how my mom responds. This is definitely not an imposter because that's exactly what she'd say.

"Why didn't you come home?" I ask.

Mom sighs and runs fingers through her hair. "That life was draining me, Sweet T."

"You had everything. A mansion, a family, a career," I counter.

"Yes. I did, Isabelle, and do you know how we even got that life?" She sounds irritated. "It was because of me. I was knocked up as a teenager, but I didn't let that stop us from having a pretty lavish life."

"Lavish?" The thought never crossed my mind, and I wish I hadn't said that out loud because now Mom answers back in a vengeance.

"Yes, lavish, Izzy," Mom shouts. "The private schools, the two-story house, the newest cars. Shit, even with your father's gambling problem, we still had a lot of money. Although you know that because we had to open that bank account together. For fuck's sake, how much life insurance did you get after the plane wreck?"

Nearly three quarters of a million, I think as my eyes look to the ground.

"Almost one million dollars." Not quite, but I don't correct her as she continues, "Even in my 'death' I was taking care of you guys, and do you know how exhausting that is? Of course you don't! I should've gotten

320

you a pet or something because then you would know what it's like to have someone rely on you twenty-four seven."

I'm hurt because I never thought of myself as much of a burden. I got good grades and stayed out of trouble. Whenever she asked me to do anything, I would never argue. I thought I was the ideal daughter. And as much as I want to probe her further about that, the real questions are still pestering me.

"Are you in love with Cain?" When I ask her this question, she instantly loses her temper and her face softens, and I can tell that she has forgotten all about her marriage to my dad.

"Yes. I do." She half smiles.

"But he wrote that book, Mom. Maybe he tricked you into loving him. He's obviously unwell, and maybe this was a way he could get close to you."

She laughs. Actual laughter. I cannot remember the last time I saw her doing so. Maybe she was miserable, because I have never seen her this genuinely entertained back at home in Austin.

"I helped write the book, Izzy." She's still laughing as my heart sinks.

"You wrote the book?" I gasp and feel like all the air has been taken out of my lungs.

Mom stops laughing when she sees how mortified I am. I can't hide those emotions.

"You're in your thirties now. How many people have been fake with you or deceived you to get their way?" Mom asks me.

"What?" Is this a trick question?

"Think about it, Isabelle. Really think." Mom's eyes pierce into my soul.

I take a moment to think about what she's just asked, and I guess I can understand the question from a philosophical point of view, but I think there's a difference between theory and practice.

Mom waits patiently. My whole life I had always agreed with her, but I don't think I can this time around.

"Yes, people are fake," I start and she smiles, "but that's a necessary function to keep the society intact." Her smile fades, and I continue.

"Mom, do you see what's happening out there? Without morality, people are going crazy. They're doing things that they normally wouldn't do."

"They're not going crazy, dear, that's just who they are, and now it's better we can recognize them." She talks to me like she's talking to a toddler.

"Dad brought home an escort—in our house!" I exclaim.

I don't know if I was expecting jealousy or for her to be offended, but she laughs again.

"Wait, really?" She's more amused than I thought. "Was she at least good looking?"

"What?!" I am caught off guard.

"He's not the best looking in the bunch and has probably been sexually pent up for a long time. I'm surprised he didn't do it sooner." Did my mom really just say that?

"Mom, people are embezzling funds, blackmailing people, raping . . . Mom, *raping*!" I have to emphasize the word more for her to get it.

"Izzy, you know that was all going on before the book came out, right? In, fact a lot of it was done in the shadows. Now everyone's secrets are out in the open for everyone else to see."

I sit with these words and realize I forgot to ask a very crucial question. The one that should've been the question I led with.

"Mom—" I begin.

She looks at me and waits for me to ask the next question.

"Did you blow up that plane?"

"Of course I did." I can tell she's not lying, and suddenly I'm nauseous. I run to the restroom and make it just in time to see the community's lunch from yesterday go in the toilet. Mom is behind me and gently pats my back.

"One of my biggest regrets, Isabelle, was never introducing you to my real self. I raised you in an environment where I was a go-getter and a provider but never embracing all of my emotions. I kept them bottled up all those years. I'm sorry you never got to meet her."

I lift my head from the toilet, vomit still staining my lips, and can see that she's genuinely trying to get through to me. I let her continue to speak.

"I'm going to vouch for you at the town hall and convince them to let you live. But I know you won't be allowed to live here," she tells me.

My head starts to spin because she just threw a lot of information at me. Am I on trial for trying to kill her new boyfriend? I didn't even do anything! If anything, Kai was the violent one. And assuming she's not lying, which she claims she's not, then she's going to try to get me out of this and let me, what, walk out of here unscathed, but then I can't move here? Is she going to come visit us back home, or am I going to be banned from this place and never see her again?

I want to ask all these questions and more, but she shushes me and tells me that I can sleep in this bed tonight. She has to get ready for the town hall the next morning.

When she leaves I notice that she doesn't lock the door. I lie next to the toilet for what seems like eternity as my mind tries to process everything.

Eventually I need to use their shower and clean myself up. I let the water hit my back as my mind races faster than I can keep up with. Mom is alive. Mom is also a new age cult leader. Except is she? What is she? Is she an anarchist who wants the world to burn? She's built a new life. Is she going to defend me, as in like, put in a good word, or will she be a public defender? I know all these questions should keep me up that night, but when I rest my head against the silk pillow in the bed, my eyes flutter and I drift off to sleep.

I dream of when Mom would take me to the music shop after school and she'd let me try out various instruments. Even in the dreams I look closer at her and can now see the exhaustion she carries in her smile and the bags that are underneath her eyes. Had I never noticed them before because I was just excited to be somewhere I wanted to be with my favorite person in the whole world?

CHAPTER TWO

A new set of clothes has been laid out for me on the bed, and it's not silky white, creepy cult clothing. Just an average pair of jeans, a T-shirt, and some underwear. It all looks brand new, which I assume must've been bought when they last went into town. When I put it on, it's a little loose, but luckily there's also a pair of leggings I fit into.

My stomach growls. It's understandable because I threw up all of yesterday's food, but I try to reason with my belly that I need to find Denise and warn her about our trial. It doesn't seem like we're being contained in a prison, and Mom definitely didn't lock me in the room. I guess it was smart on her part. Where am I going to run to even if I escape? What would I even tell the authorities?

Hey, my mom who's been dead for almost twenty years is alive and wrote a book that's getting people to do horrible things. Oh! Did I mention that she blew up a plane and her neighbors might kill my friends? I would sound hysterical, but even if they took me seriously, they'd need proof. And then they'd want me to lead them back to the supposed crime scene, which would be the last place I would want to be. My mom knows how much I hate confrontation. I should at least go check in with Denise.

I open the door to leave the room when I run into Javi. He almost drops the food he's brought for me but manages to hold on to it.

"You weren't up for breakfast so we got you some of the leftovers before feeding it to the dogs," Javi states as I look down at the ham, bacon, and eggs that are all wrapped in a tortilla.

Instantly my mouth starts to salivate, and he notices this. He smiles and hands it over along with a large cup of orange juice.

"What about Denise?" I ask, and his face contorts a little.

"Sydney thinks she should be able to swallow, but it's going to be a bit of a trial run depending on how she's recovering. So, fingers crossed," he explains.

Damn. I didn't even think about that. What happens if she can't eat? Does she need a tube until her throat recovers? I should not eat my food in solidarity with her if that's the case, but I'm too weak of a person to follow through with that kind of a pact. I grab the food and bite into it.

"I didn't see the resemblance at first, but now I cannot unsee it," Javi observes.

I know he's talking about me and my mom. I feel a bit honored to be compared to her in any way whatsoever because I always thought I looked more like my dad. The same dad who needs to pay for sex.

"Thank you," I tell him after I swallow my first few bites.

He says nothing and begins to leave when I set the food down and grab his wrist. He stops and looks at me.

"Have you heard any news on what they're going to do with me and Denise?" I ask him. His eyebrow arches.

"Don't have much love left for your boy Kai anymore, huh?" he muses.

"Fuck that guy." I haven't had much time to think about him, but that has to be the most shameful one-night stand any person has ever had.

"They're discussing him tomorrow, and today they're basically going to decide what kind of sentence you two will have," he says nonchalantly. I start to talk to him like he's the judge himself.

"We're completely innocent and wouldn't harm a fly," I plead.

"Wasn't it your guy's whole plan to come here and kill Cain?" Welp. He's got me there, and at first I think about denying it but then remember what my mom said about honesty.

"I don't know if you were born here or not, but outside of this rural community, people are doing bad things. Like really bad. This book she created is—"

"—what the world needed to read." He finishes my sentence, but we are obviously not on the same page.

My shoulders slump. I should've known that I would get no sympathy from a man who knows Cain and this version of my mom so well. He seems to come to the same conclusion that I had.

"You're not thinking about the bigger picture," he continues. "Those people were already bad human beings, but now we're seeing them for who they really are."

"Sure, the wolves are in the open. But what about the rest of the sheep?" I retorted. "Lead them to the slaughterhouse?"

His eyes narrow, and I don't know if I offended him, but he shrugs his shoulders. "You and your mom both have big hearts, I'll give you that. But something tells me that you're no different than the rest of the people who have read the book." I don't know what to make of that. I'm about to switch tactics and plead my case again when he walks off and says over his shoulder, "I see the hostility in your eyes, Isabelle. It's faint, but it's there."

When I finish eating, I go to the nearest bathroom and am able to locate a toothbrush, toothpaste, and even mouthwash. It sounds ridiculous, but I don't want Denise to judge me for eating without her when I should've gone straight to her.

329

She's up, eyes focused on the wall. With her strapped up so tight, what else could she really do? When I walk in, she lifts up her head and I see her let her guard down. I loosen her straps and she undoes her legs as well.

"Denise, I don't think that's a good idea," I begin, but she emphatically waves her hands. Her legs are shaky but they still work as she walks across the room and goes through the drawers. I try to tell her to stop snooping in their stuff, but then she finds a cell phone and her face lights up. I hover over her shoulder as she powers it on and, naturally, it has no signal and does not connect to Wi-Fi.

It's about as useless as a brick. But Denise opens the texts, and even though it seems like a burner phone with no history, she rapidly types in it and plays out the audio, which says, "Bathroom?" I am surprised she's lasted this long without asking to use it. I nod to the room that's down the hall and she quickly darts there with the phone in her hand.

She's in there for what seems like eternity. Did no one really think to let her out for a bathroom break? Although I have to keep reminding myself that this isn't a regular thing for these people. It's not like they are used to having unwanted guests for a prolonged period of time. Eventually the toilet flushes and I can hear her splashing water on her face.

330

"Want me to find you some new clothes?" I look down at the nightgown they put her in. She rolls her eyes and marches right past me. Shit. Where does she think she's going?

"Denise!" I trot next to her and try to slow her down. "They have our phones. We're in the middle of nowhere, and we're outnumbered."

Obviously she doesn't care and is willing to walk home barefoot if she needs to.

"You need to recover! And my mom is actually a really good doctor." She stops in her tracks and stares at me. If looks could kill, then I would be dead. "I-I-I obviously didn't know she was alive! And, hey, maybe me being her daughter, they'll go easier on us for our trial."

At the word "trial" her eyes widen. Right. I have not told her that part yet. Shit, this is not going well. She looks at me, and I can tell that if she could speak, she'd want me to get to the point.

"Mom said that the community was going to get together for a town hall to discuss what to do with us. She'll be in our corner, though—"

She squeaks with a humorless laugh. It's muffled, but I know she finds that amusing.

"Please. Let's stop being reckless and actually just think this through, okay?" I try to reason with her. She considers this and walks back to her room. I follow her.

She grabs the burner phone that's currently at sixty percent battery life.

She types until the message is read aloud: "Let's go to the town hall and hear what they have to say."

God. She does not like staying away from danger, does she? She continues to text the next part: "If they decide to spare our lives, then I'll go back to my room. If not—"

I stop her from texting the rest. "We hightail it out of there. Yeah, I agree. Deal."

Not a bad compromise, and honestly not that bad of a plan either.

CHAPTER THREE

We're out in the open and she texts me that they have security cameras around the place that monitor twenty-four seven. She overheard it when she was recovering from the operation. I don't know why we didn't see them before, because a lot of them are in plain sight. I wonder how the residents feel about being watched constantly. Then again, they probably all know one another and would argue something like how they don't have anything to hide.

At first we try our hardest to be in the blind spots of the cameras, but the town seems pretty deserted, and even if there were someone sitting in a room watching the footage, what would they do? We abandon stealth mode and just walk through the town, seeing no activity on the streets. There's no doubt in our minds that they are having the town hall meeting and we might already be too late to hear what they have to say about us, but we have no idea where we're going.

"It's over there," Denise texts, and my eyes follow to the big structure that looks like a municipal building. That would definitely be my best guess too. I'm about to

333

enter through the front when she grabs a hold of me and shakes her head. She directs me to follow her.

We go to the back of the building and look up to see a window that's accessible. She nods for me to help her move a garbage bin, which I do, but unfortunately it's heavier than it looks. We both grunt as we put it on the backside of the wall and then Denise pushes the window upward. It actually opens without us having to break anything. She jumps in before I ask her if this is really such a good idea.

I'm reluctant to go in, but after a moment's hesitation, Denise pops her head outside and her eyes urge me to join her. She even puts out her hand for me to get a hold of. Fuck it. We've already gone this far. I jump onto the garbage and take her hand as she helps me into the back room. From the looks of it, it was a kitchen at one point. We exit the room and notice stairs in the back. The two of us climb and don't have to worry about the boards creaking or loud sneakers because we're both barefooted.

Denise opens doors and turns on lights to see storage spaces and offices. I wonder what she's looking for when I notice that there is a room that has a window, and before she can flip the light switch, I stop her. Our eyes meet.

"That window doesn't face the outdoors. I think it overlooks the first floor," I whisper. She nods her head in agreement. The two of us go in and close the door behind us and are rewarded with a bird's-eye view of the citizens who have gathered.

Even though it's a small community, there sure are a lot of them here—at least a couple hundred. What's crazy is that they range in ages, races, and even types of people. I don't know why I thought they would be a bunch of backward hillbillies, but I assume they've probably gotten that stereotype a lot when you think about people who want to live off the grid and in the woods.

Denise is careful as she cracks the window open, and we're able to hear them just fine. To our disappointment they're talking about the maintenance that's needed in some of their houses, and it sounds more like an HOA meeting versus a trial. I'm about to suggest that we rethink what we're going to do when one of the council members speaks up.

"Next order of business is to address the intruders who have been causing disruption to Black Wolf Creek. Names: Denise Harrington and Isabelle Dunham." My heart sinks to the bottom of my stomach like they just gave me a verdict. Denise doesn't seem as rattled, though. Or if she does, she doesn't show too much emotion.

"Victoria Cross, aka Sydney, has agreed to not be a part of the council for this vote but would like to be a part of the public comments to weigh in on what should be done with these two. Also, another reminder that tomorrow we're going to be addressing the death penalty for Kai Saito."

Again I look at Denise to see if there's any reaction, and there's a smug look of satisfaction with that one. I can't say I blame her, though. If someone took away my voice, possibly forever, I would want them to suffer too.

These people are far smarter than I gave them credit for and did their due diligence with their research about us. They know where I have lived, my relation to my mom, my job, and that I'm dyslexic. Although I'm assuming the latter information they learned from her. I somehow know that this is going to play a crucial role in my sentencing. Denise is a different story.

My mouth drops when I hear about her brother and the vendetta she has against Cain. I cannot believe her brother died as a result of *Your True Colors*. For the majority of her rap sheet she remained neutral and stoic, but at the mention of her brother, I see the micro expressions in her face. I want nothing more than to hold her and comfort her, but I know her well enough now to know that she'll just push me away.

This trial is actually pretty fair, and had I been a resident, I feel like I would be sentencing both of us as guilty, but Mom paints us in a fair light and even mentions how her boyfriend was the intended target and is going to be dead within the next few days anyway. My mom

336

would've made as good of an attorney as she was a doctor, because her words portray us so positively that I would've been swayed in the other direction just as quickly.

I smile at Denise and nudge her, obviously more optimistic than she is. She's definitely not as enthused but does seem grateful that my mom is, indeed, in our corner. I feel good up until the point that Javi wants the floor. The speaker is surprised and more than willing to let him speak. I even hear a few murmurs in the crowd; he must not speak up very often.

"Denise Harrington has been nothing but a pest and has given us a few scars in the process." Uh-oh, I think. "She came here set on one thing and one thing only: to murder Cain Skaggs."

The entire room is listening and silent.

"However, she's been introduced to him, and I can see her internal conflict. This isn't to say that she wouldn't want to pull the plug on him herself, but I assume that he'd welcome that in the condition he's been in."

The man really is in bad shape, and had we started our crusade just a week later, something tells me that we'd have never meet him.

"Denise Harrington is the truest version of herself whether she wants to admit it or not. I can't say whether the book had an influence on her or not, but I do know that she follows our code of zero tolerance for lying," Javi continues. "She is not a threat to us as a whole, and I suggest we allow her to pull the plug on Cain if she wishes to do so and then let her be on her way."

I watch Denise's face the entire time, and I can see the conflicting emotions collide with one another. On one hand, this is what she came for, but now knowing he's on death's door anyway, does it mean anything? Does it take it away from her if it's his decision to leave this world? And, of course, no matter what happens, it's not going to bring her brother back. A tear forms in the corner of her eyes, but I know her well; she will refuse to cry.

"Isabelle Dunham, on the other hand—" my head snaps quickly in the direction of the speaker, so quickly that I'm surprised I don't give myself whiplash, "—she is not true to herself or us. The longer she stays in the encampment, the longer she remains a threat."

What the fuck?! Me, a threat?? I don't even think I've ever killed a bug before, let alone harm another human being. Mom objects and basically echoes what I think. She goes on about how I'm the meekest person she's ever known. It could be viewed as an insult, but I don't take it as one right now and am grateful that she's telling them about my history.

"Sydney. I know you're not thinking straight on account of this being your daughter, but you know I'm right with this. She lied to me this morning, and I do think that she also lied to herself. You mentioned how she cannot read. Without the teachings of the book, she may never learn. I motion for her to be banned from the premises and removed as swiftly as possible," Javi concludes.

Wait? That's it? Being escorted out of here? No death penalty charges? I feel so much lighter, and I hadn't realized how tense I was until my legs give out and I slump to the floor. Denise looks at me, amused, and types out on the phone, "Did you really think they'd kill you?"

"I don't know, yeah, maybe because we're witnesses." I start laughing as I realize today was probably the best I could hope for. Denise, Mom, and I can start packing our things and get cell service. I'll contact Dad and my boss and apologize for the hiatus.

The crowd seems satisfied with the oral arguments. Mom has a few closing words about how a lifetime ban cannot be put in place, and maybe for a grace period if I were to read *Your True Colors,* and they say it'll only be considered if that situation would ever arise, but for now it seems like I'm not to be permitted on these premises. Fine by me. There's nowhere else I would rather be right now than home anyway.

There are some more orders of business, and I turn to Denise, happy that we don't have to be some crazy vigilantes anymore. I can tell from her expression that she knows she should be happy with the outcome, but she obviously has some pent-up rage and doesn't know who to take it out on. We walk slowly back to the makeshift hospital, out in the open.

Many of the citizens see us, and I figure a lot of them know that we were watching them. They don't talk to us and allow us to go back to our rooms without any fuss. I'm about to go back to Denise's room when she heads straight for Cain's room. He looks up at her and is so serene. I see what looks like thousands of years of wisdom behind those eyes.

"You took away one of the most important pieces of my life," Denise text-to-speech phone speaks to the room.

"I know," Cain agrees. "I was worried that would happen when we released it."

"Then why did you let her?" I know Denise is talking about my mom, and I find that I can't really defend her, because it is a damn good question.

"I hope you never fall in love, Ms. Harrington. It clouds your judgment and allows you to look past the worst in people. It pains me to think of all of the damage that this book has caused, but I also think you're looking past all the good that it's done too," he reasons.

"You'll be in hell soon anyway, so what does it matter?" She is furious with him, and I can tell that she has a lot more to say, but her hands are shaking too much with rage.

340

"C'mon, Denise, let's go back to your room." I quietly usher her to the door where Mom is standing and observing us.

"You could've just come to the town hall," she states.

Denise's hands clench, and I take the phone out of her hand for fear of her breaking it or even typing words that might reverse their decision.

"You left before the verdict came out and missed the good part," Mom continues, and she actually looks sad. "Denise, you get to pull the plug on him tonight and then be on your way."

Denise snaps, and when she grabs the pen on the counter, I think she's going to lunge at my mom with it, but instead she writes on a notepad and Mom gives a sardonic laugh.

"I know you'd rather pull the plug on me instead. Sorry, but this is the deal. Take it or leave it." Mom lets Denise storm past her, and I'm left awkwardly looking at her new lover and his ultimate demise. What a wild ride. I cannot wait to put this chapter of my life behind me and for us to go back home.

"Oh, and Isabelle, you are allowed to leave under one condition," Mom addresses me, and I already know what she is going to request.

"Yeah, I heard. I'll read the damn book." I shrug my shoulders.

"Oh no, that's just potentially what you'll have to do to be allowed to be back here on Black Wolf Creek premises, which I know you'll do because it's going to be the only way you'll ever see me again." I feel the room get colder as she says this.

"Wait, what?! Mom!" I feel like a child again as I plead with her. "But you're coming back home with me. Dad is waiting for us and this man will be dead by the end of the day—"

My mom slaps my face so hard that I feel it immediately start to swell.

"You will respect Cain in his final hours. This man has done more for the world than you could ever accomplish in ten lifetimes," Mom spits at me.

"Sydney, easy." Cain holds her wrist from lifting her hand again.

I'm discombobulated but continue to press her. "You can't stay here, Mom."

"Why not?" She sounds surprised that I would even ask that question. "Isabelle, this place is my home. My real home. I should've been born here but will settle for these last twenty years."

"I can't lose you again," I croak out. A lump swells in my throat, and this hurts more than the slap—the thought that this will be the last time I'll see Mom for a long time.

"You'll be fine." Her voice is flat. "Go rest up. You have a big day tomorrow."

One more day with Mom? This is actually worse than death, and I am conflicted about what to do from here. I need a moment and start walking to my room.

"Isabelle, you didn't hear about the one condition," Mom calls after me. Whatever. They can tell me they're going to take me in the center of town and give me ten lashes for all I care. This stupid cult just took my mom. What's the worst thing they can throw at me now? "Tomorrow we're going to determine the fate of Kai Saito. Should he be found guilty and charged with death, you are to carry out the execution."

CHAPTER FOUR

I'm nauseous and the world tilts as I collapse face down into my bed. I start to hyperventilate without even realizing I'm doing so. I just got Mom back and now she's being taken away. My closest friend I have ever had in years lost her voice, and now I might have to kill the last guy I slept with. The whole world is burning down, and there are far more societal issues because of that damn book, but right now all I can focus on is what I'm going to do. Should I run? What would that accomplish? Even if I were to leave, do I turn these people into the authorities? We're still in a first world country the last time I checked.

If I were to rat on my own mom—you think she wouldn't talk to me before?? She'd disown me forever and may very well kill me herself, I realize. A hand gently caresses my back, and I bask in the warmth of the affection. When I turn around, it's not my mom, but Denise. She looks down at me and texts in her phone, which then speaks for her: "Tough break. I wanted to be the one to kill that asshole."

I can't help but stifle a laugh. Of course she heard us talking and, no surprise, she wants to be the one to kill Kai. Why can't they just let her have this? I guess she will already have enough blood on her hands as she is the one that goes through with the deed. I now realize I'm a horrible friend because I haven't even asked her how she feels about that.

"Will pulling his plug help you get closure?" I ask, and she stops caressing my back and genuinely thinks about the question.

"I'll take what I can get at this point." She stops and thinks before typing again. "But I really hate your mom."

I flinch.

"I understand that, but she's all I got," I reason with her.

Denise scrunches her face and doesn't hold back. "All you got? Isabelle, she abandoned you when you were a teenager. She urges people to do horrible things if it serves them. You have a great job and watch out for your father. You did all of that on your own, and she can take zero credit for any of that. You are better off without her."

I know that there are a lot of good points in there, but she doesn't know what it was like growing up having a strong, independent woman in your life who was never afraid to call people out. She was an inspiration, and I marveled at how much I wanted to be like her. I guess even when she was gone I never really moved out of her shadow and took life by the horns.

345

My job is okay. Not glamorous, and I could've jumped ship a long time ago and made even more money, but I had settled more than anything into a routine. Dad has been easy to manage and take care of, for the most part, so it's not like I should get brownie points for that one either. This trip was the most spontaneous thing I've done, and I'm conflicted whether it was worth it or not.

On one hand I got her back. On the other hand, oh my God . . . I'm most likely going to have to kill someone. Jesus Christ. It's starting to set in again and I forget that Denise is even there when I speak again.

"I don't think I can kill anyone." My eyes fixate on one spot in the room.

Denise starts texting rapidly and has a lot to say on the subject, but then she puts her phone down when she notices how genuinely sad I am. She stops and erases it all, then reaches out and grabs my hand as our fingers intertwine. Well said. We sit in silence and soak up the day. It's only the middle of the afternoon, but it has been a long one.

*   *   *

Come early evening we decide to join the community dinner and dress into nicer clothes than the casual ones we were wearing. A girl around our age, Randi, lets us go through her clothes and has good taste. Even

Denise is less angry when getting ready, and she seems happy to have a selection. It goes without saying, but I'm pretty sure that she wants to steal her outfit and never plans on returning it afterward.

I'm a couple sizes too small, but Randi shows me clothes she wore when she was younger and, sure enough, they fit easier. I am used to wearing the most basic outfits, but the two of them convince me to look a bit nicer. We relax around her and I confide that I don't really want to kill Kai, or anyone, really.

Randi suggests a more elegant dress that she used to wear when attending important events. It may get the community to see me in a different light and could sway their vote for Kai's sentence tomorrow. I'll take whatever advice is given, and it does fit comfortably. I'll admit that it complements my skinny figure, and I wouldn't be surprised to see a photo of me in this on a dating profile, if I ever choose to put myself out there.

The food is wonderful, and although Denise has winced every so often, she is able to process the softer elk meat and mashed potatoes. I have no limitations as I eat the thicker slices of elk, and the broccoli is nicer than from any restaurant I've ever been to. I should probably start making a habit of not going to fast food chains anymore. I would travel across the country just for their meals alone. I'm honestly surprised Mom hasn't gained weight while living here.

A lot of people look in our direction, and I get self-conscious that they're looking at a future killer but am reminded that they're not looking at me but are looking at Denise.

"It's not you. It's me," Denise assures me, as if reading my mind. "Cain means a lot to them, and I'm the person who is going to end his life."

"At least you'll be putting him out of his misery."

"Yeah, I know, which is why it upsets me." I hope no one overhears her text-to-speech app because I don't think that'll win me any sympathy while sitting next to her, but I also know that Denise doesn't care.

Mom is noticeably absent from the community dinner and I ask where she is, only for Javi to tell me that she's spending Cain's final hours by his side. Right. That makes sense, but I was kind of hoping I'd be able to spend some quality time with her. Maybe play a card game or even just try to catch up on what's happened the last eighteen years. I know there's not much to say, but it'd still be nice just to be next to one another. I know that I am to not bother her, though. I remember the slap vividly and could only imagine what she'd do if I tried to deprive her of her final moments with her boyfriend.

The evening comes and Denise is ready to fulfill her destiny. I ask if she wants me to accompany her, and I half expect her to tell me that she doesn't give a shit, but I think the realization sinks in and she has now transformed into a little girl who is being asked to take someone's life. She's fragile and needs support, so I abandon my own insecurities and try to be strong for her.

"We haven't known one another long, but you are one of the best people I have ever met in my life. I can see why you're scared, and that's a normal emotion to have. We're basically doing Black Wolf Creek's dirty work so they don't have to be held accountable for anything. It's not fair. Maybe they should take a better look at themselves and realize they're not better than anyone on the outside. Sorry, I'm rambling at this point." When I stop talking, I look up to see that Denise is happy to have me in her life.

We hug one another, and they allow me to accompany her as we go into Cain's room where my mom is crying. Cain shushes her and assures her that everything will be okay, and that she was the best thing to ever happen to him. That makes two of us. My mom now weighs in on the actuality of the situation and doesn't want it to happen. What kind of sick community does shit like this? And she wants to live here?

A registered nurse or some kind of doctor, Sally, instructs Denise how to administer the lethal injection, and Denise nods her head and is further asked if she needs any clarification on what to do. She shakes her head and is shown where to inject the needle. Despite her hatred for my mom, Denise scribbles on a piece of paper and asks if she needs more time.

Mom composes herself and shakes her head and allows Denise to finish what she came here for. Denise performs the task, and after she's finished with the injection, Cain gently reaches out to her and looks her in the eyes.

"I appreciate you doing this for me, and I am sorry I ruined your family's life. I'm sure your brother was a great person. Misguided, but still great on the inside." Cain's weak smile disarms her.

Denise's eyes well up with tears and she starts crying uncontrollably. I am quick to be by her side and hold her as she breaks down completely. I look over her shoulder to see that Cain begins to drift off to sleep. The machines show his heart beat slow down and eventually come to a flat line.

The presence in the air is heavy as Mom cannot let go of his hand, even though it's gone limp.

In another life I would've liked to meet this man when he was healthy because I can already see what my mom was attracted to. Denise's obligations have been completed, and it seems like she is a free woman. I wonder if this will give her peace or if that missing hole in her heart will forever be an open wound. Is Mom going to be happy that he is no longer suffering, or was she selfishly wanting more time with him no matter how much pain he was in?

Cain Skaggs's death leaves more questions than answers.

CHAPTER FIVE

In the morning we have breakfast, and I've been informed that I can attend the town hall but cannot speak or have an opinion because I am not a member of the community. I find that kind of hypocritical. I'm not allowed to have input on whether someone's life is going to be taken away or not, and I've been unwillingly selected to be the executioner. Make it make sense.

A couple of people offer some dissent on Kai's execution because of his mental health status. They argue that it's probably better to have him further examined by some specialists to see if he's on the spectrum or if he has any prior issues that cause him to act irrationally, but the majority of the people are in agreement that he's one hundred percent accountable for his actions, and the trial is definitely not going good for him. He's not getting the same grace from Javi and Mom that Denise and I got the last time around.

I feel uneasy and am just grateful that Denise allows me to hold her hand throughout the whole trial, even if she has a different point of view than mine. I'm sure all this sounds wonderful to her and she'll be skipping out of the commune when we leave. I think the trial is almost over when I discover there's a room with a door left ajar that I hadn't noticed.

Henry and his father enter the room to retrieve Kai, and I realize that he's been listening to the whole thing. He doesn't look tough anymore, and he's visibly shaking. My heart sinks down to the pit of my stomach when we lock eyes.

The council asks Kai if he has anything to say for his actions. The gag is taken from his mouth, and he looks around like a nervous child.

"I-I-I am so sorry for being reckless. I should've known better than to bring violence into your community," he pleads with them. "I only wanted to impress him and thought I should look inward to my inner self. You know? My true colors?"

Denise is livid and she's about to get up, but I hold her down and the council speaks in her place.

"Is it in your true colors to kill anyone who disagrees with the book?" one of the members asks him, and he happily jumps to agree.

"Of course! You all read his teachings, right? The man is a genius, and I'm sure if you ask him—" He is about to justify his actions when a member interrupts him.

"He's dead. Cain Skaggs passed away last night."

"He is?" Kai looks more upset about this news than potentially dying. "I never got to meet him."

"Mr. Saito, if you have anything you'd like to say to Denise Harrington, she's in the front row over to your right," another member of the council says.

His eyes search, and when he sees the two of us alive, well, and unchained, he's confused. "Denise? Isabelle?"

Denise flips him off, which gets a few laughs from those in attendance.

"If you have nothing further to say, then we will proceed with the votes," one of the council members informs him. He, of course, starts rambling whichever angles he thinks he might work, and I can't help but notice how pathetic he looks.

It's so odd that only three days ago I thought he was one of the most attractive men on this planet because of his confidence and his passion for the book. Now I see a mumbling idiot who's selling out his values in an attempt to save his ass. Maybe this'll be easier than I thought, because I just don't see him getting out of this one.

Sure enough, after ten minute's time (more time than I thought he'd get), they gag him again and put it to a vote. If Denise and I could vote I already know which way she would sway, and normally I would be with her if I didn't have to be the one to carry on the sentence. We watch in fascination as the members write on pieces of paper and put them in a ballot box.

Kai is escorted back to wherever it was they were keeping him, and it doesn't take long for the votes to be counted. Guilty. I knew it was going to be a miracle to expect anything different, but now I have to live with the idea of taking another man's life. Javi was wrong about me. He was probably just projecting himself onto me, but I'll argue that I don't have any dark side of me.

What now? I feel lethal injection wasn't that bad, and I hope that that's what's going to happen, but then they inform me that they'll give me a quick training on which firearm I will be using. A gun?! That wasn't a part of the deal! Although I know I really have no say in the deal. They are going to drive me further out into the woods where a couple of the community members will supervise me.

"Why can't I just give him the lethal injection?" I plead.

"The autopsy report," Mom tells me. "We've already planted a gun on him, and this will be a case of self-defense. It'll be far enough off of our premises where it won't lead back to us, and it'll look like an end to his small crime spree."

Oh right. We did technically steal a car, and I don't know how well he covered his tracks with the people that he said he killed. Of course they want it far away from their community. No harm, no foul. You have a resident who died of cancer and now an outsider who will be taken care of away from Black Wolf Creek. Society will know no better. And who are Denise and I going to tell? It would only incriminate ourselves with the murders, and this isn't even mentioning our intentions we had when coming here in the first place.

I hate to say it, but it's kind of genius on their part. We came in and caused some trouble, and now they're going to be completely absolved of any misdoings.

"Javi and Azul will take you to the location and afterward dispose of the firearm. They're then instructed to drop you off at the airport where you two will be flown back to Austin," Mom continues.

"We're not coming back here?" I ask.

"Your phones have been charging and you'll get them back when the task is done." Mom ignores the question. "Of course you will not mention Black Wolf Creek to anyone; your time here never happened."

"So much for telling the truth." I sulk.

"Izzy, you should be kissing every one of the council members out there. You could've been sentenced to so much worse, *and* they had the decency to buy your plane tickets." She uses her irritated tone that I remember all too well from my childhood.

"You're abandoning me again." I refuse to leave without telling her this. I don't care what tone she uses with me anymore.

"That's up to you, kiddo." Mom doesn't sound offended. "Are you going to read the book all the way through and then reach out to see if you can visit me again?"

Unbelievable. Again with this stupid fucking book. I'm conflicted whether to slap her or hold her one last time.

"Mom—" my voice cracks, but I don't have anything to say after that.

"I sincerely hope you read *Your True Colors* and then afterward we can talk." Mom hugs me, and even though I sense it's out of pity more than anything, I accept her embrace.

*　　　　　　　*　　　　　　　*

The ride is long as she promised, and even Denise has dozed off in the back seat. Of course she has. Her hard part is done, and now it's time for me to take my medicine. I wonder if she'll sleep better at night with her demons exorcised. Did she bring justice to her brother, or will she go behind my back and try to come back for my mom?

Javi and Azul chatter the entire time, switching from English to Spanish, and talk about the effects the book has had on the rest of the world. There are rumors that some national leaders have read copies and that nuclear war could be in our near future. The two of them seem genuinely excited to see the world tear itself from the inside out, and I begin to wonder if they have bunkers in place in case the worst does happen.

Denise is asleep, and the two of them almost treat me like a prisoner they're escorting, so I'm alone with my thoughts and wonder how Kai is feeling right now. He's tied up and blindfolded. If he is still nervous about everything, he's an excellent actor, because he, too, isn't resisting and lies motionless in the back seat.

I wonder how thorough their community is. Will they scrub all areas the three of us were in to further erase our existence of ever having been there? How much work will go into his murder? Is there any chance whatsoever that it'll be traced back to me? Can I claim coercion if I were to be found guilty in an actual court of law, or will my claim be bogus considering that Black Wolf Creek probably has good legal representation?

Then again, if the world is in as bad of shape as they claim it is, then I'm sure a killer would be the last of the authorities' worries. The truck bumps along a path for a while before coming to a halt, and we walk out to a clearing in the woods.

I was briefed earlier how to use this gun, a Canik 9mm. It's pretty user-friendly, and there's not much to it other than pulling the trigger. They tell me that I don't have to face him, and it's optional whether he remains

358

gagged or not. I am also reminded that if I go rogue on the plan, Javi and Azul are well-equipped with firearms and could easily take me and Denise down with no hesitation.

Denise is allowed to join me, and I appreciate that small gesture since I was there for her when she killed Cain.

"Are we allowed to have privacy during this whole thing?" I ask.

Javi and Azul look at one another, and I can tell there were bets made whether I'd ask this or not, but they actually tell me that it would be okay.

"We'll be over by the truck," Azul assures us. "When we hear the gunshot, we'll come over to inspect that the deed is done, and that will be that."

"What about the body?" I ask.

"After we drop you guys off at the airport, we'll dispose of it. We're off the beaten path enough, but there are still avid hikers in the area and dogs that could easily find it. We'd rather if it were to be discovered anytime soon that it be much further from us," Javi explains to us.

"We've got a long day on our hands," Azul agrees, "so pronto."

Okay. Here's the moment of truth.

I grip Denise's hand so hard that I worry she'll lose circulation. My other hand with the gun is limp. It's so cold and heavy, and I know there's going to be a recoil.

Kai is made to kneel, and he seems to be saying something. I suppose he deserves last words. Before Azul retreats, I call out to her.

"He is trying to say something." I explain. When I look over at Denise, her eyes seem to say "So?"

"Would you like me to take off his gag?" she asks. Against my better judgment, I nod.

Azul shrugs her shoulders and does as I ask and then walks back to the truck.

"I regret nothing." Kai explains. "I know if he were alive, he'd approve of my actions."

"You couldn't be further from the truth," I tell him. I didn't know Cain that long, but he's more complex than Kai is giving him credit for.

"If this is how I leave this world, then so be it. But at least I was true to who I really was as a person," he tells me. A chill runs through my spine, and my hands shake as I hold the gun up.

I begin to hyperventilate as I focus on the back of his head. I look over at Denise and now I'm the one that speaks with my eyes. I can't do it, they say.

She takes the gun from me, and with no hesitation and perfect precision shoots him in the back of the head. His body goes limp, and she hands the gun back to me.

CHAPTER SIX

All four of us sit in silence on the drive to the airport. A large part of me feels they suspect that Denise carried out the deed but didn't want to ask questions they didn't want to know the answers to. It dawns onto me that the first friends I made in a long time ended up being cold-blooded killers. Was I better off as a ghost?

I see that the airport is the next exit, and Denise nudges me. I look over at her and she shakes her burner phone. I almost forgot all about that.

"Um, excuse me, Azul?" I ask timidly, and Denise rolls her eyes.

"Yeah?" she asks.

"Can we get our cell phones back?" I sound like a child asking to be pulled out of timeout, but to my surprise she reaches into the dashboard and hands them back to us.

"I'd tell you not to do anything stupid, but I know you two won't." She hands over our phones, and we immediately power them up.

Denise's phone starts buzzing frantically with multiple messages making their way through. I get some work emails and a missed call from Tyreke, but the lack of

361

notifications is a little depressing. Azul notices this too and raises an eyebrow in amusement. I feel humiliated by this fact and hate that it gets to me so much. I shouldn't care what a complete stranger thinks about my personal life.

Oh yeah, well, my father texted me and asked if I'm doing okay, is what I want to say, but of course my dad's text is just him telling me that he understands why I left and that he'll be waiting whenever I choose to come back. No apologies or anything. I laugh humorlessly and I am almost certain Denise will nudge me and ask me what is so funny, but when I look at her, she's frantically texting people who are looking for her. When they start calling, she grunts in frustration and silences each call.

That's tough. I don't even know what kind of story she'll have to give them when she returns. She fell and landed on a knife that perfectly slit her throat? I suppose, knowing her, she will tell them that that's her business and no one else's, but then I remember that for her job it's necessary that she chat with her clients to help put them at ease. Has there ever been a mute stylist? I'm sure they're out there, but I think that would be awkward sitting in a chair for that long with no one to talk with.

It seems like she has a bigger problem on her hands, though; my eyes wander to her phone and there are multiple messages from both her mom and dad. It's horrible what happened with her brother, but I assume her parents couldn't fathom the idea of losing their daughter within the same year. And it's not like she can even talk with them and explain to them that she's okay and to calm down. Will she ever truly be okay after the last couple of days?

The vehicle comes to the terminals and Javi parks the car. He turns around.

"We were able to print out physical copies of your itineraries, but if you want to log on to the apps, then check your names under United Airlines." He hands over the paper copies. I can't even remember the last time I had physical copies of airline tickets, but I accept them.

He also reaches in the front seat and hands us both baggy sweatshirts.

"Wear these too." He hands them over.

"Why?" Denise asks through her phone's text-to-speech application.

"Rape has been on the rise and this hides your bodies better," he states.

"So kind of you to care," Denise texts back and gives him the finger.

"Take it, Denise," Azul orders and turns around to look us straight in the eyes. "Javi's not lying and, believe it or not, we actually do not want anything bad to happen to you two."

I think that Denise is going to protest more, but she looks outside at all the men who are departing and arriving. She sighs and takes it and puts it on, even pulling the hoodie over her head. I follow suit and do the same thing. I'm almost out of the vehicle when Javi calls out to me.

"Isabelle," he says. I stop from exiting and look back at him, "Read the damn book. I know it doesn't seem like she cares, but she really does. Don't be as stubborn as she is."

I don't know what to say, so I just curtly nod and leave. I follow Denise's lead and keep my head down but occasionally look up to see the news. Javi was right. It's barbaric out there and they really are looking out for us. I can only hope that the pilots and air traffic control staff are attentive enough to get us home in one piece.

Luckily my concerns are just paranoia, and once we're in the air, I am surprised that I am able to pass out. I think my apprehension toward plane explosions were more because of what I thought happened to my mom. Now I just have to worry about human error again. Granted, it's on the rise, but I still take my chances and don't need any drugs to subdue me this time around.

We land in Austin safely, and when I wake up, I look over at Denise, who's wide awake and in deep contemplation about her life. There's a permanent scowl on her face with a bit of a pout mixed in. She avenged her brother but at what cost? Does she take any comfort in the fact that Cain was already dying, or does that make it worse?

I reach over and grab her hand. She flinches but then sees it's me and just waves me off. While people get up to try their hardest to be the first off of the plane, I assure her that we can stay as long as she needs. She shakes her head and at first doesn't allow me to comfort her. Eventually she breaks down and the tears flow.

The cabin clears and the staff can see she's in distress, but a flight attendant pats me gently and mouths to us that we have to leave so they can get ready for the next flight. I nod my head and get Denise to stand up and join me as we leave the airplane and make our way to the ground floor.

I notice that she's ordering herself an Uber, but I stop her.

"Come stay with me," I tell her. "There are two extra spare bedrooms, and you can have your choice on whichever one you want." She shakes her head empathically, but then I remind her, "Jackie is going to be unbearable."

She laughs but then realizes that I have a point there. She sighs and hands over her phone and allows me to type in my address. I pray to God that Dad doesn't have any unwanted visitors and, even worse, that he doesn't make a move on Denise. That poor girl has been through enough. I'll have to lay down the law with him.

Of course he is home and, thankfully, there are no prostitutes in the house, but I tell Denise to wait outside while I have a talk with my dad before we do this.

"Izzy!" He embraces me. He looks deep into my eyes. "I've been watching the news and I'm sorry that I didn't reach out earlier, but I am honestly a little embarrassed by my actions."

"You are?" I'm surprised. Has he turned over a new leaf?

"Of course I am! I cannot believe how uncomfortable that night must've been for you, and from here on out, I'll set up my meetups outside of the house," he reasons, but I don't think that makes the situation any better.

There's so much to unpack there, and I want to lecture him right now about the morality of exchanging sex for money, but I realize that I'm exhausted mentally and physically. All I need to do right now is to make sure my dad doesn't perv on my friend and to let him know that she'll be staying with us.

"My friend is going to be staying with us for a while," I tell him.

"Friend?" My dad looks over my shoulder and sees Denise. I instantly regret his seeing her, because she's obviously not a bad-looking woman.

"Dad," I'm sterner than I have ever been in my entire life, "you're going to leave her alone. I cannot stress that enough."

"Of course, of course," he agrees, but I know in his tone that I cannot trust him. Isn't the whole idea of the book to go after things that are considered to be forbidden fruit? My dad gawks at her and I make sure he looks me in the eyes when I grab a hold of him.

"Promise me you'll leave her alone or, Dad, I swear to God, I will start filing the paperwork for you to vacate the house." I muster up as much conviction as I can, and he agrees.

I wave Denise inside and briefly introduce her to my dad. I keep the corner of my eye on him and do not know if I can trust him, and I certainly don't like the idea of them ever alone together, but I have to go to work eventually, and Denise has technically killed two men. She's obviously not a fan of my family, and maybe I should let her know that she has full permission to do whatever is needed if he were to ever make advances or do something worse.

She chooses the room closest to me, which is what I wanted. My father lives in the upstairs master bedroom next to the other room. Denise obviously read the situation for what it was and stayed downstairs. We have to share the bathroom, but it's no problem as I allow her to decompress with a bath while I take the shower upstairs.

  I'm glad that I never threw away clothes that were too big for me, and when I present them to her as temporary clothing, she takes them. She goes into the bathroom and locks the door. Though she blasts her music, I can hear her cry faintly.

CHAPTER SEVEN

Even though I was nearly catatonic when I lost Mom the first time around, I remember getting countless cards and support from one of her colleagues. Sure, there were neighbors and her coworkers who would come and check in on me, but one of her friends really went the extra mile.

He ended up paying for all of my schooling. I chose to go to a more affordable college and paid for all the books myself out of guilt, but he checked in frequently through email and was always telling me that he would be there if I needed anything. I remember thinking there was a chance that he may be some sort of pervert, but he never asked anything of me and, of course, I accepted the payments. If it wasn't for his kindness, I don't think I would've gone through school all the way. It's like his kind gesture gave me something to look forward to after I was so depressed about Mom.

When I did research on him, I found out that he was in the same Doctors Without Borders program as she had been. He was even down there in Colombia and was probably the last person to ever see her "alive." Why I hadn't realized this before is beyond me, but now that I

369

have seen her in the flesh and am looking back at that period in her life, it was remarkable that the only other survivor of that plane crash was also the person who didn't board the plane at all.

I book a flight to Boston to meet Dr. and Mrs. Isaac Winters. I think about calling or emailing beforehand but don't want him to turn me away, so I choose to spontaneously book the flight. I worry about Denise being alone with my dad, but she is adjusting well enough to her new mute condition, and I plan my trip around her schedule.

She, too, is leaving town to go see her parents, which is understandable. I'm sure there will be a lot of questions, and I don't know what kind of story she wants to provide for them, but I know that she needs to get in the rhythm of a new system working around how she will communicate. Plus, I'm not really sure if her days in the salon are done. I assume they are, but I never want to ask and press her on that.

I'm sure there is a lot of her life to update her parents about, and they will probably want to know more about what happened in Canada. Needless to say, it's going to be a week-long trip. Maybe longer.

Most nights we just enjoy whatever serial killer documentaries she wants to watch. She eats that shit up like candy. And in retrospect, she herself has killed more than one person, so I wonder if that would qualify her as a serial killer. It probably isn't a good idea to give her more ideas, but if this is her comfort zone, then I'm not going to deprive her of that. Denise may seem tough on the outside, but I truly know how vulnerable she is and refuse to leave her alone with my dad. He is on thin ice as it is, but if he were to mess with her in any way, I don't know if I'd change my mind about my whole "no killing" rule.

After I drop Denise off at the airport, I park my car in their lot and also go to board my flight. I already requested off of work, and it works in my favor that Denise is visiting during the middle of the week. If Isaac is working, then there is a possibility that he'll be doing a midweek shift. I could be wrong, but I remember Mom working days straight and would often use the weekend to either get away or hide herself away from the world.

But then again, I know that Isaac is not Mom, and I don't know how similar they are. Or really what his schedule would be.

The flight goes smoothly, and though I've heard that a lot of people get nauseous while reading and traveling, I'm able to focus on *Your True Colors* the best I can. I'm actually getting the hang of it after five pages and even able to finish a chapter before the plane arrives, drowning out the background with noise-canceling headphones. I'm able to get a surprising amount out of his teachings.

The allure is strong, and I'm actually annoyed when the flight comes to an end. Is this really happening? Am I no better than the others who read the book and did all those awful things? I don't want any of that to be true, but Cain's/Mom's points are actually starting to make a lot of sense, and I'm only three chapters in!

I leave the plane and order an Uber to take me to Isaac's place because I have no intention of staying that long, and I'm already paranoid about stepping foot in another rental car place. I doubt they would connect me with the last time, but in case there were security cameras that got a good look at me in Canada, it's better not to risk it. The last thing I need is to bribe some rapist with my body to get out of a sticky situation. No thank you.

I cover myself daily because it isn't uncommon to hear about sexual assault cases on the rise. A lot of women had followed suit, and it makes me stew it over in my head even more when I think about the damages Mom has caused this world. She's living her best life while a lot of us are constantly looking over our shoulders. How is that fair in any way?

A woman driver picks me up, which is a breath of fresh air. We don't make small talk, and when I settle in her back seat, I go ahead and take off the sunglasses and the hoodie. It's not terribly hot in Boston around this time, but it still feels nice to be looser with my clothes. If we ever go back to how we used to be, I vow that I'll never take fashion freedom for granted.

"Code?" the driver asks.

I had drifted off, and now I notice that Isaac lives in a gated community. I guess I should've expected that.

"Sorry, I don't know," I mutter. I can see her lips tighten and I can tell that she's annoyed. "You could just leave me here, it's okay."

I'm about to get out of the car when someone approaches from inside the community and opens the gate up. Before I can even open the door, the driver guns it and cuts the person off as they give her the finger.

"Just don't forget to tip," the woman says with a smile.

"Yes ma'am. And five stars," I tell her.

When she drops me off, I fulfill my promise and will probably leave a nice review later to top it off, but now my heart sinks as I look at the lavish house that Isaac and his wife live in. What on earth am I going to say? Why am I even here?

"Can I help you?" I realize that a beautiful woman unloading groceries is looking over at me. She's clearly expecting a kid soon, and I instinctively run over to help her out with the groceries.

"I can help you with that," I offer. At first I don't think she'll accept my help, but she exhales a sigh of relief.

"Thank you," she tells me in a thick British accent, "I was thinking I'd have to make multiple trips."

The two of us go inside the beautiful house where I see photos of her and Isaac along with their two kids. Normally I would consider him to be a goofy-looking guy, what with that nose and all, but there's a charm to him even in the photos, and I can see why his wife chose him.

"Would you like a drink for the road? I don't know where you were going, but I saw you just standing there," Mrs. Winters tells me.

"Um, actually, I was looking for Isaac," I confess to her, and when her eyes widen, I'm quick to put my hands out. "Nothing bad, of course! I just . . . he sorta knew my mom."

She studies me, and I can see the realization sink in. The woman falls back and puts her hands to her face. "Oh my goodness! You're her, aren't you? You're her daughter."

Hopefully it's just the hormones speaking, but she starts to cry, and I just stand there awkwardly, not knowing what to do. Have I upset her? I feel horrible now.

"You know, I can come back another time or just leave," I tell her and am about to go when she crosses the room and wraps her arms around me and hugs me tight.

"Your mother was one of the best people we've ever met," she tells me in between quick sobs as she struggles to catch her breath.

I wait for her to get a hold on herself. I am stunned because I have never seen anyone so ecstatic to talk about my mom. She tended to rub a lot of people the wrong way, but between the Black Wolf Creek residents and now Mrs. Winters, it makes me wonder who my mom really is.

"Please stay. I am cooking dinner soon, and maybe you can keep me company while we wait for Isaac and the kids to return?" she tells me.

"I can help," I offer, but she swats the air like I've offended her.

"I won't hear of that." She wipes her eyes and then smiles at me. "Are you a fan of steak? We were waiting until Friday, but I feel like tonight we have a special guest."

"Thank you, Mrs. Winters—" I begin.

"Andrea—please call me Andrea. And you're Isabelle, correct?" she says.

I feel myself getting slightly embarrassed. Of course she would know who I am. Her husband paid for my entire education. I nod my head.

"So will steak be okay?" she says, and I haven't realized how hungry I was until my stomach starts grumbling. I tried to be a vegetarian after Mom died, in her honor, but Dad and I were too addicted to unhealthy food and meat.

"That sounds perfect."

While we wait for Isaac to return, we make small talk, and she tells me about a younger version of my mom. It should be a woman that I sort of knew too because they met shortly after I last saw her the first time around, but the way she describes her in that hostel, it was hard to believe we were talking about the same person.

"Isaac and I were too shy to make the first move, so typical Sydney was the one to nudge us closer together with the help of teenage drinking games." She laughs when remembering, and I join in on the laughter even though I was not there.

"My goodness. I don't mean to alarm you, Isabelle, but can I tell you about the day she saved my life?" Andrea gushes and I, of course, want to know.

It's horrific. My spine tingles just from hearing the story. She was almost raped, and maybe even worse, by the sound of it. Isaac and Javier standing up for her . . . wait, Javier like Javi? Was it the same guy? My mom going toe to toe with a drug lord? I guess it really was her, because if the rumors were true about how my mom approached those loan sharks in Austin, then maybe that's the kind of person she is.

Who am I kidding? Of course that's the person she is. Her no-BS attitude bled into our household, and she was just as tough on me as she was with her Heartwood peers, those bikers, and even potential rapists. I see Andrea's eyes start watering again and I can tell that she's recalling the story fondly. She has to wipe away tears, and that's when we hear the garage door open. The sound of children noisily coming in to the kitchen begging to see their mommy melts my heart. One of the kids notices that her face is wet and asks her what's wrong.

"Nothing, nothing at all, darlings," Andrea assures them.

"Babe, that damn garage door almost jammed again. I'm going to have to call them to come back—" He stops talking when he walks in and notices me sitting there. "Oh, sorry, I didn't realize you had company."

Andrea coos to her children and tells them to go play while she and daddy talk with their new friend. She rests her head into Isaac's chest. "Honey, she's here."

He reaches out for me to shake his hand and obviously hasn't put it together yet.

"Isaac. Isaac Winters," he tells me, and I meekly shake his hand back.

"Isabelle. Isabelle Dunham." He stops shaking hands and his mouth drops.

Andrea finishes with the side dishes while Isaac cooks the steak out in the yard. Their barbecue pit looks more expensive than some of my mom's coworkers' houses. Not mine, of course, but I had a mom in the medical field too and the luxury to inherit a home just as nice.

"Your mom was the most interesting person I have ever met in my entire life," he tells me. "I really wish we spent more time with her."

If only he knew.

"Did you know she inadvertently saved my life?" Two tales of her heroics in one day? I guess it's better than seeing the world burn around us.

"You never boarded the plane," I tell him as he nods.

"I only now realize how dumb that may have been on my part. You don't want to hear about how I survived something your mom didn't." He shakes his head and is obviously disappointed in himself.

"Actually, no, quite the opposite," I tell him. "I want to know more about that day. Do you remember it well?"

"There's not a day that goes by that I don't think about everything that happened." He laughs. "I'm not a religious guy, but what are the odds that I get food poisoning so bad that I don't board a plane that explodes?"

"Food poisoning?" I tilt my head.

"Yeah. Your mom was being your typical mom, but I don't have to tell you that," he says like she and I shared the same relationship they did. "She was insistent that I eat all of my food, and I think that that backfired. I had never been sicker in my life."

"You couldn't board the plane in the condition you were in." I wasn't asking, only now realizing the lengths my mom went to.

"No way," he confirms. "I even tried but ended up collapsing. I passed out in the hotel room for a solid two days, and when I woke up and saw the news, I felt like the world had just collapsed."

The food had been done for a while, but he stares off in the distance, remembering everything so well.

"She died and saved my life." He goes silent, and I think he's done, but then he speaks up again. "I contacted Andrea and convinced her to visit me in Boston. I would've never dreamed of doing something like that, but I just thought about how precious life is and how you shouldn't let opportunities slip through your fingers."

I don't know what to say, but I am starting to see the effect that Mom has had on a lot of people's lives. It'd be nice if she were a saint who went around the world helping everyone, but it seems like she's done more harm than good. If they only knew about the pain she's unleashed . . . wait . . . They've spent this whole time

379

talking about Mom, but what about Cain? What are their thoughts about him and this book?

We go inside and enjoy the meal and, I'll be damned, this is the best dinner I have had since being an unwanted guest at Black Wolf Creek. I didn't realize how shitty of a cook I am until I ate what the Winters had to offer. Even the kids eat their entire meal without being picky or refusing. They are pretty well behaved too. The daughter's name is Kennedy and their son is Carter. I've never really been much of a kid person, but these two are well-behaved enough that it makes me start to wonder about my own biological clock.

During dinner they want to know all about me. My life, my romances (or lack of), how the schooling went . . . which I did thank them profusely numerous times throughout the night. They are eager to have me stay the night. I didn't originally plan on it, but they are insistent on me being there, and I accept their offer.

With the kids off to bed and the three of us downstairs, I know I have to get to why I had come. I need to know more about their real thoughts about my mom, and that means asking about the book.

"Cain Skaggs." Dropping his name gets both Isaac and Andrea to go rigid. The two look into each other's eyes as if I'm not there. There's a long beat before Isaac breaks the silence.

"Yeah, we know him," Isaac starts.

380

"Knew him," I correct but instantly cover my mouth.

"He's dead?" Isaac asks.

"Good riddance," Andrea retorts.

"You met him?" Isaac pushes.

I fiddle with my fingers in my lap and avoid their gaze. I already feel like I've revealed too much and tell half-truths.

"I had friends who researched the book, and when I noticed he was in Colombia around the same time you guys were, I gathered that's where he also met my mom."

Andrea frowns while Isaac rakes his fingers through his hair and exhales a long, drawn-out sigh. He struggles to look me in the eyes but eventually does so.

"Your mom was quite fond of him," he says while I think, *you're telling me.*

"No offense to your father, but I think your mom was just looking for someone to make her feel young again," Andrea interrupts.

"It's okay. My dad sucks," I agree.

"Andrea . . ." Isaac warns.

"What? The poor girl has a right to know." Andrea shoots him a look and then turns to me. "Lass, your mom was romantically involved with Cain and quite attached to his hip."

I do my best to look surprised, and she nods her head in acknowledgment.

"We didn't know what that man was capable of, and he seemed relatively harmless at the time," Isaac offers.

"Have you two read *Your True Colors*?" I ask them.

"Potent stuff." Isaac nods his head while Andrea shakes hers. "I recognize the sentence structure and awkward pauses were by design."

When I first walked in their house, I noticed the countless books they had on their shelves that ranged from classic literature to medicinal breakthroughs. Of course, it was odd that he had so much science fiction too. It should come as no surprise that he was educated and well-read.

"Why was it written?" I finally stop skirting around the question and address it head on.

"Isn't it obvious in the text?" he starts as if I've read it completely. I wait for him to continue. "It's a book of heartbreak, and when you lose everyone and everything, why go around lying anymore? Be your real self."

I've had such a thick skull that it's like a light turns on in my head. Cain started dying, and this must've been her way of punishing the world that was taking everything from her. Why wouldn't they write about letting people let their inner demons loose?

"We're not blind to what's going on out there, but you forget that not everyone has ill intentions," Isaac continues. "Now, don't get me wrong, it's been hectic at

382

work, and I'm surprised it's taken this long for government interference, but I think a lot of people are just going about their everyday lives with no intention of raping, murdering, or hurting others."

"Do you honestly believe that?" I'm taken aback by his optimism.

I'm even more surprised when he naturally laughs, which causes me to jump a little, but even his wife looks over at him incredulously.

"Throughout all of mankind's existence, we've been fighting one another, but never to the point of mass extinction. You forget that throughout all of history there has been violence, death, and destruction; but there's also been love, compassion, and hope," Isaac explains.

"Freud did theorize that the only two constructs keeping people in line were law and religion," Andrea chimes in, "but, babe, we have never seen anything like this."

Isaac scrunches up his face and tilts his head. "Of course we have."

The two of us look at one another.

"Majority of major religions want you to subscribe to their beliefs and typically segregate you from the others who don't see eye to eye. Has this new book been annoying and encouraged people to do some vile things? No doubt about it, but we're already seeing people see right through it, and life will continue to carry on."

We end up chatting more about the state of the world and how the widespread panic hasn't been as disastrous as I initially thought. Sure, there has been an increase in hostility, but we go over how we still go to work, school, and even the airport. There has been an increase in police activity over the country, and Andrea even theorizes that the government is trying to combat it with their own mass manipulation, whether it's through social media or the network news.

They let me sleep in the spare bedroom, which is well furnished. The Winters are both close to my age, but they feel more parental. Maybe it's because they have their third child on the way and have gotten used to having that instinct. I don't know if I drench myself in clinginess, but they've picked up on my uneasiness with the book, my mother, and just my overall existence.

I almost envy their children, because I wouldn't know what it would be like to be raised in such a healthy household. I am able to rest easy, and the next morning Andrea is able to take me back to the airport. We promise to keep in touch. I give them my personal phone number and tell them that they can visit whenever they would like.

After meeting with them, a large part of me is tempted to give up reading the book, but halfway through the flight it reels me back in, and I need to know what made it so successful for people to disregard the law and let their inner id take over.

384

Your True Colors

CHAPTER EIGHT

Weeks go by as we get settled in our new way of life, and I wish I could report that we've all lived together harmoniously, but dad just has to take things too far. Denise alerts me about the hidden camera that he put in our bathroom, and we take the footage as evidence to confront him with. Oh boy, does everything go to hell quickly.

When the yelling stops between me and my father, he assures us that he had no intentions of touching her, which doesn't make things better in the least. It's even more disturbing that he didn't just scrub through the footage of me and delete that right off the bat. I give him an ultimatum: if he leaves now and doesn't wait for me to file the paperwork for his removal, then we won't go to the authorities for revenge porn laws.

The way he tries to weasel his way out of everything, I am sure he'll drag the whole process out, but to my surprise he must've had contingency plans for this kind of thing because he packs his things that day and leaves with no fuss. Denise waits in her room while my father gets the last of his things and then looks up at me.

"I know who I'm becoming is selfish and wrong."
His eyes plead along with his words. "There are groups
out there for people like us who are regretting our
actions."

I become just as silent as Denise and let my dad
hug me goodbye even though my body is stiff and
unwelcoming. When he is gone, however, I do look up
online about the groups he was talking about, and
everything he said is very real.

It isn't even going too far down a rabbit hole to
find out that there are a lot of forces at hand trying to
undo the damages that book has done. Andrea is not alone
in thinking that government agencies have hired new
authors to help people be more empathetic with others, to
disregard the inner id thoughts, and to embrace whatever
compassionate sides we are now hiding as a society.

The government also locates Cain Skaggs and
wants to prosecute him for the damages he's done by
those weaponizing his teachings in the book, but the mini
documentaries I watch about him inform the audience that
he had died of natural causes recently and therefore got
off the hook with this shitstorm that we're all in.

Since it's only in English, foreign leaders send
soldiers to North America ,Great Britain, and other
developed nations to help subdue the darker side of the
public. I'm not going to say that we're on the brink of

collapse, but it was really starting to look scary out there, and I sense uneasiness when going out in public.

People stay away from one another way better than they did when the COVID pandemic hit. Many are afraid to go outside, and even Denise and I do most of our work online versus socializing. We watch as the world slowly goes back to how it was, and obviously *Your True Colors* is banned in all countries.

Even activists who don't support book bans agree that it did more harm than good in society. No, the dust is settling, and Mom's hope for ruining the outside world from the inside out failed. But I know her better now and know that the only way of returning to see her is by reading that book, so I return to the painstaking task of slowly reading every single sentence and rearranging them until it has its impact.

I only read it when Denise is for sure out of the house or asleep. You would think that after all I had been through that I would scoff at it and see right through the manipulation, but I am comforted by the words as if Mom were talking to me herself, and it does make me look very deeply inward at myself.

I've let people walk all over me my whole life, always waiting for people to do right by me, but that was never going to happen unless I went out there and took what was rightfully mine. I start calling out Tyreke for his bullshit and am able to get a much higher pay bump and my choice of working remotely if I wish to.

Santiago and I start dating. He even tells me that the first time around he wasn't as attracted to my personality, and when I further press him, he admits that he was weighing his options with three other girls and I seemed too sweet and innocent to date. I change that in the bedroom as I take over and fulfill everything I want without his getting much say in what I do to him. It's not like he complains, though.

The book really does wonders for me, so much so that I book a flight back to Nova Scotia. I rent an off-roading tinted truck and head right for Black Wolf Creek. An older version of me would've asked for permission after I did my little chore, but that was the old me. If I want to go see my mom, then I am going to. What are a bunch of hippies going to do to me anyway? Force me to kill someone again?

Mom is in one of the gardens teaching a group of younger kids how to plant rosebushes when she looks up at me, clearly startled.

"Isabelle!" Mom cries out.

"Continue your lesson," I tell her. "We have all the time in the world."

This new assertiveness is something that she isn't used to, and she does indeed finish her teaching but can't keep from glancing at me to study my body language. She doesn't need to ask me if I read the book because the proof is in the pudding.

And, to my surprise, when she is done with the kids, she hugs me like I hadn't felt since when I was a little girl. I am shocked, of course, but then gradually embrace her back. The warmth is something I realize was the missing piece in my heart all these years. What's the saying? A mother's love cures all.

I tell her that I am only in town for a couple of days, which actually upsets Sydney. Me upset her?! She tells me that I should come back in the later summer and that I can stay in her guest bedroom. I hadn't really thought about it, but I know that I own Tyreke for life with the dirt I have on him, and I have more money than I know what to do with, so I agree.

Of course I am honest with Denise and tell her everything that I am going to do. Down to the smallest detail. She's ecstatic and happy for me. It's funny how a well-executed plan is far better than a half-assed one. I leave her in charge of the house and even get the dachshund dog that Mom wanted us to have a long time ago; his name is Rex.

I don't tell dad any of my plans, and he's been doing great in his twelve-step program. I still don't let him anywhere near the house or Denise, but I have started to give him an allowance again for being true to those words and at least trying to be a better version of himself. I never find out if he's staying with a friend or had some money squirreled away, but I know he's going to be on his best behavior for his daughter dearest so the money never stops coming in.

Black Wolf Creek is nice. I was never majorly against it before and now can see why people see it as a paradise. I want Mom to teach me everything in the weeks that I am there, and she does. I learn how to garden, tend to the animals, and hunt. It's probably for the better that she never showed me that last skill set, though, because that ends up being her demise.

I sprint back to the town square, eyes watering, and my lungs screaming at me. Mom angered a moose after we almost shot an elk and it chased her down a steep hill. I tell the residents that she was heroic in making sure that I was out of the elk's path, but I urge them to go to the canyon where she fell so we can see if she is alive.

Javi and Henry notify the authorities, and there is a search party from all the neighboring villages to find where she could be. Unfortunately there is a river with a strong current that Mom's body could've fallen into, and after a week of looking they tell me that I can stay in her place and that all of her belongings will be passed onto me. I'm catatonic and shake my head and tell them that all I want to take with me is the surgical tools she had as a reminder of the remarkable life that she lived.

Dr. Sydney Nuciforo really put herself through med school while supporting a family of three and rose to power in Austin. She created an empire and willingly walked away from it only to build another empire under the guise of another name. Through tough love she raised a completely independent woman who now takes complete control of everything she wants. In her two lifetimes she accomplished more than most people would if given fifty. I want her scrubs and her medical supplies to remind me of the first period of her life and hope that her smell never fades from them.

Your True Colors

Your True Colors

SYDNEY

Your True Colors

EPILOGUE

I'm in one of the gardens teaching the children how to plant rosebushes when I look up and see Isabelle walking toward me. Oh, the relief I feel when I read Isabelle's body language and see her sense of neediness gone! Finally I'm not required to be the center of her universe. She is letting me live my life, and I wonder what the book did to her. I realize that it must've gotten her out of her shell and that she now has other outlets outside of me to hold her attention.

She still loves me, but finally in a normal, healthy way. I can have a regular conversation with my daughter without talking down to her. She is now a peer. I honestly didn't think I was ever going to see her again because I didn't think she'd have the resilience to make it through, but I stand corrected and she is here in the flesh.

And to further surprise me, she doesn't want to stay. She is only in town for a few days. Of course I beg her to stay longer because I have never met this side of Izzy and I have grown to love it! She is a fully grown, strong, independent woman. I didn't think Cain's departure from this world would ever complete me, but now I have something to live for. I invite her to return at the latter end of the summer so we can spend some quality time together.

When she leaves, I end up stalking her on Instagram, only to see that she's made friends and is even dating a goofy-looking guy named Santiago. I suppose if he makes her laugh and treats her right, he could be the hunchback of Notre Dame and I'd accept him. Maybe I can even have grandchildren one day? But I can't get too far ahead of myself. Right now, I can't wait for her to bring him here. I know that even if I travel under Victoria Cross's name, there's a huge risk of being discovered in Austin, and something tells me that my ex would have a lot of words to say.

I can't wait to show her how to garden and that certain animals are not just cut out for farm life in case she wants to raise them in the city where she lives. But when she returns, she seems adamant about wanting to hunt and be more proficient with firearms. I try telling her that it's such an odd skill set and that we don't need to learn that, but she's rather firm and persistent with it, so I eventually cave and give her the rifle.

I am on the phone with Javi, telling him he'll have a new recruit, but she tells me that she didn't come this whole way to spend time with her neighbors. I even sense a little bit of the old clinginess in her, and as much as I want to remind her that she's reverting, I bite my tongue and let this one slide. Okay, whatever, so she wants to spend more time with me hunting. I'll let it go.

We're deep in the woods when Isabelle nudges me to look at a beautiful elk off in the distance. I whisper to her that we're past our quota with elk meat for the season and that we'd only be hunting ducks, but when I turn around, she has the shotgun aimed perfectly at me.

Before I have a chance to ask her what she's doing—

BANG

White pain erupts in my whole body, and I look down and notice that a large chunk of my leg is missing. At this close range it shredded my kneecap and dislocated everything below it. I try to stay calm in the situation but scream with agony. Did Isabelle miss? Was she trying to shoot the elk?

"I brought your surgical kit," she explains with no remorse in her voice. "You better patch yourself up really quick with a tourniquet before I take care of the other one."

I follow her eyes as she looks to my leg that's still intact.

"W-w-what do you mean?" I stammer as she tosses down the equipment I am to use to stop the bleeding. She's not wrong. If I don't do something quick, then I'll bleed out and die.

"That book taught me a lot of things. Like how I never really wanted you as a mother. I just liked the idea of having you as a mom."

In a horrific turn of events, I truly believe that my daughter has gone insane. I patch myself up before she does it again to the other leg and then I pass out.

*　　　　　　　*　　　　　　　*

When I wake up I'm in the back of a tinted truck. My arms are tied behind my back and the pain is agonizing in my leg. In the front seat, Isabelle drives without saying anything.

"Isabelle?" I croak out, my throat parched.

Isabelle reaches over and turns down the stereo. "Good morning, Mom. Well actually it's close to evening again, but the drugs I gave you knocked you out good."

My mind races quickly and I don't know what she wants, but I'll try to plead with reason. "Sweet T . . the community is going to know that I'm gone. We don't want you to get in any further trouble—"

"Oh they already know. I told them you fell off a cliff. They've had a search party out for the past week." She explains this as if it were common knowledge.

"What?" I manage.

"I think Azul thought it was suspicious that I kept going to a specific part of the woods when looking for you, but she never followed me." Isabelle shrugs her shoulders. "And if she does suspect something and pays me a visit, then I'll be ready for her."

"Ready for her?" I sit up despite the pain pulsing throughout my body. "Isabelle Claire Dunham, if you even lay a finger on Azul—"

"She's not your daughter," she interrupts me. "I am."

She stares at me through the rearview mirror and her eyes are as cold as ice daggers. I have to gather my thoughts and think about all of this logically.

"Okay. So where are you taking me?" She scrunches up her face and tilts her head like it's such an odd question.

"Home, of course."

*   *   *

Six Months Later

Only now do I understand Victor Frankenstein and see the monster that I have created. They're not bluffing when they say they'll take out my tongue if I continue to scream. That is the deal that Isabelle makes with Denise, who relishes the thought of tearing it out.

401

Afterward, they allow me a mirror to patch up my mouth the best I can, but without both my legs it's hard to really plan any kind of strategic attack against them.

Denise stays home while Isabelle goes to either her boyfriend's place or work, and after a long day she comes into my room where I am chained up. On the speakers she plays an AI impersonation of my voice that, I'll admit, gets my voice inflection down.

"How was your day, Izzy?" The program speaks for me.

"Mom, you would not believe the day I had! Santi thought he was sly when I overheard him talking to one of his buddies about him proposing to me."

"Propose?!" the voice speaks for me. "This calls for a celebration!"

"Way ahead of you." Isabelle reaches into her purse and takes out champagne.

She pours me some, and I stare at her with what I hope is the worst stare a woman could give. She ignores it and tilts the alcohol to my mouth. I chug a big gulp and hold it in my mouth before spitting it back in her face, though it's hard to do so without a tongue.

She flinches and obviously gets upset. In retaliation, she strengthens my wrists straps and gets me to yelp.

"What was that, Mom?" Isabelle continues, "you want me to curl up in bed with you?"

My skin crawls as Isabelle gets in bed with me like she's done countless times since keeping me prisoner. She rests her head on my chest like she did when she was a child.

"I love you, Mom," she says.

"You are the best daughter a woman could ask for, and I'll never leave you again—"

This is a frequent misery I experience and tears well up in my eyes. What monster have I created?

KNOCK KNOCK KNOCK

At first I think it's a door-to-door salesman, but when the knocking doesn't stop, I hear a faint voice from downstairs. Isabelle groans and wants Denise to handle it. She continues to rest into my chest, and the vague words downstairs sounds so familiar, but I cannot put my finger on who it is.

Usually Denise knocks on the door when the two of us are alone together, but today she bursts through, which annoys my daughter.

"Dammit, Denise, what is it?" Isabelle lifts her head off my chest.

"This guy says he knows you. He's in the living room right now," Denise's phone translates.

She sighs and gets off me and heads downstairs. Denise stares down at me with no remorse in her eyes for what has become of me. I wish she would just end me already—wait, that voice from downstairs comes into focus . . . I could recognize it from anywhere.

Isaac?

Your True Colors

AUTHOR'S NOTE

Throughout my life I have always been obsessed with how much sleep I get. There was a period in my life where I would sleep close to nine to ten hours a day but would end up with headaches, and in recent years it has been required that I wake up earlier, which has messed with my sleep schedule, and I typically get between six to eight hours of rest.

I work at a news station in Arizona and often help with booking guests for our different segments. Sometimes I talk with them beforehand through Zoom calls. Once we booked a guest who claimed to have written a book specialized in sleeping. I was ecstatic! I told him before he went live on our show that I was going to buy his work, and I even sent him the clip of him on air. When I got around to reading it, I ended up getting pissed off.

It had maybe three pages out of over two hundred that actually talked about sleep, and the rest of it was essentially a self-help book. I've read a couple of those in my life and feel that they're all the same. So much of it is about rethinking how to approach the world or just believing in yourself more. I was kind of livid about it at the time, but then it gave me the idea of *Your True Colors*.

406

If a lot of these books are convincing people to go out there and achieve their goals, then what about a book that gets people to be the worst versions of themselves? I didn't really know how to approach this and what would happen, but I was pleasantly surprised with how easily the story came to me. I understand that a lot of people would rather focus on the chaos unfolding, but I definitely felt it was more about the relationship with a mother and her daughter.

I knew little to nothing about Isabelle Dunham and even found myself more intrigued by her "deceased" mother, Sydney. I hope you enjoyed the adventure, because it was a tale that I thought could be told. One of my biggest influences when reading is an author named Bentley Little (ironically also from Arizona) who tends to go batshit crazy with the worlds he creates where the basic rules of life are no longer applicable, and it's almost as if a lot of his characters are under a spell.

I'll admit that I wanted my story to be more grounded than that, but it truly is hard making a more realistic reality in something so absurd when in actuality a lot of people don't read, and even those who would read a book like this are usually not susceptible to that kind of manipulation (unless it's a religion), but let's pretend anyway . . . isn't that what fictional books are for?

To that guest who got me to buy your book, I will say that you did change my life forever—just not in the way you thought you would.

John Martinez
7/2/2025

ACKNOWLEDGMENTS

When I used to read books, I would always be surprised about the amount of people that the author thanked and didn't think that that many people would take a part in helping create a book. But now that I have been through the process, it opened my eyes about how much of a village really goes into it!

My Martinez side of my family is the world to me, and their endless support for all of my endeavors in life does not go unnoticed. There's been more than a handful who had an even greater helping hand in this book.

Aunt Anna Martinez was the first person to read it and, bless you, it had so many errors in it that she actually thought I was slightly dyslexic! My cousins Randi Martinez and Julia Downs are avid readers and really helped me get in the psyche of a woman's perspective. It doesn't hurt that they are some of the coolest women I know! Their notes were extensive, and I loved their brutally honest opinions on the characters in the novel. (Yes, Randi did get a character named after her in the book.)

Lhea Carbajal has been a cheerleader of mine since our high school years, and I am glad she shares the same enthusiasm as my mom. Their support has never gone unnoticed in life, and I hope they know that they help me believe in myself.

Darryl Dawson may have been too busy to have fingers in this project, but his writing has been inspirational to me, so for him to even have kind words about my work was more than good enough for me.

E.J. Becker tried where he could to get around to the book, and I love that he would give his two cents outside of the grammar when he could.

Monica Davis for getting it so late and fixing what you could grammatically in such a short notice and giving your insights.

Amy Martinsen has been a mentor that I am lucky enough to have found. I honestly don't think I would have gotten this far without her expertise. I am just some kid from Mesa who has no idea what he's doing.

Allison Kartchner who took me on and made sure that the edits were clean and readable. It's always great to go with professionals. I also cannot reiterate how lucky I am that I was connected to her. Loved her thoughts. She made it better.

Amanda Rojas who actually likes my screenplays and has been a fan of my writing for quite some time now. I always appreciate her brutal honesty.

Ricardo and Kendra Olivares for being the biggest cheerleaders and for making me look somewhat decent in a photo. I'll never be the true Guapo.

Anyone to everyone who has told me that they would buy a copy or given me insights, from the book cover design to ways to market it is an endless list, but I'll try to include everyone that I can: Austin Hilliard; Hayden Hilliard and his partner, Jason Stoner; Audrey Stoner; Darrell Cunningham; Whitney Clark; Laura Ard; Kelsie Hagglund; Liana Phoenix; Shane Jenkins; Cooper Van Wey; Anthony Canales; Pierre Xavier; Sheyenne Martinez; Aaron Thew; Rocio Yerpes; Reese Kowalski; AJ Janos; Nicole Crites, Sean Hennessy . . . you know what, really all of my coworkers at KTVK/KPHO; all of my former screenwriting group who taught me I'm a shit screenwriter but maybe I have a knack for this; my Barro's coworkers, not so much with the book but hey you hooligans put a smile on a face; the small and mighty support of my father's side of the family along with his wife and two daughters. Friends that I skateboard with, have met traveling, play basketball with, listen to pop-punk music and sing along with, share a bond over horror movies with . . . even just a simple "good job" is more than enough of support that I need.

    If you're still reading this: you. I don't know if I'm that good of a writer, but I hope it at least appealed to some of you, and as long as you'll have me, I'll continue writing. There are still a lot of stories to tell, and I appreciate you took time out of your day and some money out of your bank account to take a chance on this.

But of course the most important person I need to thank for this whole process is . . . my dog, Murrow. Just kidding, Mom!

My mother ingrained reading into my life since I was a child. She read to me. She had a custom picture book with monkeys made for me. She didn't forbid me to read *Goosebumps* when it was controversial with some schools. She always encouraged me to be nose deep in a book, and I love that even to this day we exchange books and talk in depth about stories.

She's also the complete boss woman who sees enough potential in me to have gotten the ball rolling with this piece. She has helped in more ways than most of you could even know, and I can confidently say that I have the best mother a person could ask for. It's basically the opposite relationship Isabelle has with Sydney. I love you, Mom. This one was definitely for you.

Your True Colors

John Martinez currently resides in Phoenix, Arizona. Not Black Wolf Creek. *Your True Colors* is his first novel. His second book, *unWanted*, is expected to be released in late 2026.

www.ingramcontent.com/pod-product-compliance
Lightning Source LLC
Chambersburg PA
CBHW030541260626
47157CB00006B/2143